STEFANIE LOZINSKI

Magnify

Storm & Spire Book One

*To everyone, young or old, who has ever imagined
that an ordinary rock was a dragon's egg.*

"Courage is almost a contradiction in terms. It means a strong desire to live taking the form of a readiness to die."

G. K. Chesterton

Contents

Foreword

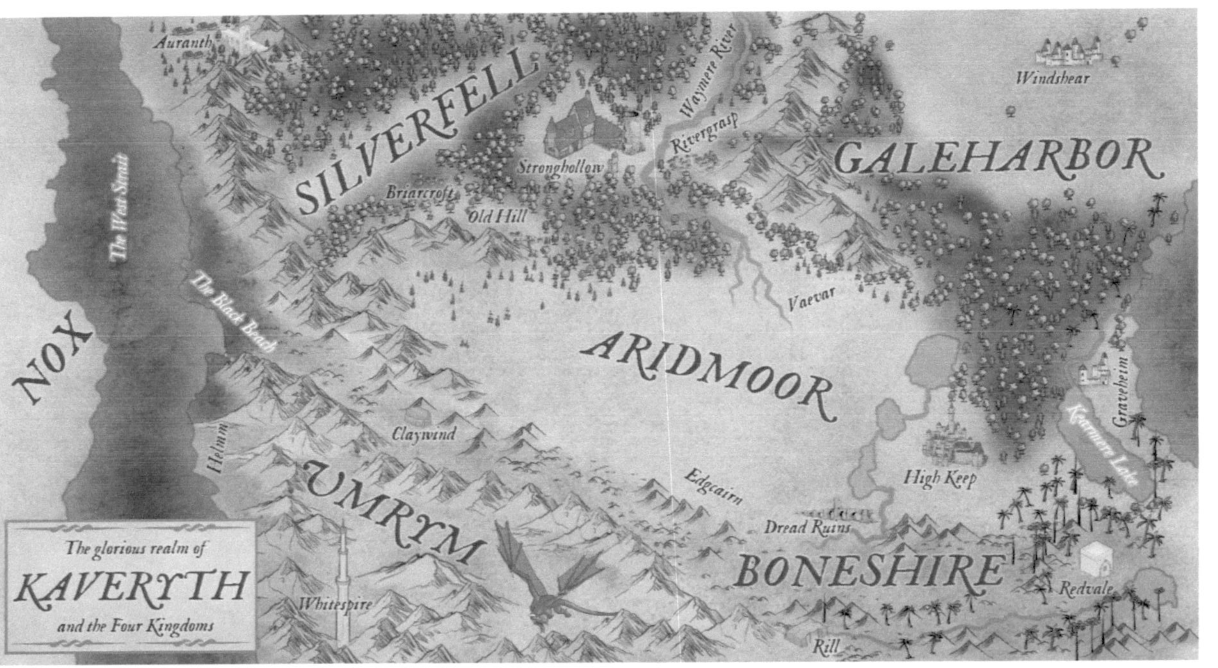

Auranth
SILVERFELL
Waymere River
Windshear
Rivergrasp
GALEHARBOR
Stronghollow
Briarcroft
Old Hill
Vaevar
The West Strait
The Black Beach
NOX
ARIDMOOR
Gravebeim
Kearmere Lake
Helmm
Claywind
Edgcairn
High Keep
UMRYM
Dread Ruins
BONESHIRE
The glorious realm of
KAVERYTH
and the Four Kingdoms
Whitespire
Redvale
Rill

Chapter One

The spire stood at the center of the world, watching everything, presiding over the birth of babies and the death of old men.

Wes Cervos looked toward it, across the city of Whitespire, as he crested the craggy gray ridge. He should have been waiting for his two companions—a Witness by the name of Odrigh, this time from Galeharbor, and his own Deermaster—but he had gone on ahead.

It was a special place. He needed to look upon it alone, even if only for a moment.

They would reach him soon, their ascent up the mountain burdened by the vast amount of wealth they carried in gold and jewel, but it was enough. Wes had been making the journey to the only overground city in Umrym once a season for as long as he could remember, but it never lost its magic.

For a moment, just a breath or two, standing there at the edge of divine things, the slightly pudgy boy of seventeen felt himself the hero that an Envoy was supposed to be.

The kind of hero who didn't so often preside over scenes of death.

The kind of hero who won.

"Wait, sir, if you would," came the Witness's voice from behind him as he scrabbled up the well-worn dirt track. Odrigh was a thin man, his slight stature belied by the corded muscles that rippled along his forearms. Like many who lived by the South sea that drew up against the edge of the Kingdom of Galeharbor, he was a sailor foremost, more at home in the sunshine on the tilting deck of a ship than he was climbing the cool, stony mountains of Umrym.

"Sorry, Odrigh. Is Deermaster Lev alright?" Wes asked, forcing himself to look away from the majestic spire, his lofty thoughts of heroes and grand deeds dragged back down to earth.

"Fine," the Witness said, giving his hand a loose wave of dismissal as the third member of their party came clomping onto the top of the ridge.

"The deer have been stubborn, I think."

"You think?" The Deermaster said, looking out from beneath his one beefy arm at Wes and Odrigh as he half-dragged the lead deer up onto the flat ground by the bridle. The three remaining deer needed no further encouragement. They were attached loosely by leather straps to the lead animal's saddle and followed him with evident relief onto the top of the mountain.

"I need a new profession. These beasts are more demanding than the Elf-Queen Manta herself ever was!"

Wes grinned at that, handing the bearded man a full water-skin from his own pack. He'd known the Deermaster since childhood, and he had been making such threats for years. The deer of Silverfell were renowned for their strength as well as their beauty all across Kaveryth, and none knew more about their care and breeding than Lev did.

After a brief rest for the deer and the men, they returned to the path on the far side of the flat bit of mountaintop, facing the valley floor that lay below.

"It never feels nearly as far as it looks," Wes heard Lev say to Odrigh as they began their descent. It was true. The journey into the heart of Umrym was a long one, but they were close now.

"Hail, Envoy! Wes Cervos, what a sight for these tired eyes!"

As if on cue, a deep voice called out to them, its owner seeming almost to materialize out of the rocks as he stepped onto the path. He was shorter than Wes by about a foot and a half, making him somewhat tall for a dwarf.

His hair was curly, bubbling out of the bottom of the black leather cap he wore like white soap foaming in a bath. His beard was combed into a complex braided design and dotted with gleaming black and silver beads. It hid most of his smile, but could not hide the gleam of mischief in his eyes.

"Hello, Ozmeak," Wes said, giving a slight bow which his companions repeated. "I trust that everything is prepared?"

"Of course," the dwarf said, falling into step beside Wes as they continued on. The steep road had already begun to even out, and as they drew closer to the floor of the valley, it became evident that Whitespire was no ordinary city.

The great spire at the eastern side was the only building that stood above ground, though the rear of it pressed against a mountainside. The rest of the block-like structures always reminded Wes of the lids of great stone caskets, buried halfway in the rocky valley floor.

The bulk of the city was underground, the tops of buildings poking through the stone only for the purpose of ventilation and surface entrances. Dwarves did not much like to spend time overground.

Neither did the dragons—not in these days.

The dwarven guide spoke with his companions, pointing out various stone peaks of the Severed Summits in the distance.

Not a single dragon in the sky this time. He found the whole thing disconcerting.

While it was true that the dragons spent much of their time in their vast underground caverns, they normally spent time in the air as well, patrolling the skies of Umrym and flying over the rest of Kaveryth now and then.

They used to, anyway. Until five years ago. I would swear it was nearly to the day... He refused to think about it, refused to dwell upon the evils that had befallen him.

He couldn't bear to. Especially now.

"You look poorly, boy," the dwarf said, giving Wes a nudge on the lower part of his arm. "I promise we'll give you some decent food before sending you off home."

"I don't think my belly is much in need," Wes said, forcing himself to smile at the pleasant old fellow, pushing his sadness aside for the time being. "Turns out even a march as long as this is not enough to make one thin and handsome when it's only done once a season."

"I'd advise against deer training as a fitness regime, as well," Deermaster Lev said, gazing down at his own bulging stomach. "Doesn't quite do."

"Right," Odrigh said, swallowing. "Right. Well, I think you look like... a fine man of your Kingdom."

Wes couldn't tell if he wanted to blush or to laugh. With his brown muscles and easy step, Odrigh made him look even more like a lump of bread dough than usual. As far as his looks went, he liked his brown eyes, his thick dark hair, and nothing else.

The moon-shaped scar running across his right cheek he liked perhaps least of all.

"Thank you, Odrigh," He said, walking a little bit faster.

They had reached the edge of the city now, the building-tops that had looked so haphazard from above stretching out neatly along the main path leading to the base of the central spire. There was a moment of eerie silence as they made their way along the path.

Even the winds that usually screamed across the mountains had gone quiet, dulled by the walls of the valley. The dwarf guide did not attempt any jokes or spouting of trivia, perhaps sensing the general mood that had settled over the Envoy's company.

Will our sacrifice be accepted? The worries rushed over him before he could stop them.

Has it been accepted at all in these five dark years? Or have the Dracodei turned away from us?

He had no way of knowing. For the moment, there was only the steady march of man, dwarf, and deer, the chime of clinking treasures, and the silent sky uninterrupted by the beat of dragon's wings.

* * *

Wes squinted as the sinking sun dipped below the western peaks that lay ahead. Now that the great spire stood behind them, he was content to take up a slower pace at the rear of the little convoy, half-listening to the conversation of Lev and Odrigh as they forged ahead along the path toward home.

Ozmeak had guided them to the final incline that lead out of the valley, just as he always did. Wes accepted the hearty handshake he offered, the pat on the shoulder, and the promise that he would see "the fine Envoy" again in a few months' time.

He reached into the front pocket of his trousers and fingered the small metal Claim that lay there.

The sacrifice had gone well.

It had been routine, at any rate. The men had reached the base of the dizzying spire and Wes had left them and the dwarf outside, leaving him to fend for himself with only the caravan of deer for company on the final leg of the journey.

There was no real danger—only the dwarf women who worked as temple servants were allowed into the upper part of the spire. Wes always found the ladies pleasant enough, though they were not comfortable with a great deal of conversation.

As Wes ascended the great spiraling staircase, leading the four deer behind him, he felt the silence press against him like a heavy cloak.

No one else but the Envoy was allowed to approach the sacred cavern itself.

More than once throughout history, Envoys had died there, their bodies left to rot until the next Envoy came who was strong enough to move them. Sometimes, it took years. Envoys began to follow their calling from the day of their birth, but training and physical growth was not instantaneous. Wes himself had taken his first trip to Whitespire when he was six years old.

He could still remember what it was like to be Envoy as a child, the cold empty tower, the crushing silence. Fear always threatened to drive him out empty-handed, but he had never failed to acquire the Claim.

Wes shivered despite the burning in his legs as he continued upwards. The stairs had no doubt been grand once, thousands of pounds of marble gleaming in the rays of sunlight that poured in through the small, open windows along the walls.

Now, the entire place stank of must and age. Wes rarely dared to glance out the windows, not wanting to be reminded of how far he was from those who were tasked with keeping him safe.

The cavern entrance itself had never been magnificent. Each time that Wes made it up the final turn of the staircase, sweat pooling on his forehead, body aching, he was underwhelmed.

The fine marble walls seemed to jut directly into the rough stone face opposite the staircase, with no mark of workmanship to be seen. In the center of the stone was a hole just big enough for a man to walk through, the sides pressed in so tight that he could only see blackness within.

Off to one side was a dry stone fountain that pressed against the wall, a round bowl standing atop a thick pillar covered with intricately sculpted curves and flowing lines. In the center of the basin, there was a second column in miniature with a small depression on top, also empty.

Wes could see the thick coating of dust that covered the surface, as well as the cobwebs that hid in the corners beneath. He suspected that whatever its purpose was had been lost to legend a very long time ago.

Wes began unloading the deer's burdens, wrestling great

bags of treasure over his meaty shoulders one by one until they formed a large pile on the worn marble floor.

The animals stared off into the cavern's mouth, transfixed, their tails twitching as Wes patted their muscled shoulders, bidding them to wait. The first bag of treasure was one from his own Kingdom, Silverfell; he could tell by the thick green cloth and the swirling designs in silver thread along the top edge.

Drawing a breath, he heaved it behind him and entered into the darkness.

* * *

"Wes, what do you think about stopping once we reach the brook?" Lev's voice tore him from his memories.

Though the Deermaster turned back to look at him from his saddle, Wes could scarcely make out his face in the gleam of the reddish evening sunlight. He pressed a hand to his forehead, blinking away the harsh glow from behind his eyelids.

"Sounds perfect. I swear the tower has gotten taller since last time," he said. "That, and we haven't eaten in hours. I'm starving."

Lev nodded and turned back toward the sunset and the seemingly endless stretch of mountain peaks. It was true, too. After climbing the staircase, unloading the treasure, and placing each bag one at a time on the great stone altar hidden in the shadows of the cave, he was exhausted.

And then he'd had to make his way back down on foot, keeping the newly unburdened deer from taking off toward ground level in a rush of exuberance. They'd been traveling since first light that morning.

It felt like a very long time ago.

"Thank you, Envoy, sir," Odrigh said. Wes had asked him to stop with the formality, to no avail. It seemed that the Kingdom of Galeharbor's Witness took his role rather seriously. "I saved some of the finest salted fish for our return journey."

Wes made a face, grateful that the man was not looking in his direction. He'd been treated to such seaside fare many times since leaving Silverfell and had been hopeful that the provisions had finally run out.

They made a good pace, now that they were able to ride the quick-footed deer themselves. The promise of a warm fire and a little dwarvish wine served as further motivation as they made their way up hills, down gorges, and through tight stone passageways where they could only ride in single file.

Wes liked those portions of the path least of all.

They reminded him of the sacred cave which held the altar of the Dracodei, all shadow and stale, ancient air. He longed for the lush forests of Silverfell. He could almost smell the damp moss and taste the crystalline water that poured abundantly through his Kingdoms' streams.

He hated to leave it, but leave it he would, again and again, until the day that he died.

"Will we make it by dark?" Odrigh asked, looking back at Wes. The sun no longer stung his eyes. The light that remained was a mottled haze of blue and purple, fighting to push the orange sunshine beneath the shadow of the mountains.

"Don't worry. We're not far," Wes said, giving a smile that took more effort than he expected. Odrigh's unease had reminded him of how tired he was, and of how foreboding the mountains of Umrym were when night fell.

He was relieved when Deermaster Lev rushed into one of his

numerous tales, no doubt hoping to keep up a jovial mood until they could make camp.

"Now, Witness, do they talk much of history over in the East?" Lev asked, letting his deer draw up next to Odrigh's. Wes was only a couple of feet behind, now that the path had widened. He was not so eager for solitude beneath the drawing curtain of dusk.

"Some," Odrigh shrugged.

"The Elf-Queens?"

"Of course."

"The Song of Vavoren Brewmantle?"

"The dwarf sang it while handing out bottles of wine. Twice."

"The fall of Noctua?"

Odrigh did not dignify this with a response. Wes grinned at his indignation. Everyone in Kaveryth knew about the history of Boneshire, not least of all a well-traveled sailor-son of Galeharbor.

"Well, I suppose you know all about the origin of the dragons, and even the Dracodei, then," Lev said slowly.

"Of course," Odrigh said, the bravado gone from his voice. "The basics, at any rate. But it would be a good one to pass the time. Especially here," He gestured ahead of them, where the path narrowed once more, forcing them to return to riding single-file. The walls stretched far above their heads, blocking nearly all of the remaining light. Wes was relieved to know that their planned campsite was just past this unpleasant mountain corridor. He rubbed his hands together, eager to warm them over a cheerful, sparking fire.

"Very well," said Lev, as though very much put out. He paused for barely two breaths before diving into the familiar story of vain Elf-Queens, valiant men, strong dwarves, and all-powerful dragons.

Wes tried to listen, but his tiredness was pressing in more strongly on him now, lulling him momentarily into sleep before he was inevitably woken by the shifting of his mount beneath him. The cycle repeated as time passed, and he found himself quite content, resting on the very edge of dreaming.

"The Dracodei could have crushed the dwarf resistance with only a thought. They're gods!" Lev was saying, taking one of his hands off the reins and waving it around wildly. "The shorn peaks of the Severed Summits testify to their power. Instead, they chose alliance, chose to preside over Kaveryth with the help of even the humblest of races—"

Before the man could finish his thought, Wes heard something that forced the air from his lungs.

A great yell rang out along the stone passage, many rough voices tumbling together into a single roar.

Dwarves appeared, first three, and then five. No one could see where they came from as they surrounded the three travelers. They poured down the passage, axes in their thick hands, heavy helmets covering their heads. The shouting echoed against the cliffs, their words sounding more like the snarling of dogs than proper speech.

Wes was awake now, trying in vain to urge his mount forward, the shock of meeting anyone at all having rendered him unable to move for several moments.

Bandits? Dwarf bandits? Here? Such a thing was unheard of. It was the task of the dwarves to serve the dragons and the Dracodei, not to rob their Envoy. *Surely they know they will be executed immediately for this treason.*

"The Feast of Offering is ended! You're too late!" Lev yelled from up ahead, his voice barely audible over the endless shrieking of the dwarves. "We have nothing to steal, let us alone!"

Wes drew his sword, trying in vain to turn the deer around in the narrow passageway. *They will still take our deer if we let them, Lev.* He closed his eyes for a moment, feeling his heart hammering in his chest as he tried to think of a plan. The noise was disorienting. He felt as though he was being tossed along by rapids, unable to come up for air. It was too dark to see very far ahead. All he could make out was a mass of dwarves, shoving each other and screaming at his companions.

"Leave us!" Shouted Odrigh, his voice quavering.

"Get him! Come on, Barrl, get him," said one. Wes caught a glimpse of the whites of the speaker's eye as he drew closer, ax aloft in both hands.

Hearing movement from behind, he tried again to get the terrified deer to move. The animal was hemmed in on both sides and had begun to panic, rearing into the air. Wes only managed to hold on for a few rounds before he was sent sliding from the saddle and toward the hard ground. Wes gritted his teeth against the pain that shot up his spine as he landed on his rear end, his sword flying out of his hands with a clang as it hit the rock wall. The deer reared again, his hooves crashing to the ground mere inches from Wes' head.

"Barrl!" Sneered the voice again. This time it was closer. "Put the deer down, at the least."

Before Wes had a chance to think, he heard the telltale whoosh of an arrow flying through the air. The deer stumbled, stepping on Wes' foot for a moment before collapsing to the ground. He dove after it, trying to blink away the growing darkness as he made for the passage wall, each step leaving him exposed.

He heard more arrows flying over his head, more shouting coming from all directions. There was another thick thumping sound as one of the other deer was shot. Wes continued to shuffle through the open space, half crawling until finally he collapsed against the far wall.

"Wes! Wes!" Odrigh's voice came from somewhere ahead of him. More arrows. The clank of metal on metal. Another heavy thump, followed by a cry from Lev and the sound of running hooves. "Get to him!" Lev yelled.

Wes fumbled at the pack attached to his belt, his hands shaking as he made for the small tinderbox that he kept there. Even if he found his sword, the night had covered the mountains, leaving him helpless to fight back in the dark. He was still fully exposed on one side.

Before he could get anything lit, he heard a dwarf behind him.

He turned, finding himself barely a foot away from the intruder. "Come honorably, and we will treat you likewise," he said, his voice a low hiss. *You must be Barrl.*

The shouting had nearly ceased ahead of him, leaving a disorienting ring in his ears punctuated with the harsh battle sounds.

"Surrender, Wes Cervos, Envoy of the Four Kingdoms. Surrender and I promise I will see that you live."

Chapter Two

The edge of the paper crumbled away, sending several flakes of brittle parchment tumbling like snowflakes toward the stone floor. After so many hundreds of years hidden away between thick leather covers, it seemed it could no longer bear to be read.

Celesyria swore, drawing back her clawed fingers as though she'd been burned.

The Codex Veritatis is not the work of dragon-pen, that much is clear. She stretched her huge head toward the floor, hoping to make out at least a few of the words on the scattered bits of paper. *Nevermind. It was only a corner. What's important will be there still.*

It has to be.

As she drew back up to the edge of the table, she managed

to bump her head against the dark wood, narrowly avoiding sending the entire book flying. The temptation to swear again was immense, but instead she decided to close her great yellow eyes, waiting a moment for the annoyance to pass.

It didn't, not completely, but it was enough. She found it rather hard to be cheerful, stuffed as she was into a too-small corner of the Great Library. The name alone had given her certain expectations.

They were not met.

If only Gramnok had a taste for adventure. This would be much easier for one in possession of hands. And thumbs. As it was, her best friend did not care very much for adventure, at least, not for anything that would take him past the caverns of Whitespire.

When Celesyria had told him of her plans to travel to Helmm in search of more books from the Codex, he had responded in his usual anxious fashion, refusing to have any part in her plans.

Fortunately for her, he had agreed to keep her designs to himself, with much hand-wringing and a few toothless threats. At least, she hoped they were toothless.

She looked at the open book before her once more, marveling at the small size of the elven writing. As carefully as she could, she nudged the large, mounted magnifying glass with her nose until it was placed neatly over the page.

Careful to keep her wings furled tight, she turned a single page with the tips of her claws, surprised at the amount of dust that puffed up into her nostrils. *Don't sneeze.* She feared even to breathe lest she cause more damage.

The female dwarves who kept watch of the Great Library had been wary of allowing her to access the old reading caverns as it was.

As the dust settled and the urge to sneeze passed, she began to read.

She was not quick to do so—the Old Language was not commonly used in Umrym, and she had little practice deciphering it—but she was determined. Within moments, she had fallen into a near trance, the black slit in the center of her gleaming yellow eyes moving ever so slightly over the page as she took in the words.

When she found what she was looking for, she paused, translating it again, and then once more. She had to be certain.

It's true.

The truth of what she'd read finally began to sink in and become real.

I know what's happening to my race. I know why we are dying.

* * *

I surrender, Wes thought to himself.

The words rested on the edge of his tongue as he lay there in the darkness, scrambling for his sword, trying to make out where the dwarves were. He felt the hot, slick feeling of fresh blood on his fingertips.

I wish I could. I wish I could let this curse pass from me. I don't want to be the cause of any more death.

"What say you, Envoy!" Barrl's sneering voice continued as he bent down close to Wes' face. Wes could feel his breath against his nose, hot and smelling of meat and ale.

He fumbled once again with his belt, knowing how pointless it would be to light a flame but longing to do it anyway. He wanted to see the face of the traitor.

Just kill me. Let a new Envoy take my place. A strange sense of peace washed over him as he felt the cool edge of a blade against his thick neck. If he died before he could marry a woman, making her Queen of Silverfell by custom, his noble House would die with him.

All of my ancestors would be forgotten, even… He couldn't bear to think of it. In any case, they were dead. It was he who had been forced to endure these five terrible years, feeling the pain. Why shouldn't he be allowed to escape it?

If he were taken alive, the people of the Four Kingdoms would be left without anyone to bring their sacrifices to the Dracodei.

It would ensure destruction on a scale never yet seen. But if he were to die…

"If you—" he started to say.

There was another whoosh of air. A whimper which rose until it became a yell. The smell of blood was stronger now, making him want to vomit.

If you want to kill me, kill me.

The blow did not come.

For a moment, there was a pause in the action, a breath inhaled across the small battlefield, as though time had stopped.

He wasn't sure if everyone else could feel it, or if he was going mad with the shock, but he drew a couple of slow breaths, gulping at the night air as Barrl stood before him.

He tried to think, desperate to figure out what to do, how to get away.

A second later there was another thump. The dwarf hit the ground, spitting blood and whimpering.

The sounds of violence rushed back into his ringing ears.

He was glad he had not had a chance to wish for death out loud.

His parents and his brother had not died as heroes only for him to become a wicked coward before his own end came.

There were more yells, more clanking metal, the harsh sounds echoing against the stone, making his ears ache.

Finally managing to get hold of the hilt of his sword, he drew back against the wall, his body partially protected by a small outcropping of rock. His head hurt, and there was a heavy feeling between his ears. Had he smacked his head when he'd fallen off his deer? He couldn't remember.

"Odrigh!"

Lev cried out from farther down the passage. It seemed that the fight had moved away from him. More cries followed, more banging, more chaos. *How many are they? How many are we?* Struggling to his feet, he finally managed to get the pouch on his belt opened.

He drew out the tinderbox, his hands shaking as he tried to coax a spark from the steel and flint. Finally, he managed to light the little wooden match-stick.

In the small pool of light it provided, he could see the gleam of his sword laying on the ground nearby. Before he could grab it, however, he noticed the thick blood on his fingertips. There was more of it now, so much that the match-stick slipped loose, the tiny flame turning end over end before being extinguished in the dirt below.

The darkness seemed even more total than it had been before.

"Wes! Run!" Came a voice from ahead. He couldn't tell if it was Lev or Odrigh. Or had there been someone else? He couldn't think straight.

The sword, I need my sword. He tried to force his legs to move toward where he had seen it. It was only a few steps away.

There. He felt his outstretched fingertips brushing against the other side of the passageway. He heard his name being called again, repeated over and over. It sounded far away. He knelt down, nearly falling onto his hands and knees as he groped for his weapon.

Everything was spinning now.

He couldn't figure out where Lev and Odrigh were, couldn't figure out what the noises hammering between his ears were.

Suddenly, his stomach began to roil. His head was pounding now, the headache so intense that he forgot completely about the weapon. He half-fell, half-rolled onto his side, breathing hard, clutching at his skull.

It stings. He had a bizarre sensation that he was outside of his body looking in, an observer with only minor interest in the subject at hand.

It stings.

I see, the blood is from my head, not my hands.

He thought no other thought.

He could not hear the other dwarves, could not hear his friends.

He could not hear anything at all.

Chapter Three

Wes thought that the sun felt very good.

It glowed behind his eyelids, enveloping his world in orange and pink. It was an agreeable sunlight, not so hot as to be unpleasant, but not cool enough to belong to dawn.

The air was cool, however, and before long he found himself wincing as a heavy gust blew over him.

No. He opened his eyes and sat bolt upright.

Not again. Please, no.

He felt dizzy and disoriented, his body remembering where he was and what had happened before his mind could catch up to it. He looked at his hands. They were covered in flaking, dried blood.

He reached up to investigate the back of his head, relieved to note that his skull seemed to be largely intact. He reached for his sword, which lay barely three feet away from where he had passed out. Fumbling in his front pocket, he drew out the round piece of gold.

The Claim is with me. He turned it over in his hands without much interest, watching the way the sun reflected off of the crossed lines carved into its surface.

"That's all that matters in the Four Kingdoms, right?" He said aloud. "Never mind how many have died, as long as the Dracodei receive their sacrifices."

He would bring the Claim to Silverfell, presenting it to the council known as the Septemvirate, as proof that the celebration of the Feast of Offering was complete. It would remain with them until the next Feast came, a few months from now, when he would take it with him to Whitespire and leave it with the sacrifices, receiving another in return.

Each Claim, one for each of the four Feasts of Offering, had a slightly different design carved upon it, too complex to be faked by treasure thieves.

He began to call for Lev and Odrigh, knowing it would make no difference, but taking strange pleasure in the sting of his dry throat as he yelled their names.

His voice echoed up the passage. He counted the fallen. There were eight dwarves here, more than he'd seen the night before. All were heavily armed but wore the usual apparel of Umrym.

"Death at the hands of my men was a mercy, you filth," he said, reaching down to examine an arrow that was stuck into one of their burly chests.

"The Guardians do not take kindly to those who threaten the sacrifices."

The passage was eerily quiet every time that the wind stilled.

Realizing that his head was feeling much better, he made his way up the passageway, stepping over the bodies of the fallen dwarves.

The one who he assumed was Barrl had been so close when he'd fallen that he'd practically slept on top of him.

If one of my men hadn't shot him, I'd be dead. And had a better man been chosen as Envoy, Odrigh and Lev would still be alive. The thought brought the threat of tears to his eyes.

"Lev! Odrigh!" He cried out again, pausing to wrap a piece of cloth torn from his shirt around his wounded head. He felt much better than the amount of blood would seem to indicate, but he did not want to take chances. There would be no help here, none for many miles, if his friends were indeed dead.

The only reply was the distant skittering sound of some animal.

Wes pressed on, relieved as he stepped over the final fallen dwarf a few yards further up. The bodies disturbed him, and he would be happy to emerge at the end of the passage.

The sun was high enough overhead that the center of the path was well-lit, but the sides were bathed mostly in shadow. Wes shivered.

The deer, he remembered, a flicker of hope filling him as he moved forward, the passage curving tightly to the left.

Perhaps they stopped at the pool.

He made his way around another outcropping of rock before stopping short, the nausea of last night bubbling up once more.

Unlike the dwarves, the bodies of Lev and Odrigh were not hidden in the cool shadows.

Flies swarmed over the men's faces and necks. Wes kept a hand over his mouth and nose as he bent down to examine them, certain that he would vomit if he inhaled at all.

The buzzing filled his ears, convincing him that the insects would swarm down his shirt and over his own face at any moment.

He closed his eyes for a couple of moments, his chest tight and aching, forcing himself to be calm.

"I'm so sorry, Deermaster," he said as he reached into the mob of wings and feet, pressing his fingers to Lev's thick neck in search of a pulse. There was none.

Odrigh lay nearly on top of the other man, his chest a bloom of red.

Wes was certain he was dead, but he checked anyway, dozens of the flies landing on his arm as he pressed his fingers against the sailor's neck.

He could see the bow still clasped in Odrigh's thin fingers.

Wes began to cry then, warm tears and snot covering his face as the flies hummed.

It was the Witness from Galeharbor who had saved his life in the end.

Lev he had known forever. Lev had cared for him not only as Envoy, but as a long-time friend of his family.

Odrigh was different.

Every Feast, one of the Four Kingdoms, in turn, was required to send a man of fighting age to accompany the Envoy on his journey to Whitespire. They were selected by lot. Odrigh had been chosen as Witness of Galeharbor. He did not merely accept his duty to his people, but had stood with Wes even when he could have fled. Even to the very end.

Odrigh and Lev were heroes.

And Wes, once again, wished that he was dead.

* * *

The candles burned like tiny stars.

Set into thousands upon thousands of alcoves, the flicker of the lights made it seem as though the vast walls of the cavern were moving. Celesyria glanced around as she landed on the smooth stone floor of the eastern entrance cave. She shivered. Some thought that the subterranean city of Whitespire was beautiful at night, but she'd always found it eerie.

The illusion of the rippling walls made her feel like she was inside the bowels of some impossibly large creature, unable to escape. She looked behind her a final time, drawing in a deep breath, enjoying the feeling of the cold night air pouring into her vast lungs.

She had flown from Helmm as fast as she could, but still, she had arrived home later than she'd intended. The Feast of Offering was tomorrow, and her mother and father were not going to be impressed that she'd nearly missed it. *Oh well.* She gave one last wistful glance at the moon before making her way into the larger halls of the city. *I found what I needed. It's more important.*

Unfortunately, she didn't think that her parents—both Guardians, servants of the Dracodei and protectors of all Kaveryth—would see it that way. They did not share her interest in dusty old books. They were content to serve the Dracodei, never feeling the need to go after the nagging questions that swirled around in their heads at night. That is, if they even had such thoughts. It was hard for Celesyria to be sure.

Suppressing what was sure to be a thunderous yawn, she made her way toward the Guardian's quarters, not seeing or hearing anyone. It was very, very late, and any who were still awake, dragon or dwarf, were likely to be in another district.

There's also less of us than there was before, she reminded herself, her sadness about their present circumstance mingling with her relief.

At least I finally know why. And if I know why, I can do something to stop it.

There were several living areas scattered throughout Whitespire, but the cavern that housed the Guardians was by far the largest and most beautiful.

Celesyria stood in the middle of the center room, the vaulted ceiling stretching high enough above her head to make even her great stature seem small. Here in this district, there were no candles. Instead, there were hundreds of glowing orbs of green and blue, hung from the ceiling supports on thick black cords. They gave the whole room a soft, dreamy feeling.

It was her favorite place in all of Whitespire. The Dracodei were said to live above the great spire itself, somewhere in the clouds, a place where they never even have to land. She found it hard to believe that any place, real or even imagined, could be more beautiful than her own home, either within the earth or over it.

Celesyria walked as quietly as she could, her claws tapping against the floor as she moved. There were dozens of hallways leading off of the main room in all directions. To her right, she could see the faint glow of the vast communal kitchen at the end of one of the longest passageways, where dwarf chefs prepared meals for the dragons who made up the rank of Guardians. Usually, the tempting smells poured out even into the main hall, but lately, meat had been in rather short supply.

A moment later she reached the passage that led to several of the family-sized sleeping areas. She could hear snoring from within various rooms, low and rumbling, heavy enough to make the walls tremble. Though the sound would no doubt be annoying to anyone who was not accustomed to it, she found it comforting.

All of a sudden, she was tired, the long journey from Helmm having finally settled into her muscles and bones. *Sleep will be good.* She made her way toward the entrance of her family's quarters and pushed the huge swinging privacy door inwards with her nose. *As much as I love the skies, there is something so lovely about a tight little place to curl up and dream.*

"*Have you finally lost your head?*" Came a sudden voice within her mind, loud and biting.

Celesyria jumped backward, nearly doing just that on the edge of the frame that held the door.

"*Mother— Let me explain—*"

"*The Feast of Offering is tomorrow, and you're off playing archivist!*" Her mother snapped, her voice harsh between Celesyria's ears.

"*I know. I'm sorry, I didn't mean to be late. I'm sorry,*" Celesyria pleaded, feeling even more tired now that the moment of surprise had worn off. It was fortunate that dragons communicated primarily by telepathic means, at least when speaking to one another. Her mother was angry enough to wake up the entire district were she to speak audibly.

"*You may very well be called upon tomorrow, to assist with laying up the sacrifices,*" her mother said, her voice a little softer after taking a few breaths.

"*Your father and uncle have both tried to pull some strings. It's an honor to be picked, the sort of thing befitting a future Guardian.*" Her mother narrowed her yellow eyes pointedly, her dark orange scales gleaming in the glow of the orbs.

"*Thank you,*" Celesyria said. *It's an honor to you, not to me.*

She felt a rush of anger and pushed it down as quickly as it came. She knew things that her mother did not. She had to make them understand but now was not the time.

"Please tell uncle thank you, as well."

"Alright. Get some rest," her mother said, turning her back and heading toward her own sleeping area, which was little more than a hollow in the stone, piled full with soft pillows and blankets.

"But you should know something. Three more have died since you left. This time, all of the dead were Guardians."

Celesyria did not answer her as she made for her own identical bed. The implication of her mother's words could not be more clear. The Guardian commander would soon begin another training period, and if she was going to be asked to join, it would happen soon. It was her chance to be a part of her family legacy and to serve her race.

Most of all, perhaps, it's my chance to fit in with the rest, for the first time in my life.

As strong as the temptation was, she had already made up her mind about what she had to do.

She only wished that she didn't have to break her father and mother's hearts to do it.

* * *

As Wes drank from the clear pool, hidden deep in the Severed Summits of Umrym, he couldn't help but glance over his shoulder. The birds were singing again, and the buzz of insects filled the air from time to time, but those were the only sounds of life.

Without a deer, he'd had no choice but to leave the bodies of his friends on the path behind him. He thought of them there, the sun beaming down on faces that would never smile again, and swore to himself that no matter what, he would ensure their bones were retrieved for an honorable burial.

The water felt good on his dry throat, cold and bracing. There was a thin layer of ice resting near the edges of the pool, the stubborn remnant of Umrym's winter stretching out into the season of the spring Feast. The promise of the coming warmth brought Wes little comfort, however. It was a long way home, the distance all the more overwhelming now that he was so utterly alone.

Perhaps I will be able to send a message once I reach Aridmoor. The Kingdom of Boneshire was closer—he would reach the border within two days if he pushed himself—but he doubted there would be any suitable messenger to be found there. *The Septemvirate will send out men to bring home the bodies, and I can request that someone accompany me.*

After taking a few more minutes to fill his waterskins and hoping that one of the deer would materialize, he continued along the path, keeping his hand against his sword. He smiled to himself, humorless. If there were more bandits, whether dwarf, human, or elf—at this point, nothing would surprise him—he would not be able to fight them off.

Despite his earlier thoughts of hopelessness, there was a nagging will to survive that went beyond mere fear of pain. He reached up to his cheek, feeling the pale, crescent-shaped scar with his fingertips, lost in memory.

Five years. Five long, aching years.

Wes had been twelve, and he had been alone.

He had been brought to the deepest halls of the Citadel in his home city of Stronghollow, where he was left alone for hours, unsure what was happening or what to do. The walls of the city had been breached, the guards said, nearly dragging him off to safety. He had protested, of course, demanded that he was practically a man, trained in the sword and able to fight, but they ignored him.

The room where he had been hidden away was more pleasant than a dungeon, but only just. The walls were made of gray stone, unbroken but for a single wooden door that Wes knew was heavily guarded on the outside.

As he was taken away he was able to hear the cacophony of battle above his head, but once the door closed, there was nothing. The screams of women and children were quashed by the thickness of the walls. The screech of clashing metal could not slither through the imperceptible cracks.

He was left alone with his thoughts. As the Envoy, he was himself the greatest treasure in all the Four Kingdoms.

Only he could deliver the sacrifices to the Dracodei. Only he could ensure their favor and protect the people.

Finally, there had been a knock on the door.

Elder Dorold himself, head of the Septemvirate, had come. He entered the room, raising a hand to the guards, who gave the two of them privacy. Wes was already crying as Dorold began to speak, his bravado collapsing as the bearded man enveloped him in a hug.

"I'm sorry, Wes," he said, trying unsuccessfully to hold back his own tears. "The elves made it over the wall. We tried to fight them off, but they were able to breach the Citadel."

Wes pressed his head into Dorold's chest, refusing to breathe. He wanted to stay in that moment forever. If he didn't acknowledge what was happening, surely it wouldn't be real.

"We tried to get the King and the Queen into the safety of the lower Citadel," he continued, his voice shaking now as tears flowed freely. "But there was a complication."

"A complication," Wes said flatly, as though the whole thing was ridiculous. One spoke of complications when it came to tending hedges or ordering food for a harvest banquet. This was about human lives, snuffed out, destroyed by their enemies.

He thought of the elves, so alien with their gray-blue skin and dark eyes, pouring out of their land of Nox like a river of evil and hate.

"The Princess was with your family. One of the elf-warriors managed to get hold of her and put a knife to her throat. Our soldiers were trying to stop the elves who were pouring into the Citadel."

Dorold paused, and Wes attempted to wipe his eyes as fresh tears filled them again. He knew what was coming, but was powerless to stop it.

He could only stand there as the avalanche buried him.

"Prince Roven was willing to do anything to save his be-trothed. His courage was commendable. With the help of the King and Queen, they managed to slay the kidnapper and free Princess Kessara."

Another pause.

Wes pulled away from Dorold then, unable to bear another minute.

"And then what, Dorold," he said, his voice a whisper against the stone. "Tell me."

He could never recall the exact words that were said afterward, though the rest of the exchange was burned permanently into his memory.

They were all dead. Mother, father, older brother.

The House of Cervos had been decimated, reduced to a single twelve-year-old who was forbidden to rule and many years too young to find a wife to make queen.

Wes remembered in detail the stinging of his skin as he clawed at his moonscar, trying to rip it from his face with his fingernails. No matter how much he managed to make himself bleed, the mark of the Envoy stayed where it was, his fate written in dead flesh.

Chapter Four

"Do you ever wonder what it is the Dracodei do with all of this treasure?" Celesyria asked as she hefted chunks of stone into the opening of the small tunnel. Through the remaining spaces between the rocks, she could see the gleam of gold coin, piles of it, more than could reasonably be spent.

"Would you be careful what you say, please?" Gramnok Beastbane hissed as he stood back, admiring their handiwork and directing Celesyria as she moved the last few large stones into place.

"Oh, come on," Celesyria said, rolling her eyes as she pulled her large head back out into the open part of the cavern. *"The Dracodei can't read minds."* Her neck ached, and she was relieved that the work of laying up the treasure was almost over, at least until the next Feast of Offering.

If there is another Feast. One way or another, she hoped that she would not be involved.

She felt guilty participating in the rituals of the sacrifice, but what else could she do? When she'd awoken that morning, her mother had been thrilled to tell her that she'd been assigned to such an important task.

More than that, she was able to work alongside her best friend—her only friend. How could she have said no?

Instead, she decided to go along with it for one more day, hoping that she could breach the topic with Gramnok, at least.

So far, she was not having a great deal of success.

Like most dwarves, Gramnok faithfully served the Dracodei. He had complete trust in their every word, brought to the citizens of Umrym every so often from the mysterious, secretive great tower.

Thinking about it now, Celesyria wondered why she'd never found it suspicious before that gods would require the hand of dwarf women to pass on their decrees.

"Even so," Gramnok said, patting at the completed tunnel with one of his large, hairy hands. "It's not for us to worry about such high things, little sister."

Celesyria smiled, showing the tips of her sharp teeth.

At 137 years of age, she was older than any dwarf in Umrym, and so large compared to Gramnok that she could swallow him whole. Still, she found herself treating him like a big brother, someone who was wise and prone to get in the way of her plans more often than she would like.

As they set to work on another tunnel, they fell into a comfortable silence.

Gramnok, having long since proved his characteristic dwarven loyalty, was tasked with carrying the sacks, boxes, and piles of treasure into the tunnel and ensuring they were placed in a careful manner. Celesyria followed, using the strength of her jaws to lift huge rocks that would be nearly impossible to move without the help of one of her kind.

"They asked me today, you know," she said after a few moments, helping Gramnok to situate one of the larger chests of treasure upon a rolling cart. *"They wish for me to begin training as a Guardian. The Commander spoke to me herself."*

"That's wonderful!" Gramnok said, a smile lighting up his bearded face. "Even though you're a member of an old Guardian family, not everyone is chosen. The Commander sees something in you."

"Right," Celesyria said, picking at a piece of dirt on the cavern floor with a front claw. *Not everyone is chosen, except perhaps when our race is dying out,* she thought to herself.

She appreciated Gramnok's faith in her, but she couldn't shake the feeling that most of the dragons she knew seemed to see her as a problem, a nuisance that never fit in in Whitespire. She doubted much had changed in that regard, whether she was being recruited for the Guardians or not.

As a hatchling, she'd dreamed of visiting other far-off cities, hoping that somewhere in Umrym she would find those who were like her, interested in knowledge rather than brute strength.

Unfortunately, having done a fair bit of travel since, she had come to realize that dragons were mostly the same everywhere. Still, late at night, as she tried to fall asleep in her nest, she would imagine places that rested off of the edge of the map, beyond the North Sea.

There, perhaps, there was something more.

"You really should be honored, little sister. I heard that

Jaconial was passed over for recruiting once again," Gramnok added, his brown eyes gleaming. Jaconial was a female dragon near Celesyria's age that had made fun of her for much of their time in hatchling training. Gramnok, ever loyal, was not a fan of hers, even though he often worked with her father in the mines. "She'll be very happy for you."

"Ha. Well, I feel a bit bad for her," Celesyria said, trying to figure out the best way to put her feelings into words. Gramnok was a good friend, but that didn't mean that he always understood how she saw their world. In any case, it was strange for anyone remotely competent to be passed over in their present situation.

"She works so hard to become a Guardian. She believes in the cause."

"And?" Gramnok said, hefting another bag of treasure into the new tunnel they were working on. There were beads of sweat on his brow, and he was getting to the point of exertion where she was beginning to smell him.

"I don't. Not anymore. Not the way that I should, if I'm going to serve the Dracodei," Celesyria said, her words tumbling out in a rush. She was thankful that she could speak directly into Gramnok's head. She would have gotten her tongue tangled up otherwise. *"I've learned things about them. Things that you—"*

Before she could finish, she noticed another dwarf passing behind them, wheeling two carts fastened together, heavy with treasure.

"Hello," Gramnok said, tipping his felt cap and giving a slight bow. The other dwarf returned the gesture, breaking into a whistling song as he made his way down another large hall, the wheels clattering on the stone as he went.

"Even if the Dracodei cannot read our thoughts, you do

not know where their eyes and ears are," he snapped in a whisper, turning to Celesyria and wagging a finger in front of her enormous face. "You may wish to be some sort of revolutionary, but I am quite content with my work. And my life, for that matter!"

"I know. I'm sorry," she said, hoping that the softness of her tone would serve to quiet his own. The stereotype was true: dwarves were prone to very hot tempers, and Gramnok was no exception.

"I mean it, Celesyria," he said, the red flush leaving his cheeks as he took a few breaths. "Whatever it is you're getting yourself tangled up in, I do not wish to be involved."

"I know why the dragons are dying, Gramnok."

* * *

Celesyria explained what she had read in Helmm as Gramnok kept watch.

Though no one could hear her speaking to Gramnok unless she wished it, they could still hear his responses. They mostly consisted of grunts, harrumphs, and an occasional vague follow-up question, but for once he was probably right to be careful.

"I see," he said, finally, his words hanging in the air.

They had finished the tunnel, and would soon be expected to report to one of the dining halls for dinner, but they lingered in the privacy of the treasure caves for a few moments longer.

"So? Will you come?" She asked, trying to make her voice sound hopeful despite her well-earned pessimism.

"Little sister," Gramnok started, looking down at his heavy black work boots. "You have not seen all of the Codex Veritatis yourself. What if you are wrong?"

"I know what I saw."

"I'm sure that you thought you saw just that," Gramnok crooned. Celesyria puffed hot air out of her nostrils, wishing that she was high above the Severed Summits where she would be free to let forth a burst of flame. Would it kill him to treat her as an equal rather than a misfit he'd taken under his wing? Just once?

"So you think I'm a liar. Or crazy."

"No!" Gramnok exclaimed, a little too loudly, shaking his head. He gestured toward the hall that led upward out of the treasure caves, making his way slowly as he talked. Fortunately, no one seemed to have heard his outburst. "I think you're reading things in old languages you don't understand very well, and in your quest for answers, you may be getting things wrong."

"I'm not wrong, Gramnok. I don't have all of the details, but I'm not wrong."

"How will you prove this to the Envoy? Can you find a complete copy of the Codex?" Gramnok whispered as he nodded to a couple of dwarf-women heading in the other direction, their dresses sweeping against the stone floor.

Despite the fact that they were still underground, the air tasted somehow better as they made their way closer to the surface.

"Do you even know that a complete copy exists at all?" He prodded. "I thought it was a myth."

"That's what the humans say."

"But you're certain you've seen at least parts of it."

"Yes. And I think that the Dracodei have the rest. Somewhere."

Gramnok put his fingers over his ears for a moment, as

though he could prevent her words from reaching his brain.

"You need to respect the gods. Who knows what will happen if you don't?" His voice was low and rumbling now, even as he smiled at another group of dwarves and a dragon who walked passed them.

"I knew you wouldn't come. But can I trust you to keep quiet about this?" She pleaded, lowering her head until her eyes met his. It was no easy task - she had to press the bottom of her jaw against the floor.

"Please?"

Gramnok looked around, giving a clumsy bow to another dwarf-woman called Cingra that Celesyria suspected he fancied. She refrained from making fun, for once, though Gramnok it seemed could not resist a final longing gaze as she walked out of sight.

"Fine. I will say nothing. But you had better be careful."

"Careful of what? Who can threaten a dragon?"

"The courts, for one. Blasphemy is a crime."

"I'm going to be careful, alright?"

"Just remember how Boneshire got its name," Gramnok said.

They had reached the huge hall at the end of the passageway, where dozens of dwarves and several dragons were milling about, talking amongst themselves. He gave her a nod before walking off to visit a few of his friends, probably nervous that being seen with her might somehow implicate him in her plot.

The Elves would not dare to leave Nox again. It was they whom she feared even more than the courts and prisons of dragons, dwarves, and men.

She hoped that she was right. She had to be.

Soon, she would tell her mother and father that she was

joining the Guardian training that began tomorrow. She hated to lie to them, but outweighing the guilt was the resentment she felt.

Why couldn't they at least try to understand? She left the crowded room and headed down an empty, echoing passage, a shortcut that led to one of the smaller dining halls.

They've always treated me like some freak, like nothing that I care about means anything. But I hate to lie to them. If I had courage, I would tell them the truth, no matter the cost.

She shivered slightly in the dark shadows of the little-used tunnel. Most of the dragons had no reason to come this way, and she had hoped that it would be a good place to be alone to think. But she couldn't shake the feeling that she was being watched, even though she had yet to do anything wrong.

The guilt sat coiled in the pit of her stomach, insistent and burning, but she ignored the feeling. *I have no choice. I have to act, and I have to do it now.*

As she made her way into the larger hall at the end of the dank passage, she took a large breath. Tomorrow, she would go to Boneshire, and if she was lucky, she would find the Envoy on his way home.

* * *

Wes stared into the orange flames as sparks and smoke drifted off into the dusky sky. The air was drier here than in the mountains, and the snaps and hisses from the fire seemed dangerously loud.

Ahead of him, just over a small, dusty ridge of red stone, lay a vast ribcage sticking out of the dirt. If the sudden change in the color and feel of the place was not enough, Wes was now certain that he had crossed into Boneshire.

The last two days had been lonely, but he had experienced a bit of good luck, at last.

As he made his way out of the mountains, he'd found one of the deer, drinking from a shallow creek. The final stretch of his journey through Umrym was easier, after so much time spent on foot, but he was not particularly relieved to have reached his usual camping spot.

Boneshire was an unfriendly land.

Wes had heard many magnificent tales about the place, once a great Kingdom ruled by the House of Noctua. Ever since the royal House had fallen two hundred years ago, it had become the most dangerous and largely lawless place in Kaveryth.

The bureaucratic administration that remained was dedicated to collecting treasure for the sacrifices to the Dracodei, as well as selecting Witnesses when Boneshire's turn came up.

Beyond that, the various cities and towns were left to their own devices, with varying degrees of success. Many of the good people of Boneshire were effectively ruled by roving gangs of criminals, gambling lords, or worse.

"Alright, boy," Wes said, giving his stag a pat as the animal nibbled at a patch of dry grass sticking out from between two red rocks. "Let's hope the ironwolves stay in their dens tonight, hey?"

He listened to the lonely sound of his own words, small in the vast darkening sky above him. He had taken to speaking with his deer more and more that day, feeling a bit better about it than when he was talking to himself.

It alarmed him that only a few days alone with his thoughts was enough to make him feel not only depressed but slightly mad.

On the steady fire was a pot of soup, fashioned with the meat of a skinny rabbit he had managed to catch and various dry foods he was growing tired of eating. It looked appetizing, but Wes thought only of his dead companions, and how he would happily eat Odrigh's seaside fare every night if it could bring them back.

You can't bring them back. He reached his hands out over the edge of the fire and rubbed them together. Though Boneshire had a look of heat about it, the nights were often frigid.

There was a sound then, far away, but loud enough to be heard over the hungry, crackling fire. He cupped an ear with his hand, trying to make it out. *Not ironwolves, at least.*

No, this was a bigger sound, like a wind that had gone rogue and broken away from its brothers. He heard it again, closer now, and watched as the sparks from his fire were tossed in all directions.

His deer looked up from the grass he'd been eating, the whites of his eyes showing as he gazed up into the darkness. Suddenly Wes wished that there was no fire, as it was making everything that lay beyond it difficult to see.

How fast the night falls. He squinted at the sky overhead. The lost wind had gone quiet. Wes felt the pounding of his heart within his chest, several beats punctuating the sudden silence before he allowed himself to breathe.

Before he could think of anything else, there was the sound again, a great rush of air crashing into him so hard that he tumbled backward, landing on his bottom for the second time in recent memory.

His deer was rearing again.

Wes could hear the pounding of hooves hitting the edge of the makeshift fire pit and sending sparks flying. He felt the sting of hot liquid on his fingertips. The soup pot had been knocked to the ground, the liquid spreading out as Wes stumbled to his feet, turning in circles and blinking at the sky.

The fire was regaining some of its strength, and he could see that other than the soup, his little camp was still intact. To his dismay, however, the deer had bolted in the tumult, leaving no sign as to which direction he had run. The darkness that lay beyond the camp was so complete that the animal may as well have run off into another world.

"I'm so sorry," came a voice that was not a voice. *"I nearly hit that big rock, and I misjudged my landing. It won't happen again."*

Wes, not knowing exactly what else to do, continued to turn around in clumsy circles, trying to find the source of the words, or the deer, or both.

"Hello? Show yourself!" He said, a slight waver in his voice. He reached down, grasping a long stick that stuck out of the edge of the fire, raising the flaming end like a torch.

"Right. Sorry. Here... I'm right here." The voice had moved outside of his head. "Don't be afraid."

Wes spun again, facing the direction of the sound. He lowered his stick, blinking as he tried to drive the brightness of the flame from behind his eyelids.

There, just beyond the fire, was a dragon.

Chapter Five

The dragon was speaking again, her gentle, girlish voice sounding within his head, but Wes struggled to focus on her words.

He could not stop staring at the huge creature, her head alone nearly as large as he was. Her skin was a burnt orange color, rather similar to the reddish sand that covered most of Boneshire, and it was covered with thousands and thousands of tiny scales that glimmered in the firelight.

Her eyes reminded him of the stray cats that lurked about on the streets of Stronghollow, yellow with slits that narrowed every time she looked into the light of the fire.

"I know that this is not the most polite way to introduce myself, but I didn't have many good options," the dragon said.

"Er—that's alright," Wes said. "What's your name?" He

wished that he had a more intelligent question to ask, but in his shock, it was the best that he could do.

It seemed that the dragon could only speak into his mind within close proximity, and that her powers did not extend to hearing his thoughts. As far as he could tell, he still had to speak the normal way, out loud, feeling rather foolish as he did so.

"*Celesyria. And you're the Envoy Wes, of the House of Cervos, rulers of the Kingdom of Silverfell,*" she said, without any need to take a breath or pause.

"You know a lot about me."

"*Not really. The dragons don't tend to concern themselves very much with human affairs. Most of us, anyway,*" she amended, curling her tail around her body as she rested near the fire. Wes was certain that it was too small to make much of a difference in warming her, but he got up from his seat anyway, stuffing another of the small logs he had scavenged into the burning coals.

"*The dwarves keep their libraries, though, even if most of them care more for gems than books.*"

"You can fit in a dwarf library?" he asked, unable to quell his curiosity.

"*Not well. But let us get to the point. There will be time for questions on the daily lives of dragons later.*"

"While we're on the topic, I do have one question. No one seems to have seen many dragons in recent years. Ever since the elves came over from Nox..." Wes let the sentence fade away. *Nothing has been the same since Silverfell lost its monarchy.*

Nothing has been the same since I lost everything.

Celesyria's yellow eyes blinked a couple of times as she looked off beyond the fire, lost in thought.

"What happened to them?" Wes prompted.

"That is why I've come," Celesyria said finally. There was sadness in her voice. *"Well, part of the reason."*

"Okay."

Wes settled back on the stump he was using as a seat, taking a bite of dried meat. It was not as good as the ruined soup, but he was famished. He felt rude not offering his guest anything, but he resisted the urge to be polite. She'd eat his entire supply in a single bite.

"Have you ever heard of the High One?" Celesyria asked.

"No, I don't think so," Wes answered, mouth still partially full.

"What about the Codex Veritatis?"

"The books? I've heard of them, yes. Written at the beginning of the world, by the pen of the Dracodei themselves. A legend, nothing more."

"What you have been told of the Codex is a lie," Celesyria said slowly. Her voice had gone rather cold, the cheerfulness extinguished like a snuffed fire. *"You have been taught other lies, as well. So have essentially all humans, dwarves, and even dragons, as far as I can tell."*

"Except you?" Wes said, a little harsher than he'd meant it to sound. "I may not look the part, but I've received the finest education in the Four Kingdoms. The head of the Septemvirate is like a father to me. I think he of all people would know about it if the Codex actually existed."

"I don't mean to impugn your knowledge, or elevate my own," Celesyria said, lifting her head from the ground and sending a puff of dust into the fire. *"Everyone in Whitespire thinks I'm a fool. If I thought they would listen, I would have gone to them. If there had been another way but this—"* she raised a claw,

gesturing around the dark campsite "*—I would have done it already. I came to you because there is no one else I can turn to. There is no one else who has the power to make things right.*"

Wes laughed a little at this, shaking his head at the dragon perched across the fire from him, her scales glittering like jewels. "If you think that the Envoy has power, perhaps it is your education that was deficient."

"*You carry the sacrifices of the Four Kingdoms, Wes Cervos. Every man, woman, and child relies upon you fulfilling your calling. There is only one person in all Kaveryth that bears the moonscar,*" Celesyria said, her tone forceful as she sent another accidental cloud of dust into the fire, choking the flames.

The night seemed to close in around them, embracing the strange pair in their shared loneliness. There was a pause for several breaths as Wes tried to gather his thoughts.

It had been only days ago that he had stopped at this very same campsite, joking and laughing with Lev and Odrigh. Now, they were gone. His deer was gone for the second time. And a dragon had appeared out of nowhere to demand that he help her change the world. It was all too much.

"*Wes. I need your help. You're the only one with the power to—*"

"The power to bring death wherever I go?" he snapped, jumping up from his seat. "I am destined to watch everyone I care about be killed so that I can continue to act as a beast of burden, carrying treasure off into the darkness. That isn't power. It's slavery."

"*You sell yourself short,*" Celesyria said. She gestured a claw toward the log he had been sitting on, and with a roll of his eyes, he sat back down. "*But even if that were true, it doesn't mean that you can't help me to make things better for all of Kaveryth. It is upon you that the lie of all lies currently rests. And it is upon your*" *shoulders that the truth can once more be carried, if you decide to bear it."*

Wes opened his mouth to speak, the dwindling fire and encroaching chill momentarily forgotten, but he did not get the chance. Celesyria pressed on, her eyes flashing in the ember light.

"Listen to me. The Dracodei are not the true gods of Kaveryth. They are not gods at all."

* * *

Whatever Wes had expected Celesyria to say, this was not it.

It sounded fantastical, like one of the stories that the children in the villages on the edge of Stronghollow might tell. Unlike those tales, however, hers was blasphemous.

"How dare you say such a thing," Wes said, trying to keep his voice level. "In Silverfell, even a dragon would be sent to the dungeons for that, if not executed!"

"I know. That's why I had to find you before you returned."

"What makes you think that I won't tell the Septemvirate?"

"Faith," Celesyria said, her voice soft.

A moment of silence stretched out between them before she continued.

"I found a portion of the Codex Veritatis that I was not sure existed. I'd heard it mentioned in other books, but I had to see it for myself. I went to the Great Library at Helmm, and there it was, seemingly forgotten. I believe it to be authentic."

She glanced at Wes, as though expecting an interruption, but he remained quiet.

Whatever faith you have, you misplace it by turning to me.

Celesyria continued.

"There is a prophecy. It was given by the High One, one thousand years ago."

"Who is this so-called god?" Wes said, feeling a nervous twinge in the pit of his stomach. Until a few moments before, he had never heard of such a being. Though there was no one around to report him for blasphemy against the Dracodei, the instinct to keep quiet about such things was well ingrained.

"He is the creator of all Kaveryth. And according to this prophecy, He made a promise to the remnant—"

"Who is the remnant?"

"I don't know, exactly," Celesyria said, closing her eyes momentarily as though waiting for him to interrupt again. *"If you would allow me to finish—"*

"You don't know who this remnant is, yet you're sure this prophecy is authentic?"

"It would seem my reading on the temperament of humans in Silverfell was accurate, after all," she quipped, sending a small plume of smoke out of her nostrils. Wes had never seen a dragon breathe fire before, and he decided that he no longer wanted to.

"The High One made a promise. For one thousand years, He would allow all Kaveryth to persist in their evils, but at the end of that period, He would bring his people back to the truth."

"How?"

Celesyria lowered her head, looking down at the red sand beneath her claws.

"The portion of the Codex that I read did not detail the entire plan, but I've seen enough to act. The High One promised that after the thousand years has ended, He will bring death and corruption to those who have usurped his throne, and life to those who continue to serve Him."

Wes thought of the dwarves that had ambushed him and murdered Lev and Odrigh. Never before had he heard of dwarves daring to violate their alliance with the dragons. Had it been going on for a while already, or was it something just beginning?

His mind was spinning.

All his life, he had cast the history of Kaveryth in a certain light. His people, the people of the Kingdom of Silverfell had their place in the world, and so did everyone else.

The other Kingdoms were their allies, the dragons—with the help of dwarves—were their protectors, and the elves of Nox were their enemy.

What Celesyria was telling him threatened to upend the way he looked at the world. Of course, there had always been small factions of human enemies within, especially in Boneshire, but even they usually had deep ties with Nox.

If dwarves were seeking the help of the elves... It was absurd. It had never happened, *could* never happen. The Guardians relied upon the dwarves to craft their armor, to breed their meat, to mine their materials.

If there was a dwarf uprising against the dragons, the elves might actually have a chance to take over the Four Kingdoms. It was unthinkable.

The entire story was preposterous. So why did he feel such terror at the thought that could be true?

"Have you noticed anything about the dragons?" Celesyria asked. Wes nodded, feeling unable to speak. He stared at the dying embers, deep in thought.

Though he could hear Celesyria's voice in his mind, his ears had heard nothing but the rush of cold wind and the coo of far-off birdsong. *She is mad. She must be mad. None of this makes any sense at all. How could four entire Kingdoms and even the Septemvirate be wrong about something so central to our existence?* He wondered. He could hear the birds drawing closer now, their cheerful music a strange backdrop to the even stranger conversation.

"*We're dying, Wes. When my parents were young, there were many thousands of us in Umrym. When I was a hatchling, not long after the fall of the House of Noctua, there were perhaps four thousand left.*

"And how many remain now?" Wes asked, rubbing the top of his dry mouth with his tongue.

"*There are less than two thousand of us left,*" Celesyria said.

There were tears pooling at the corners of her eyes. As she blinked, they dripped onto the ground, creating little puddles of red mud. "*Every day, nearly, someone dies. We have not told our human allies, though they must have their suspicions, but the dwarves know.*"

She gave him a knowing look. He was certain she had made the same inferences he had.

"That doesn't mean the prophecy is true," Wes said, trying to keep from crying himself. He hated how easily he cried whenever someone else did. His older brother Roven had seldom cried, let alone his father. It was an embarrassing trait, a remnant of his childhood, reminding him that even at seventeen, he was still a boy in so many ways.

"There could be a sickness," he continued. "Or a poison. Surely your leaders—or the Dracodei—" he stammered.

"*No one has ever seen them!*" Celesyria snapped. Wes could see the remaining snot in her cavernous nostrils, but the tears were gone in an instant. "*Don't you understand? We speak of them living in the skies above the spire, where they never need to land. Isn't that convenient? They speak to us only by letter. They use dwarven women to deliver their messages to our leaders."*

"So you're saying they don't exist?"

"I'm saying that they are not gods. They are imposters, eager to keep the treasures of the Four Kingdoms pouring into Umrym. Now perhaps more than ever. We can scarcely manage to protect our own borders, let alone the dwarven mining industry. Someone is doing this, probably a group of someones. It could be dragons, sure, but they are not gods."

Wes felt his anger bubbling over then, leaping off of the stump and striding over to the dragon, standing so close that his face nearly touched hers.

For once in his life, he felt courageous, his rage dulling all sense of fear. He could hear the hammering of his heart and the rush of blood pounding in his ears.

Celesyria was silent, drawing her head back slightly as he leaned even closer. He could smell the breath whooshing from her nostrils as it formed white clouds in the cold night air.

"My father, mother, and brother did not die to protect me so that I may continue to deliver treasure to a group of bureaucrats!"

He yelled in the dragon's face, feeling a gravelly sting as the words tore forth from the back of his throat. "You're a liar. Go back to Umrym, or I will tell the Septemvirate everything you have said."

* * *

Celesyria stepped back as Wes walked toward her. His face was as red as a beet, and for a moment she thought that he may reach out and strike her with his fists.

"I'm so sorry about your family," she started, pulling her tail closer to her body, a needless protective instinct. Wes would only hurt himself if he struck out in a rage.

She had read about what happened to the King, Queen, and Prince of the House of Cervos. It had saddened her, but it was a whole other thing to meet the one who had been left behind, all alone, with the weight of the Four Kingdoms upon his shoulders.

If only I could make him see that I weep not only for my dead, but for his, as well.

"What does it matter? According to you, they died for nothing," Wes spat. His dark brown eyes flashed with fury. Until that moment, there had been a decided lack of confidence in the way that he carried himself. It made him look like a boy.

Now, in his anger, Celesyria could see the handsome young man that lay beneath.

She had to make him see the truth.

She had to make him see the possibility that she saw.

Somehow, she had to make him listen.

"Never say that!" She said, loud enough to make Wes cover his ears, though it would do no good. *"Your family did not die for corruption and greed. They died to protect someone special. Someone unique, important to the future of the whole world."*

Wes laughed again, the same bitter chuckle as before.

"Who, me? A fat sad-sack with an accident of birth? I'm nothing. Being a part of the royal house has brought me nothing but pain."

"But being the Envoy can bring joy. Not only for yourself or Silverfell, but for all creatures of Kaveryth—"

"It's a lie. You said so yourself."

"The Dracodei may be, but the High One isn't. The Envoy isn't.

The Envoy serves him!"

"How do you know? How do you know any of this? You find it in another one of your dwarf libraries?" Wes spat.

"I've found several portions of the Codex. I don't know how, exactly, but it's very clear that the Envoy has an important role in service of the High One," Celesyria said in a rush, the booming strength gone from her voice.

She was growing tired. She wondered how long it would be before her father and mother realized that she had not gone to Ancora Canyon for training like she'd agreed to do.

"I will find out more, I promise. But I need your help."

For a moment, Wes hesitated.

He stood there looking at her, his gaze unrelenting. She felt that she might blush if dragons were capable of it.

It was clear to her that noble blood flowed in his veins. He was not merely an overweight boy from the forest Kingdom.

He was a son of the fathers and mothers of that great land, the inheritance of generations. Even if his words denied his importance, his countenance betrayed him. And it went deeper than the moonscar that rested on his right cheek.

"Please. Please, listen. Help us," she pleaded, lowering her head into a bow that nearly touched his boots.

"If what you say is true, the dragons deserve what is happening to them," Wes said, stepping forward, his voice as cold and biting as the wind that swirled around them.

He grabbed the sides of Celesyria's face in his hands, yanking her nose upwards until she was looking into his fierce, raging eyes.

She flinched but was too stunned to move. He was angry, and anger made him reckless.

"Wes, I know that what I'm claiming about my race is terrible,

but not everyone—"

"Go. Now."

She pulled away from the roughness of his touch, knocking over one of his packs. She heard the gurgle of liquid running out of a burst waterskin. It would be seeped up by the sand in seconds.

"Wes—"

"Go! Fly!" Wes yelled at her.

He was fumbling in his pocket for something. He found whatever it was and tossed it on the ground, where the darkness shrouded it from her view.

"I quit. Wait for the next Envoy and try your chances with," he said, his voice suddenly small. She watched as he began to weep, great sobs wracking his body as he collapsed near the remains of the fire and leaned against a large rock.

"Wes. Why won't you listen to me?" Celesyria tried again. She hadn't thought about what knowing the truth would mean for him, after everything that he'd lost. *You should have been gentle,* she chided herself. *What good is it to tell the truth if the person cannot hear it?*

"Just leave," he said, putting his head in his hands.

High One, if you listen to dragons, please help me find a way to make him see. She attempted to pray, unsure if it would do any good.

With a few quick pumps of her wings, Celesyria lifted herself into the air and made off into the night, leaving only silence behind.

Chapter Six

A howl sounded from far across the desert, sending a chill deep into Wes' bones. He pressed his eyes shut for a moment as he walked aimlessly, wishing to be anywhere else.

His last words to Celesyria echoed in his mind, over and over. They felt unreal, like someone else had said them.

But she was gone, and it was too late for him to make amends. He had watched as she flew away into the night, moving so fast that within less than a minute she was out of sight.

He wasn't sure how far behind him his camp was, or exactly where he might return to the road, but he couldn't stop to think about it. It was too dark to see very well, but at least he could tell by the visible constellations that he was headed in a north-easterly direction.

The fat white moon had disappeared, lost behind a patch of

thick clouds. His thoughts continued to churn as he took one step, and then another, and then another, lost in the rhythm of simple, forward motion.

He would reach the Kingdom of Aridmoor eventually, but beyond that, he had no plans.

Before storming off, he had thrown the Claim on the ground, more certain than ever before that being born Envoy had been a terrible mistake.

A mistake by whom? He wondered, nearly tripping over several rocks that lay in front of him as he marched on. *The Dracodei? This High One the dragon speaks of? If she's right, this High One of hers is no more genuine than the dragon usurpers. If He was the true God, He would have known to pick someone else.*

Despite his indignation, he couldn't help but feel a pang of familiar guilt rising within him as he walked. The slow, relentless use of his overtired leg muscles had blunted the edges of his anger, leaving him exhausted. Finding a suitable rock nearby, of which there were many to choose from, he decided to take a few moments to breathe.

The moon escaped from the clouds, high overhead, and he shivered as the chill of midnight gripped the dry, windy clime. He looked down at his hands in the gleam of the moonlight, noticing that a few droplets of Odrigh's, or perhaps Lev's, blood had fallen on the fingers of his gloves.

Whether Celesyria is right or wrong, I do not know what will happen if I... abandon the people as Envoy. He turned over the familiar dilemma in his mind as though he would stumble upon the perfect solution if only he considered it enough.

It was hard to believe how much the world had changed in his short lifetime. He thought of before, of a time when he wasn't so very alone. He had not resented his calling then. It wasn't always easy—the life of an Envoy is set apart, and that brings its own difficulties—but it hadn't always felt so hopeless.

There had been a time when he was able to take pride in what the Dracodei had chosen him to do. He would visit the palace gallery with his father, looking at paintings of the Envoys who had come before him, listening to his father's tales about their lives. And then, his father would show him the small gold marker that lay beneath an empty portrait frame, reminding him that when he reached the end of his life, he would be remembered.

Now, the thought of his face hanging in the palace for centuries only made him ache. He didn't want this anymore. His face, his name, would forever bring forth memories of tragedy and death.

The question drifted into his mind like smoke. He had asked it of himself many times, often while fingering the hilt of a blade, and that was as far as it had gone.

Could I bring myself to draw my own blood and escape my fate forever?

It was at that moment that a fresh howl sounded, much closer now. There was a strange, cooing sort of sound at the very end of it that brought Wes onto his feet at once.

Only ironwolves howled like that.

Wes looked up at the stars, trying to focus long enough to find the familiar constellations he had been following as several more howls rang out. He pressed the fingertips of his blood-stained gloves into the sides of his forehead, closing his eyes, trying to calm himself as the calls of the predators continued.

He took off in the chosen direction at a run, the forbidden question echoing in his mind, taunting him.

He imagined a great pack of ironwolves, their ashen fur thick and shiny upon their huge frames, their sharp teeth bared. He could hear their calls, taunting him as he ran. His chest heaved with effort, and twice he fell, tearing the knees of his pants as he landed on sharp gravel. The howls had been joined by growling, a deep sound that reminded him of thick cloth being torn.

He cried out as he jumped over a bush that lay in his way, not noticing the thick spines of the plant until they were biting into his flesh.

He cursed, tears pricking at his eyes as he stumbled once more, the new puncture wounds from the nasty plant stinging as his knees smashed into stone. He was at the base of a steep, stony hill that hid the light from the moon.

He scrabbled in the dirt for a moment before getting to his feet. He could hear the howls again, and the deep rumbles of hungry mouths, so close that he feared they could snap at his heels.

He fought his way up the hill as best he could, wrenching an ankle in a space between two rocks, desperate to return to the glow of the moonlight above.

He imagined one of the ironwolves taking hold of his ankle and dragging him down the way he came, followed by a great press of furry bodies as the pack descended on him, ready to rip him limb from limb.

It would not be a quick death.

It would not be the simple bite of a knife in the right place.

It would be torture.

"Okay, I admit it. I don't have the guts. I take it back, gods!" he cried out, his voice barely loud enough to compete with the howling behind him. His throat was ragged. It hurt him to yell, but he continued, his words tumbling out in a torrent. "I'm sorry. I'm sorry. I do not want to die. Please! Let me live, O great Dracodei. Give me another chance. I will bring an extra portion of treasure. Okay, two extra portions. Forgive me!"

He listened for a moment, chest heaving, ankle throbbing. He wished more than anything to hear the flap of Celesyria's wings, but she was gone, and it was his fault. The cry of the wolves was the only thing that existed in all the world, pressing out everything else, leaving him wrapped in a cocoon of cold fear.

Wes found a gap in the stones and began to shuffle inside.

His belt caught on the edge of a rock, but he managed to yank it free, diving head-first into the darkness. He didn't know if it was a cave or only a depression in the hill face, but he was out of options. He felt the warmth of blood on his left arm as he went deeper, his body too big for the space, the walls straining to keep him out.

The howling was relentless.

In the brief moments between the wolf cries, he could hear the smaller yip of pups, the sound of shifting rocks bearing the weight of large bodies. He curled up until his thick figure was squished as small as it would go, his nose pressed against the dark dirt of the back wall, certain that some horrid desert bug would crawl into his nostrils. He pressed his hands over his ears, tears falling freely once again, and closed his eyes. He could see nothing but blackness.

"High One," he whispered, tucking his chin toward his heaving chest and pulling his sore knees inward. "If You are the true God, allow me to live."

* * *

The morning sun was bright against the back wall of the cave. Wes could see that it was smaller than it had seemed last night, a burrow for some unknown desert creature. There were tiny bits of bone on the floor, and a pile of foul-smelling feathers in the opposite corner from where he had fallen asleep.

In the light of day, he could see that the hard-packed red sand wall that rested at the tip of his nose could not possibly have held any sneaking insect, a fact for which he was very grateful.

How am I alive? He attempted to stretch out his arms and legs, trying to release the cramping and get his blood flowing.

There was enough room to turn around, but only barely, and his muscles ached from the awkward position in which he had slept. The floor was hard, and bits of jagged bone had pricked at his back, leaving sore spots.

The events of the prior night were fuzzy, removed.

He remembered the scream of the wolves and the desperate attempt to get over the hill and back into the moonlight. It had been terrifying, and then the cave had appeared just in time, a miracle cut into the landscape.

Providential, almost.

He remembered crawling in, and he remembered ranting madly at the darkness, but after that, his memories felt slippery and uncertain.

He gave his head a turn back and forth, attempting to get the crick out from his neck. *I had best get out of here before the burrow-owner returns.*

As he emerged into the harsh sunlight, he shielded his eyes, looking down at his feet. One ankle was swollen in its boot, and both of his pant legs were torn in multiple places, but he looked decent enough.

Aside from the ache, and the filth of dried blood, he was well enough to continue.

I need to find the camp. I need to retrieve the Claim. Urgent guilt twisted around in his belly.

What if it's lost? What will Dorold think? How could I have been so impulsive and foolish?

He attempted to set aside his worries as he turned to face in the direction from which he had come, his eyes aching in the rays of light that cast themselves across the desert.

As far as he could see, there were red stones, small desert bushes, and the dried husks of last summer's flowers.

Every so often the natural landscape was interrupted by some long-dead dragons' bone, poking up toward the impossibly blue sky.

It was beautiful and terrifying at once, and in that moment, he remembered.

I asked the High One to spare my life.

He squinted toward the northern edge of the world, looking for anything that would indicate the distance to Aridmoor and safety.

He remembered curling up, desperate, praying to a new God.

A God that was not the Dracodei.

He felt like throwing up.

Such an offense was punishable not merely by imprisonment or exile, but by death.

How could he have said such a thing, even in the height of such terror? It was the Dracodei who had always been loyal, fighting for all of the people of the Four Kingdoms, keeping the elves from destroying Kaveryth.

I wasn't in my right mind. He turned toward the top of the hill and began to climb, taking a drink of water from his almost-empty waterskin.

He was desperately hungry, but it would have to wait. Finding the Claim was his sole focus now.

No one will ever know what I have said. I will retrieve the Claim, and I will make for Aridmoor as planned. All will be well.

It was much easier to climb the hill in daylight. As he crested the peak, he could see the shadows that lay on the western side, the early morning sun too low to reach it. He felt a rush of wind as he made his way downward, careful not to turn his ankle in one of the many small spaces between the rocks.

He felt safer now that the night had passed, and he could hear nothing but the pleasant chirp of birds, though he could not see any nearby. The calls of the ironwolves seemed like a distant dream.

It was a coincidence. He descended into the cool shadows where the wind had gone silent. *The High One, real or imagined, had nothing to do with anything. Perhaps the Dracodei helped me, or perhaps the wolves simply gave up.*

It was already growing much warmer, even without the heat of the sun at his back.

In the safety of daylight, he could almost believe his own words.

He could see a familiar ridge, not so far away, and began to make for it as he reached the flat bottom of sand. He felt a brief glimmer of hope at the thought that Celesyria would be back at the camp, after all.

He shook his head, sending his curls bobbing out from where he'd tucked them behind his ears.

None of that matters now. She's gone, it's too late. I need to find the Claim and escape this cruel desert.

* * *

The camp looked different in the daylight. Wes could see the remnant of his fire and three socks that he had left behind by mistake, but alas, his deer was nowhere to be seen.

He suppressed the urge to swear. Though he hadn't expected a sudden shift in his fate, the lingering hope had been there nonetheless, and the loss of it pained him.

Before he could begin to mope, he felt a sudden intuition that something was amiss. He took a few steps toward the ashen remains of the fire, stooping down to pick up the mismatched socks and shaking them until they were free of the red sand that covered every inch of the area.

He listened.

He could hear nothing but the gentle swish of wind, punctuated every few minutes by birdsong. The breeze was pleasant now, carrying a scent that he associated with the coming of spring.

The whole desert looked much more pleasant when it was cast in sunshine. Even the distant protrusions of old dragon bones could have passed for cheery.

He imagined how much Silverfell would have changed while he was away, the pine trees free of snow, the barren oak branches beginning to grow the buds that brought forth green leaves.

Spring was so close.

All he had to do was make it home, or make it even into Aridmoor, and everything would go back to normal.

Shaking off the chill that continued to press upon the top of his spine, he began to search for the Claim. He couldn't remember exactly where he had thrown it. The basic layout of the camp confused him now that it was no longer dark.

Had Celesyria stood on the north side? Had he been to the west, or the south? He closed his eyes for a moment, rubbing away the beads of sweat that were beginning to gather on his brow. The day promised to be blazing hot.

Perhaps there. He noticed a thick stand of bushes of a sort common to Boneshire, all spiny gray branches and twisting vine in the off-season.

For a few weeks, right around the summer Feast of Offering, he knew that they would be covered in bright pink flowers, smelling like the finest perfume in Windshear. Wes knelt at the base of the bushes, carefully pressing his gloved hand beneath the nearest one and feeling about for the piece of metal, avoiding the thorns.

He searched for several minutes, pressing further with the help of his sheathed sword, but he could not see even a glimmer that would indicate the location of the missing Claim.

The sun was screaming hot upon his back, and he could feel sweat beading at the bottom of his spine and dripping into his pants.

How could I have been so stupid? He tore his already damaged gloves on one of the thorns as his search became more frantic.

What did I think was going to happen? I bear the Moonscar. I cannot take the throne of Silverfell. My duty to my people is to be the Envoy, nothing else.

Having reached the end of the row of plants, he stood, trying to shake the endless specks of red sand from his trousers, boots, and cloak. Somehow, bits of it had ended up in the skin of his neck, transforming his sweat into a gritty mud that chafed against his flesh whenever he turned his head.

He had never longed for a bath so much in his life, but the

sky remained stubbornly blue, free of even the smallest cloud. As he took off his gloves, trying to clean yet more sand from one of the cuts he had accumulated, he heard a sound.

He felt the chill return. It was not a cry, exactly, nor was it the sound of footsteps. It sounded muffled, like it was coming from very far away. He stepped around the barrier of thorny bushes, noticing a hollow behind them that he had not seen the evening before.

In the hidden space between the bushes and the sunset-colored stone behind them was another fire pit, a small leather pack of dwarven make, and two small children, bound and gagged.

One of them was trying to cry out, terror in her eyes, as Wes stepped between the children and the fierce sunlight, basking them in shadow. Their skin was a smooth, dark brown, and they were dressed in decent clothes that had seen far better days.

"Shh, shh, it's alright," Wes said, stammering, as he knelt and tried to untie the gags. His heart was pounding as he looked over his shoulder, seeing nothing but the bushes and the blue sky over their heads. "Sit still. Let me help," he continued, trying to get his fingers into the knot at the back of the female child's gag. Beside her was a boy, who looked somewhat younger and perhaps even more terrified.

It was no use. They had been gagged with rough, unfinished leather straps, knotted multiple times. Wes cringed at the red welts on the edges of the children's lips, wondering how long they had suffered.

More than ever, he wished for the presence of his companions, or even Celesyria. Instead, he was alone, unsure who had captured the poor children or when they would return. He thought of the dwarf-made bag sitting by the fire as he began to work on the thinner straps that held the girl's hands and feet bound.

He knew that human slave-sellers were known to capture people throughout the Four Kingdoms and lead them through Boneshire on their way to Nox, but dwarves? Such a thing had never been seen before.

Then again, neither had dwarf bandits in Umrym ever attacked and killed an Envoy's companions.

He drew one of his knives from where it hung on his belt, the heat and effort pushing all of his questions from his mind as he began to saw at the girl's restraints. His father had given him the twin blades when he was a young child, long before he'd learned to use the sword. They were curved and sharp, with little flowers carved into their silvery hilts. "A reminder that true strength is not found in cruelty, but mercy," he'd said.

The sleek knife was not well suited for cutting leather bonds in a hurry, but he continued, tearing away at the straps a little at a time.

Just as he began to get the girl's legs free, he heard the muffled screams again as the little ones cried out.

He went still, sunlight glinting off of the curved blade.

Somewhere beyond the bushes, across the other side of the camp, he could hear the sound of men's banter.

Chapter Seven

Celesyria counted the great constellations as she flew, naming them one by one. *Manta. The Shield. Vavoren.* Ever since she was a hatchling, she had loved the stars. Her father had taught her how to navigate the sky, where the only map available was painted in pinpricks of light. Now, she knew them all by instinct. It calmed her, though she could still feel the ache of Wes' rejection, heavy upon her heart.

Perhaps Gramnok is right. The portion of the Codex could be fake. Even if it is authentic, I was a fool to think that I could do something about it.

She looked down, watching as the Severed Summits came into view beneath her feet. The air was very cold, but it was a comforting sort, the kind of chill that made her eager to curl up in her nest with a hot drink. In Boneshire, she felt stripped naked by the cold, dry night air, like it was trying to push her out of the sky and back to where she had come from.

Despite the many ways that she felt like she could never quite fit in, Umrym was home. She had to remember that, even as her thirst for adventure so often lured her away.

As far as her eyes could see were the sheared tops of the mountains where the dragons had fought the invading dwarves, thousands of years ago.

The dragons had at that time been so numerous and so strong that the very rocks of the world bowed to their will. She had grown up hearing tales of those golden days, when her noble race had forged a friendship with the dwarves rather than annihilating them when it was clear that their attempt to take Umrym had failed

A memory surfaced then, several years old, one that she had wanted to bury but never could.

The first time that she had read a portion of the Codex, she had been at home in Whitespire, poring over the selection of books and documents in one of the small, private dwarven libraries that were housed near the mining district.

The owner was a relative of Gramnok Beastbane, and he had been amused that a dragon would take such an interest in his old, dusty writings.

At first, the old dwarf had watched over Celesyria on her vis-its, anxious that she would ruin something with an accidental flick of her tail or turn of a claw. After a while, though, he began to see her as a friend, trusting her to be alone with the ancient history of his race and hers.

She had taken to the study more than anyone expected her to, even Celesyria herself. She would go home at the end of her research sessions, teeming with interesting bits of knowledge that her parents tried to humor, until one day when she read something that she feared she could never share with anyone.

She had spent months holed up, day after day, reading everything that she could get her claws on. In that time, she had torn two books and one part of a scroll, but by then the old dwarf was so used to her presence that he couldn't bear to see her go, even if the rumors of her clumsiness were rather well-founded.

Her old dwarf friend always said that the history of Umrym and all Kaveryth was something that should be kept alive, treasured and carried by everyone, not left as it so often was to the moths and the dust.

It was in a particularly cobweb-infested corner of the library where Celesyria made her great and terrible discovery.

Hidden beneath a corner desk, in a damp part of the room that always smelled strangely of mushrooms, there was a scroll.

She spotted it with her sharp eyes as she was looking over an old map of Ancora Canyon, marveling at the trees that had once spread across its bottom like a blanket of green. She reached for it, managing to catch the bit of ribbon that held it shut with the tip of her claw and pulling it free.

She remembered that she had almost called for the dwarf who owned the library, knowing somehow without even opening the scroll that it was old and forgotten and important.

Instead, she glanced over her shoulder, nearly knocking the hanging ceiling lamp to the floor, and plucked the ribbon loose.

Most of the scroll was written in an old language, likely elven, that she could not read. She marveled over the intricate curling letters, thinking that perhaps she would ask the old dwarf if he knew what it said while suspecting that he likely had no better idea than she did.

As she read a little further down, however, she was surprised to see the familiar, angular strokes of the common tongue, with a few black droplets where the pen had leaked dotting the edges. It was a quote, a couple of lines, encased in little dashes.

The fire-breathers have come to us out of the Farplace, and to the Farplace again they must return. The worst among them and the best alike have no place in this world the High One has made. A soul is necessary for all who belong here, and a soul that race will never possess.

Celesyria pumped her wings with renewed energy, feeling the mountain air wash over her scales, bathing her in cold. She had already reached the edge of Ancora Canyon, barely noticing the passing of time as she flew, lost in her memories.

The Canyon was no longer lush and green, but silvery and barren. The once-great river that had brought life to the vast bottom had dried up into no more than a little slip of water, just passing through.

She imagined the future Guardians that would fill the space as soon as dawn broke, training and honing their skills in flight and combat.

She was supposed to be there.

She *should* be there. For hundreds of years, her family had bred Guardians, offering their lives to the highest cause her race knew.

Deep within her heart, she felt a stirring as she flew.

First soft, and then insistent, a second heartbeat imposing upon her own. She could not bear to join the Guardians, not now, not even to pretend everything was alright. She could not fight for such a cause as theirs. Their wars were built upon nothing but lies.

Umrym was her home by birth, dragons her race by chance, but it was through the race of men that she was meant to fulfill her purpose.

Perhaps in doing so, she would learn about the Farplace. Perhaps it was her true home after all.

"Whether I have a soul or not, I will serve the High One, the true and only lord of all Kaveryth and all the world," she said to the stars, looking up at the familiar constellations that led toward Whitespire.

Soon, the dawn would break free of the eastern mountains.

She turned to face the coming day and flew with all of her might.

* * *

The footsteps were heavy.

Wes could hear the crack of dry branches breaking and the sound of boots on stone. The children moaned from behind their gags, their eyes wide as he continued to hack away at the older girl's bonds.

"Shh," he attempted to whisper, the sound catching on his dry tongue. *Please, please be quiet,* he pleaded to no one in particular as he finally got the captive's legs loose. He looked into her eyes, willing her to understand that she could not move or make a sound.

Not yet.

The voices of the men began to carry on the breeze that had been so pleasant before. Instead of bird song, Wes caught snatches of rough speech. He couldn't make any of it out.

Perhaps they were not using the common tongue, or perhaps they were not as close by as he thought.

He hoped it was the latter.

He jammed his knife under the bands that held the small boy's legs, sawing back and forth against the rough leather with the smooth, curved blade. He thought of his cooking and skinning knives, somewhere in a pack that had been lashed to the runaway deer. This would have to do.

"—A fair price, for the boy," Came a snippet of speech before it was lost to the wind.

"The lovely ones can—"

"Won't be missed—"

Wes began to saw faster, the sweat from his palms soaking into his gloves, making the knife slip.

They're too close.

He got one of the thin bands free. There were several more to get through.

I'll never make it. They'll never make it.

The little boy made another sound as Wes accidentally slashed into his trousers, leaving a small gash that began to bleed. He swore under his breath, fumbling with the knife, trying to get the rest of the leather loose.

"It's okay, it's okay. Be still."

He could see tears pouring onto the boy's cheeks, his eyes closed against the evils that surrounded him. He looked no older than five or six. *What kind of a monster saw an innocent child as a target.*

"The ships won't wait, Belzhdor!" This voice was closer and hard as stone.

The older girl had gotten to her feet with some difficulty. She looked over Wes' shoulder toward the approaching men. He got one of the boy's legs free, sparing a brief glance himself. He saw only scrub bushes, red stones, and clouds of dust where the sand had been shaken loose by the breeze. The men were still far enough away that they couldn't see what their prisoners were doing.

He returned to his work, forcing his hands to slow as he continued. Sweat flowed from beneath his curls, stinging his eyes. He thought of what would happen when the men caught him. He imagined the feeling of swords slicing into his flesh, or perhaps arrows burying themselves in his chest, the final sucking breath as his lungs collapsed like a pierced water bladder.

I would be free of my duty as Envoy. He felt the urge to laugh. How often he had wished for it, safe from the reality of what his death would truly mean.

"We need to make it before the ironwolves come out." This man sounded calmer than the others. *Probably he's the man in charge.*

Wes realized that death was not the worst thing that could befall him. If these were slavers, he knew he would wish for the brief pain of death rather than what they had in store if they allowed him to live.

The girl standing beside him dropped to her knees. Wes could see the rise and fall of her chest as she breathed, the fear in her eyes.

They were coming.

He let the knife go still for a moment, listening, the panic in his gut so strong that he feared he would vomit into the sand. Before him was a small hill of stone. He could climb over it, run, and he would make it.

The slavers would assume the children had gotten themselves loose.

I would make it. I would. His chest shuddered with breath as all went quiet for a moment. *My people need me, don't they?*

It had always been said that before death, a person saw their life flash before their eyes.

It was true.

He saw his mother, her gentle, lined face and shining brown eyes. His father, dressed in his ceremonial robes for court, his dark mustache shining with oil, his cheeks red and cheerful from dinner wine. His brother, Roven, so handsome that he seemed cut from stone, patting a much younger Wes on the head and letting him play with his best toys.

"We could stop at Claywind."

"There's a friendly place there, an inn."

"Right. And the women, prettiest in Boneshire!"

"Not saying much, is it?"

A laugh. A belch. More footsteps, enough that Wes had lost count of how many were coming for them. Three? Five? The boy began to whimper again. The girl, who Wes supposed must be his sister, had sat down beside him, cradling his head in her hands, stroking his smooth black bangs away from his sweaty forehead.

She had no tears in her eyes as she stared at Wes, only resignation, as though she knew he would be a coward in the end.

He clamped his eyes shut, listening to the footsteps, imagining the puffs of sand sent up into the air as they drew nearer.

He imagined Odrigh standing before them, his skin tan and healthy and alive, singing one of his sea songs.

He thought of Lev, pushing his glasses back up onto his nose, telling him in excruciating detail how he adjusted a deer harness incorrectly.

He let the knife fall into the sand. Grabbing hold of the remaining straps of leather, thinned by his blade, he began to tear at them with his hands.

He felt the red pain of blistering fingers, followed by a snap so loud that he was sure the entire desert heard it.

He looked into the little boy's eyes as he helped him to his feet. Unlike his sister, his gaze held nothing but impenetrable, childish hope. They betrayed a blind confidence in Wes that he had done nothing to deserve.

It drove him forward, taking the child's hand and urging the sister to follow.

He and the two children began to clamber over the ridge, the heavy sand gripping at their feet, not wanting to let them go.

* * *

They were heading south. At least, Wes was fairly certain that they were.

As the sun drew ever higher in the cloudless blue sky, it became harder to tell. Pools of shadow receded slowly, bringing clarity to the landscape which only made it more difficult to differentiate where they were going from where they'd already been.

Not long after escaping the immediate vicinity of the camp, he'd managed to get the children's arms free, but the gags would require more time to remove. Time they didn't have as long as the men were still chasing them.

He could not tell how long they had been running.

His muscles burned, his throat crying out for water. He could only imagine the agony that the gagged young ones were feeling, the edges of their bleeding lips cracking open in the dry heat.

They had kept pace well, considering their size. He thought of the knife, abandoned at the foot of the hill. Its twin was still safely hung at his belt, but never before had the blades been separated. It made him uneasy.

There was a bigger problem. The Claim was still missing, and he didn't see any way he could ever hope to find it. He wasn't sure what the loss of such an ancient treasure would mean to the Septemvirate. Worse, he wasn't sure how the sacrifice would be proved—no Envoy had ever returned without it.

And, of course, the slavers will know exactly who has freed their bounty. A chill ran along his sweat-covered neck.

Finally, after crawling over a particularly nasty pile of stone with thorns growing between them, Wes decided to call for rest. He had hoped for shade, but as far as the eye could see, there was none. The scrubby bushes were barely tall enough to cast a shadow in the noonday sun, and most had spines that prevented one from getting too close anyway.

"Let's get those gags off," he said to the little boy, looking back in the direction they had come, listening for several moments. "We should be safe here."

He could not hear any footsteps or shouts, but it was hard to be truly sure. The sounds of the wind scouring the desert played tricks on his ears. Part of him wanted to keep going, to keep rushing off toward a mirage of perfect safety around the next outcropping of red rock, but he knew that none of them could continue in their current state.

He brought his full-sized sword out of its sheath and carefully slipped it under the gag at the back of the boy's head.

"Stay still, child," he said as he felt the boy flinch. He

couldn't blame him – he could feel his hand shaking slightly as he began to cut away at the leather. He was not a confident swordsman as it was, and this was an especially delicate use of the deadly weapon. "It's alright."

There was no snap this time. The leather merely fell away, falling to the ground where it would soon be covered over by the shifting sands.

The boy began working his jaw, tears forming in his eyes as he looked down at the dirt. "Shh, don't speak yet," Wes said, placing a hand on his shoulder. "Take your time."

Before he could start on the older girl, the boy rushed against his legs, nearly knocking into the sharp sword as he embraced him. Wes stood stiffly for a moment before letting his hand rest against the back of the boy's matted, dirty hair, feeling the child's heart thumping against his own and the sound of quiet sobs.

He was not used to children. At the palace in Stronghollow, there were only a handful, even among the servants and craftsmen. The city itself was not much more fruitful. Rich and poor alike had few, if any, little ones.

In better times long since passed, all of Silverfell was filled with large families.

The royal House of Cervos, especially, had borne many sons and daughters. The future had been hopeful then, full of promise.

Nowadays, Wes was the only child left of his House, and he was nearly a man. The rest of the people had grown poor and fearful of the bad times to come, unwilling to bring a generation forward that would only inherit their despair.

"It's okay," Wes said as the boy finally pulled away, giving him a shy smile. "Let me get her loose and perhaps I can help you with your wounds."

In the same manner, he freed the girl from her bonds, though her cord was done up even tighter and took several minutes to loose. There was a fire in her eyes that Wes suspected had been there long before now. Perhaps she had talked back, angering the slavers in some way that warranted a firmer guard against her ability to speak.

He watched as she worked her mouth closed as the boy had, bits of dried blood flaking onto the ground as she moved. She did not cry, but hugged her brother for several moments, letting her mouth rest in silence.

Wes, not knowing what else to do, sat down and began to look in his pack for the meager supplies he carried on his person. He found nothing of use for medical care, but there was a little water and some dried meat that he almost gobbled up without bothering to share. The run and the heat had made him ravenous.

"A gift," said the girl finally. He turned to face her, leaving the food and water for when they were ready to all eat together. Without the gag, he could see she was a very pretty girl, perhaps twelve or thirteen, with the same gentle smile as the boy he was now certain was indeed her brother.

"It was nothing. You don't need—"

She stretched out a hand toward him, her wrist still red from where her bonds had been tied.

In her palm was the Claim.

Chapter Eight

They ate as they walked, Wes ensuring that the children got larger portions than he. The water they had was only sufficient to tease at their thirst, but it had to be enough. This area of Boneshire was unfamiliar to Wes, and the children seemed to have little idea of their location, either. Wes was simmering over with questions, but he bit his tongue, giving the children a few minutes to eat in peace. Instead, he kept watch, looking back over his shoulders every few moments.

He found out that the girl was called Holga, and the boy—indeed her younger brother— was called Gohr. He had yet to hear Gohr say even a word, but he could tell that he enjoyed the dried meat he was given by the sparkle in his dark green eyes.

Without the gag in his mouth, Wes could see that the boy

shared his sister's handsome features. They did not look like the kind of people who belonged in the rough deserts of Boneshire, but they had assured him that they were indeed from a relatively local village near the edge of the South Sea.

"Our papa taught us about the Envoy, and the Septemvirate," Holga began without preamble, slowing her pace so that she walked alongside Wes, her brother a few steps ahead of them. The boy was looking at his feet, for the most part, but seemed happy enough, kicking at bits of dried summer flowers and bug husks as they went. "I believe that we were destined to meet."

Looking at her somber green eyes, Wes couldn't entirely suppress his laughter.

"Being near the Envoy is usually a good way to get yourself killed. Me, especially."

"But you saved our lives."

She gestured to her brother, who was poking at his sleeve with a broken piece of thorn.

"About a week ago, a band of four dwarves came to our village. They snatched us from a path where we play, and we've been with them since. I never found out where we were going. I thought we were heading west toward Umrym and other dwarves, but it was hard to be sure."

"You were a miracle. A mysterious figure rising out of a dust cloud, come to free us," Gohr cut in, the first words Wes had heard him speak. He looked very young, but his elocution betrayed a solid education. The girl spoke well, too, with the hint of an accent that Wes couldn't place.

"Right," Holga continued. "I was beginning to lose hope. And then when you couldn't get the straps free..." She trailed off, looking forward at the path as she walked. She didn't appear to be injured from her time spent in bondage, if anything, she and her brother looked to be in a far healthier state than Wes himself.

"Sorry," Wes said, wanting to fill the silence. *You were right to doubt me. You should continue to do so.* "We still don't have any food or water. And if you've been traveling away from your village for a week—"

"Not good, right?" Gohr chimed in again.

"No," said Holga, smiling at her brother's back as though he was simply the most charming child in all the world. "But Papa has taught us well. There are lots of things one can do to survive in the desert. In any case, the coast cannot be that far away. There will be villages with people. We will find help."

"Would your father have gotten far looking for you?" Wes asked, trying not to think of all he had heard about the particularly dangerous coastal regions of Boneshire. He imagined their father, a handsome man who shared their deep brown complexion, picking his way across the stone and sand on horseback.

"He's joined our dear mother in the Eternal Lands," Holga added, her smile faltering only slightly. "Not very long ago. In fact, I suspect that's why we were taken away."

* * *

"The slavers sought you out because you have no parents to come looking for you?" Wes asked, feeling the pang in his chest that he always did when he met another who was orphaned. He hated how many children in the Four Kingdoms understood the pain that he felt.

Holga shook her head, her tight brown braids whipping

against her cheek.

"No. Because of what we know that others in Rill do not."

"Rill is our village," Gohr put in, not looking up from the path before him.

Wes' head hurt. Clearly, the little boy understood a good deal more than he did about what was going on. He thought of Celesyria. He hadn't so much as given her a chance to explain herself, and now she was long gone. He decided that the best course of action was to keep his mouth shut for once.

"Well, 'Rill' is not really a proper name for it, Gohr. Though if there is a more official one, I suppose no one knows it. The river gorge where Redvale stands moves southwest toward us until it becomes a little rill, hence the name," Holga said, beaming, as though she was sharing a geography lesson. Wes wondered if Gohr was rolling his eyes, but all he could see was the back of his head, his little braids bouncing merrily as he stepped along.

Wes was familiar with Redvale. It was the only city in Boneshire that retained any level of administrative control. They frequently sent a delegation to Silverfell when it came time to discuss matters of the Feast of Offering, especially when it was the Kingdom of Boneshire's turn to produce a Witness. Apparently, the river that flowed beneath its citadel continued farther than he thought, bringing a source of life to the harsh landscape.

"Anyway," she continued. "Our family line goes back a long way in our village, back before the fall of the House of Noctua. We were never nobles, but my people once lived in the old capital, where we were renowned for our tapestry-making. My ancestors crafted the most marvelous scenes, keeping historical knowledge alive even for those without letters! The horses of Aridmoor looked so perfect, it was said that they could jump straight out of the image…"

"Hmm. Interesting. Please continue," Wes said as she trailed off, trying not to allow the frustration to show on his face. He did not wish to lose his temper, especially toward someone so young who had been through so much, but he feared he might not be able to help himself if she did not approach her point soon. Already he could see that the sun was moving lower in the sky. He wanted some idea of where they stood before they came across an unfriendly village, an ironwolf, or worse.

Holga tittered. "Of course, I wouldn't bore you with a history lesson,"

"You already have," Gohr said brightly.

"Well. Anyway, those who crafted the tapestries used many sources for their historical research. There were those in the royal House of Noctua who possessed copies of various portions of the Codex Veritatis, in secret. One of our distant uncles, who I'm told was rather handsome, fell in love with a House noble. She entrusted him with the ancient writings, and he told their tales in the threads of his tapestries," Holga paused again, her fingers clasped in front of her as she looked up at the bright sky as though enraptured.

Wes was listening intently now, jolted out of his exhaustion and hunger by the second mention of the Codex Veritatis he'd heard in as many days. It seemed impossible to dismiss as coincidence.

"After the Envoy attempted to take the crown, all Wrathland broke loose. Most of my ancestors were killed in bloody battle."

Wes thought that Holga sounded rather too pleased at this. Gohr, for his part, had slowed until he was just ahead of them, not wanting to miss any of the more exciting parts of their family history.

"When the elves came from Nox, they had nearly every tapestry burned, permitting only those which depicted geometric patterns or typography to be preserved."

"That's tragic," Wes said, filled with a sudden longing for the beautiful landscape paintings that hung around the palace at Stronghollow.

"Why would they want to destroy such important history?"

"What do you know of the Codex?" Holga asked instead.

"I've always been taught that it was a myth. The legend is that it was written by the Dracodei and was later lost," Wes said, deciding not to mention what the dragon had alleged about it, for the time being.

He hoped that the children could be trusted—after all, Holga was herself coming dangerously near blasphemy already—but he couldn't be sure. The world was not the same world as the one he'd grown up in. There were more dangers to think about now.

More secrets that could be betrayed.

"That," Holga said, turning to Wes, a sad smile on her pink lips. "Is exactly why the elves sought to destroy the record of history in Boneshire, with the aid of corrupt men, dragons, and even dwarves, depending on the time period in question. They want the citizens of the Four Kingdoms to think that the Codex Veritatis is unimportant, a story, no more."

"But why? What is there to be gained?"

"Because what the Codex Veritatis says is a threat to power. In the case of the elves, it is a threat to their very survival."

"Are you sure about this, sister?" Gohr asked, not turning to face them. There was a quaver in his voice. "Can you trust him?"

"We could have been lost forever, our knowledge lost with us, and then there he was. Like you said. Like a miracle," she said. Wes thought he heard a slight catch in her throat as she went on. "I hope we can trust him. If not, there is no one else to turn to."

Gohr nodded, satisfied, as he allowed himself to walk a little further ahead once more.

An uncomfortable silence fell over the group, broken only by the shush-shush of boots against sand.

"What does the Codex say?" Wes asked.

This time, he would wait for the full answer, whatever it may be. Whatever it meant for his future.

He had to know.

"Most of it has been forgotten, despite the efforts of my ancestors. But there is one thing, a prophecy, that we were taught to guard with our very lives. Gohr?"

The boy slowed until he was keeping pace with his sister and Wes again, tucking the piece of dried flower he had been fiddling with into his shirtsleeve. He began to recite, his childish voice clear and strong as it carried on the desert winds, with no one else to hear it but the stones.

"Stripped of all help, stricken with thirst, he will come. His tongue will be as sharp as his antlers, his eyes cast down with grief. He will leave his token to the earth, he will set the hopeless little ones free. He will bestow a crown, he will reverse the oath. He will bring the bread of hope to all Kaveryth, even to a Kingdom long thought dead. The usurpers will be cast out, the mighty will be brought to lowliness, and the High One will rule forever."

* * *

The sun felt incredibly close.

Celesyria gazed down at the desert landscape below, her keen eyes searching the shadow of every crag and between every rocky pass for Wes Cervos. She was nervous to be flying in the daylight, but she had no choice. Even if she could spot Wes' camp more easily at night if he lit a fire, she was better off finding him before he reached Aridmoor.

There were more people there, more villages.

Even at night, she would need to be exceedingly careful when she left Boneshire's borders. She did not doubt that her parents were already furious with her for failing to appear at Ancora Canyon, but they most likely assumed that she'd only taken off to some distant library within Umrym.

As the dragons dwindled in numbers, being spotted by humans had slowly become more and more noteworthy. If the wrong person was to see her, it could very well make its way back to Whitespire. And if it did, she would have more than the rage of her parents to deal with. She would be seen as a traitor, perhaps even tried as a criminal in court. Most of her fellow dragons treated her eccentric interests as being rather harmless, but she couldn't count on that perception to paper over a blatant act of treason against the Dracodei.

Wes, you better have stuck to the usual route. She flew higher, allowing her eyes to rest from her hunt for a few moments.

She turned a few loops in the air, relishing the warmth of the sun. Spring was very near, and she could imagine the change that even a single rainfall would bring to the desert, the brief shift in weather enough to bring millions of flowers into bloom around thousands of sudden water sources.

Until following Wes, she'd only ever traveled to the northwest edge of Boneshire, near the city of Claywind. There, the entire desert reminded her of a harsher-looking Umrym, the same sort of mountains cast in red stone instead of gray, the winter snow replaced by dry wind cold enough to make your lungs ache.

Here in the wilderlands, near the ancestral path the Envoys treaded, the broken Kingdom of Boneshire felt alive, even though the plants and animals were hidden.

As she dipped back down through the cloudless sky, she spotted one of the huge dragon skeletons that dotted the landscape from time to time. She bowed her head.

Rest, brother. She flew over the remains, checking behind every rib for a sign of Wes. She had always been taught that the display of dragon remains in Boneshire was wicked, one of the most grievous insults that could be directed toward her race.

When she had visited Claywind, she found it hard to argue with the idea. There, a large skull—female, by the look of the eye sockets—had been turned into a bawdy tavern, with various riff-raff pouring in and out of its mouth like sour wine.

On the whole, it did not seem that the humans of Boneshire were particularly appreciative of the dragons for what they had done.

The war had been short, but brutal. Never before had so many dragons spilled their blood in combat.

Celesyria found the whole matter particularly distasteful when she considered the cause.

In those days, not long before she had hatched, there had been an Envoy who carried the blood of the royal House of Noctua in his veins. Like Wes Cervos, calamity had befallen his family in a time of great turmoil, leaving him the only heir of the entire House.

Despite the pleas of the Septemvirate of the time, and despite the tradition of time immemorial barring anyone who bore the moonscar from the throne, the Envoy had declared himself King of Boneshire.

On the third day of his rule, he had been struck dead, leaving his people without a ruler and all of the Four Kingdoms waiting for a new Envoy to be born.

Into the power vacuum that had been left behind stepped the usual bandits, slavers, and crime lords, turning the desert Kingdom into even more of a Wrathland than it had been before. Worse, the elves who had been exiled to Nox became aware of Boneshire's weakness.

In they came, crossing the West Strait and pouring onto the Black Beach in their thousands, seeking to retake what they considered to be theirs.

It was then that the Dracodei commanded the Guardians to take up their oath and protect the Four Kingdoms.

Both of Celesyria's parents fought in that conflict, driving the elves back to Nox. But it had not been enough. Boneshire was never the same after the war, even with the attempts of the other Kingdoms to maintain law and order.

And in the process, hundreds of dragons and men had lost their lives. Celesyria's aunt and two older cousins were among the dead. She had never gotten the chance to meet them.

Still, despite all of the terrible things that had happened in this desert land, she could not be so sure that it would be right to remove the skeletons from view. Though the ribcage below was the largest structure that could be seen for miles and miles, it looked almost as though it was meant to be there.

Dusty-looking vines and bushes trailed up each tree-sized piece of bone, preparing to bring forth the prettiest summer blooms. Birds preened atop them, singing merrily in the late-morning light.

Was it really so terrible to leave one's body behind in death, when it would be so appreciated by the world that kept it? Besides, even if they could somehow scrub away the violence of the place, the common tongue moniker of Boneshire would remain.

I think I'd rather be buried here than burned in the great tower.

Celesyria flew on, adjusting her route slightly to follow the Envoy's ancestral path once more. The great bones receded behind her, gone from view in mere minutes.

Then again, if the High One does not wish us to be a part of this world, perhaps it would be better to be turned to ash.

As she pondered this thought, she noticed a flash of movement below.

She flew closer, allowing the wind to carry her on silent wings.

It was a deer.

Even if it was not wearing a pack across its back, she would have known it was one of the mounts from Silverfell, with their broad shoulders and impressive antlers. They were famous across Kaveryth for their agility and stamina.

Perhaps you're looking for him, too, little guy. She swept back upwards so as not to terrify the creature a second time.

"Can you hear me, Wes?" She asked in her mind, letting the words flow out as far away as she could get them to reach. She waited a few moments, hearing only the rush of wind past her ears as she flew further along the route. Speaking this way was often an exercise in frustration. It was far from an exact

science.

She could only hope that he was close enough.

Even if he was, what good would it do if he could only hear her? How would they find one another in this vast land?

"I could use a pair of wings right now, Celesyria. On the east side of the Dread Ruins, if you wouldn't mind."

She curled her right lip upwards in an approximation of a smile, making a sharp turn and flapping her wings as hard as she could, her concern over the deer forgotten.

* * *

"I'll be there in a few moments. I assume the ruins are not so difficult to find."

"You won't miss them," Wes said to Celesyria, trying to get used to the strange sensation of speaking within his mind. He had not realized it was possible until, suddenly, he was already doing it.

Could any human do this? Or was it dependent on some other factor? He shook off his questions. There would be time to ask her more about it later. In the meantime, he would enjoy it. It was nice to feel special about something other than the scar across his cheek and the fate he'd been given.

"Look for a waterfall," he added.

Wes stood at the top of a large cliff, the pounding sound of falling water filling his ears.

Holga and Gohr had walked a little way along the river at the base of the waterfall, Gohr returning to his habit of examining various local plant life.

He did not have time to tell the children that they were about to meet a dragon, however, he was confident that they would react to her far better than he himself had.

He could scarcely believe that she had come back to find him at all.

After the way he had spoken to her, he would not have blamed her for flying back to Umrym, never to seek him out again, exactly as he had demanded. He looked up at the sky, squinting into the sunlight, waiting, looking for the telltale outline of orange wings against the blue.

She wasn't there yet, so he stooped near the edge of the water, letting his hands fill up and drinking deeply. It felt so good, every drop the most delicious drink that he had ever tasted after such a long time spent thirsty. He could scarcely believe that the water he'd drank back home in the palace had ever been so pure or clean.

Most in Silverfell assumed that the Dread Ruins were frightening or terrible, but Wes had always imagined otherwise, having ridden past the place dozens of times on his journey as Envoy.

He was pleased to have been vindicated. It was beautiful here, an oasis in a sea of harsh desert land. He knew he would be almost sad to leave it behind.

A couple of hours before, he and the children had been walking toward the South Sea coast, their hunger and thirst consuming them until by chance he had seen a sharp hill in the northern sky that he recognized.

Though he was remiss to backtrack, fearful that want of provisions would lead to their death, he knew that if they could only reach the Dread Ruins, they would survive. From there, Aridmoor—and thanks to the small settlements there, the promise of food—was only mere hours away.

More important, though, was the river that thread its way

through the middle of the old capital. Though it was not very large or impressive compared with the lakes of Silverfell and Galeharbor, it was still the largest water source in Boneshire.

Now, at the start of springtime, it was flowing especially fiercely, white rapids blooming like clouds at the bottom of the waterfall on the eastern edge of the city. He and the children had made it there before dinner hour, shouting with joy as they lay on their stomachs, lapping up the fast-moving, crystal water as quickly as they could. All around them were the remains of a city that had been abandoned two hundred years ago, at the start of the war, before the dragons came to save Boneshire. Of course, it had not been called Boneshire then. The former name of the Kingdom had been lost to history.

Wes looked from the harsh blue sky to the tops of the buildings, each one sharing the classical Noctua-style architecture that many villages in the south of Aridmoor still tried to emulate. They were stunning, even in their state of decay, all tall spires and tight, curling designs, with owl motifs common throughout.

The river had provided sufficient water for the areas outside the city walls to grow abundant crops, enough to feed all of the old Kingdom and export even more. Wes could almost hear the sounds of the thriving city that the Dread Ruins had once been, her marketplaces alive with the ting of lyres and the heady scent of spices.

He found it difficult to reconcile the present name of the city with what it had been not so very long ago. Wes knew that many had fled the destruction loosed from Nox, seeking smaller and safer enclaves in which to hide, and still more had died attempting to hold the capital city. Still, why had no one returned after the war ended? The whole thing was unnerving.

Wes felt a shiver run down his spine as he continued to watch the sky for signs of Celesyria. *Why throw away such a wonderful place rather than rebuild it?*

Before he could give it any further thought, however, Wes saw the dragon nearing the city, her orange scales glimmering like fire in the light of the setting sun. *Thank the Dracodei.* The thought rose to mind without him beckoning it, the remnant of a lifelong habit.

He felt a smile spread across his face, unbidden, as he waited for Holga and Gohr to notice their visitor.

Chapter Nine

Wes lay on his back near the remains of his fire, unconcerned with the chill that was beginning to pour over his body.

Never before had he seen so many stars.

The little pinpricks of light flickered from their place behind the great black cloak of the sky. Here in the Dread Ruins, the desert felt alive. The waterfall sang without ceasing, but every so often a night bird came near enough that her song could be heard over the crashing of the water. The stones were not so unfriendly anymore. Wes could imagine they were cradling him like warm bedcoverings as he waited.

Dawn was near.

Celesyria had been delighted with Holga and Gohr, and they had in turn been delighted to meet her. They had never seen a dragon before, but knew enough of Boneshire's history to feel very much indebted to her race.

Before either Wes or Celesyria could explain the circumstances of their meeting, Holga had made quick work of telling tales and singing songs of their people, with Gohr revealing a rather impressive skill at ceremonial dance. Wes had made a fire, and the four of them had enjoyed each other's company and good cheer so much that the pangs in their bellies seemed to subside.

Before long, of course, Holga had asked the kind of questions that drew one away from merriment, and between Wes and Celesyria, the whole story had come out.

Celesyria had been especially delighted at the line in the children's prophecy that spoke of Wes' sharp antlers. Upon hearing it, she had taken off without warning for a few minutes, only to return with a terrified, screeching deer hanging from her claws.

Though Wes was happy to have the creature back—especially since the food and supplies it carried were still intact—the return of the deer struck him with melancholy.

After the party had taken food from the packs and drank from the waterfall, they all began to stall, moving as slowly as possible to put away the remnants of their breakfast and tidy up the makeshift camp.

They knew that it was time.

Wes helped the children onto the dragon's great orange back, Gohr sitting in front of his sister, looking even smaller than he did on the ground.

The children bid Wes goodbye more than twice, but still, when Celesyria carried them away to the southeast, toward their home in Rill, Wes was astonished by the sudden depth of grief that he felt.

He had stumbled upon these two children without meaning to, and had very nearly abandoned them in their hour of need. Yet, he felt a deep connection to them, forged in the fire of a difficult journey together, however brief it had been.

Now, they were gone, and he had no reason to assume he'd ever see them again.

Wes looked for the constellation of the great deer that lay to the northwest, tracing the six stars that made up the animal's horns with an extended finger. *Cervos. The deer.*

He'd always assumed that prophecies of old would be mysterious, contradictory, almost impossible to understand as they came to pass. Perhaps most of them were that way, only making complete sense after they had been fulfilled.

But he could not deny that he fit the prophecy that the children had brought. He could not deny that his meeting of three separate people, who all believed impossible things, was difficult to dismiss as mere coincidence.

Far off in the distance, he heard the wailing of an ironwolf. The call was not answered. It was a lonely sound, but it was beautiful, too.

He thought of his childhood in Stronghollow, his life in the palace before the dark days began. His father and mother in their ceremonial dress, standing at the palace gates before the great treed courtyard, giving an address to the people. He remembered how he always stood off to the side with Roven, trying not to fidget in his uncomfortable clothes as his older brother looked every bit the future king that he was.

When they had died, the head of the Septemvirate, Elder Dorold, had become almost a second father to Wes, the familiar anchor in a life that had become unrecognizable overnight.

"It is you who the Kingdom must now hope in, my boy," he'd

said, more than once, placing a hand on Wes' shoulder, looking at him with pride in his eyes. "Everything will be alright in the end. As long as we are loyal to the Dracodei, as long as we put the sacrifices first, they will take care of everything else."

He hoped that his mentor was not too worried about him. Certainly, he would be missed by now, as would his companions. He was sure that more than a few soldiers would have been spared to begin a search for them.

Still, as much as he missed Dorold, he couldn't help but remember something else the man had said to him. A very long time ago, at a time when such thoughts were too big and far away for him to understand.

He'd told Wes that he needn't worry too much about finding a queen and continuing his family line. That there was plenty of time for that when he was an older man, when things were better in Silverfell, when a good match could be made. He had reminded young Wes that, as it stood, he did not have anything to offer a young noble from another of the Four Kingdoms.

In any case, he said, life in Silverfell would not be so different without the rule of the House of Cervos. After all, most of what a king and queen did, important as it was, was symbolic. In day-to-day matters, the Septemvirate already managed a great deal, along with the lower nobles and local magistrates.

The decimation of the House was indeed a calamity, a tragedy the likes of which had never been experienced in Silverfell, but it was a tragedy that could be overcome.

Wes pondered this as the first slivers of dawn light broke on the eastern edge of the desert. He thought of Holga and Gohr, sent off to an uncertain future without a father or mother, in a land ravaged by chaos.

He'd always figured that the Septemvirate were indeed

capable of ruling the people of Silverfell. Things had grown more difficult, but there was certainly not lawlessness on the scale of what was seen in Boneshire. The traditions and history of the people were intact, indeed, they were celebrated. The Feast of Offering was always observed with care and dedication from virtually every citizen.

But is that enough to protect my Kingdom from eventual ruin if we never again have a monarch to rule us?

His breath was coming in plumes of mist now, night having long since fallen, but he didn't mind the cold. His deer stood nearby, asleep on his hooves, nickering at some disturbance in a dream. The bracing air that filled his lungs felt as though it was washing him clean, purifying him from the inside out. Everything that he thought he knew felt like it was being torn apart, but there was a new determination welling up within him.

Despite the fear that he felt, despite his certainty that anyone would be better suited for the task that lay before him, he could no longer deny the truth. Dorold Eli was right about one thing: The hope of the Kingdom rested on his shoulders.

But that hope would not be fulfilled in sacrifices to false gods. He knew that now. Despite all of the education he had received, the best that the Kingdom of Silverfell had to offer, he had never been able to understand. He had been lied to, about the biggest questions that man could fathom to ask. The women who had been his teachers had no doubt been lied to by those who taught them.

Whether or not Celesyria had all of the right answers, whether or not he was ready to believe in the High One, that didn't matter to him at the moment. What mattered was that the whole system of the Dracodei, the rules which he had never been allowed to doubt or question, had been brought before him in the light of day, and he was not sure that he would ever be able to unsee the blemishes he'd found.

He listened as the fire crackled, bits of spark and the scent of ash catching in the air.

For once, he was thankful for the moment alone, the chance to think.

To decide.

The blood of the House of Cervos would not die in his veins, and the treasures of the people would no longer be offered to the usurpers.

No matter what it took.

* * *

"I got them close to Rill," Celesyria said, lapping up great mouthfuls of freezing water from the river, the roar of the waterfall behind her making her glad that she could speak within her mind.

Now, Wes could not only hear what she said but speak back himself as well.

She knew it was possible the upright races could project their words as dragons did, but it was difficult to learn, and some seemed forever unable, even with practice. Not even Gramnok was able to do it.

"How close? Did you see that they made it?"

Wes stood a few paces away, resting against a large piece of red stone. The sockets of his eyes were baggy and hollow, no doubt due to the combination of hunger and lack of sleep.

Celesyria was happy that she'd found and eaten an ironwolf on the way back from taking the children to Rill, but she had not found any game suitable for human consumption.

"They'll be alright, Wes," she said firmly, licking droplets of water from her lips.

She had arrived as the sun was cresting the horizon. Now, a few minutes later, the entire lower part of the Dread Ruins lay before her along the sides of the river, bathed in an orange glow.

The former capital city of Boneshire looked as desolate as the rest of the desert, but still, the light made her nervous. *"They assured me that they knew the rest of the way into the village. They will have quite a tale to tell, even if they don't admit the part about the Envoy and the dragon."*

She watched Wes for a moment as he gazed out at the sprawling spires and block buildings. He looked a little skinnier than when she first laid eyes on him, but there was something else different about him, something that went beyond the weariness he wore on his face.

"Is everything alright?"

Wes looked up, surprised, his smile coming a little too quick, not reaching his eyes. *"Yes. Just hungry. It's distracting. I kind of always thought being fat would come in handy in this type of situation, but that doesn't seem to be the case."*

"You could eat the deer. You've been getting along without him so far," she pointed out, adopting his joking tone. It was more than his hunger.

Something behind his eyes was different. She wasn't sure he could explain it himself even if she asked.

"That would mess up the prophecy," he said, meeting her eyes, his voice suddenly solemn. The sun reflected off of the river, leaving speckles of yellow light dancing on the back of Celesyria's eyelids every time she blinked.

"Perhaps."

"I did not sleep last night. I had much to think about," Wes started. She said nothing, instead curling herself against the side of a large, squarish building that blocked some of the harsh morning sunlight. *Could the High One be at work in his heart, as it seems He is in mine?*

"Being here—" He gestured to the Dread Ruins surrounding them. *"—I've come to realize things that I couldn't make sense of before. If the House of Cervos ceases to rule Silverfell permanently, we will fall, in time. Just as Boneshire has. I'm sure of it. And yet, the Septemvirate is unconcerned."*

She waited for a moment before responding, gathering her thoughts. She had feared as much all along, but the prophecy that Holga and Gohr had passed to them confirmed it.

"I think you're right. It is not a coincidence that you are both Envoy and the last person to carry the royal blood in your veins," she said, choosing each word carefully. *"You must 'bestow a crown'."*

"Finding a queen is the only way that the House of Cervos will continue to exist. If I don't, we will die, just as the House of Noctua did."

"Do you know what the part about reversing the oath means?"

"No. Actually, I was hoping that you did."

Celesyria shook her head. *"I've studied the political history of Silverfell, including recent history,"* she paused before continuing, resisting the urge to look at her feet. *"In regard to the calamity that befell the royal family. But I've never seen any reference to an oath. I guess we'll have to find a queen, and worry about the rest later. That's the clearest answer I can give you."*

"It won't be easy," Wes said. *"Compared to Boneshire, it seems Silverfell is prosperous. But in reality, we are in deep decline.*

Poverty has never been worse, and crime has never been so vicious as it is now. Any attempt at competent governance is thwarted by the endless squabbling of the nobles of the Lesser Houses. They are consigned to rule only lower territories, but believe me, that does not restrain their appetite for power. Many of them have become tyrants."

"*If the High One desires to preserve the House of Cervos, we will find someone."* Celesyria put in.

"*Finding a woman willing to marry me will prove more difficult than you think. I always thought I had more time. I can't do much about the state of the Kingdom she'd be inheriting, but I could work on myself,"* Wes said, taking his turn to gaze at his feet, a blush rising to his cheeks. Before Celesyria could protest or offer some word of encouragement, he continued.

"*In any case, mere willingness is not enough. I am barred by the most ancient laws of the Four Kingdoms never to take up the authority of the throne myself. I will not become king just because my name can make a woman queen. I'll be able to advise, nothing more. We must find a woman capable of ruling my people. If not, things could end up even worse than they were before."*

"*Such a girl does exist,"* Celesyria said, hoping that she sounded more confident than she felt. "*And don't sell yourself short, Wes. Matters of the heart are more complicated than you think. True love is not based upon who is most fair."*

"*My brother Roven fell in love,"* Wes said, rubbing at his chin and looking off to a point far away. "*Before he died. She was very beautiful, and he was very handsome, but I suppose you're right. There was something deeper between them than shared fairness."*

"*You speak of the Princess of Galeharbor?"*

"*Yes. She was captured by one of the elves. It didn't surprise me that my brother would have done anything to save her, but my parents went beyond their duty."*

Wes continued to look away. She could see the telltale reddening at the corners of his eyes, the pain of his past threatening to set tears flowing.

"The King and Queen of Silverfell were some of the most honorable leaders that the Four Kingdoms have ever known," Celesyria said firmly, wishing she could offer some condolence from her race as a whole. It saddened her to admit that the death of Wes' parents had been met with indifference by most of the dragons she knew.

Hidden in their caverns, it was easy to forget the comings and goings of the rest of the world. But even they could not deny that since the murder of those two great monarchs, the decline of the dragons had increased precipitously. *If only we cared about outside events for reasons that go beyond saving our own scaly hides.*

"I miss them so much," Wes said, meeting her eyes with obvious effort. *"I would do anything to hug my mother one more time. To tell my father that I'm thankful for all that he taught me, for all of the ways that he sought to make me a virtuous noble, even if I will never follow in his footsteps as a ruler."*

"You will do them a great honor by finding a queen," Celesyria said after a moment. *"They will look on you from the Eternal Lands with great pride. They will watch their grandchildren grow up, bringing forth a new generation of Cervos that will rebuild your homeland."*

She had to blink a few times to avoid allowing her tears to fall. Was it possible that one day her parents would be proud of her, too? Even after all of the times she had deceived them?

* * *

The rest of the day passed in the mundane details of preparation, such as they were, and Wes found himself retreating into his own head, grappling with decisions that bit at his conscience.

With the recovery of his deer and his supplies, he'd had a little bit to eat, but it was not enough to replenish the energy that he had spent.

Fortunately, there had been plenty of empty watersacks, and he'd set himself to the task of filling them with fresh river water for the remaining journey.

He'd repaired one of his boots with the help of a bit of cactusvine that grew against an old market stall, and he'd been able to find a bit of live aloe that had survived the winter in an abandoned house and used it to make a salve for his various small wounds. He'd given his deer a thorough grooming, and taken out maps of the Four Kingdoms that he carried in his main pack.

What he could not seem to decide on was exactly where they would be going. After several hours of poring over the various maps, the detailed lines of ink and pigment had begun to blend together. He set them aside in frustration, deciding that pacing around their makeshift camp near the side of the river was just as productive.

Celesyria had made it clear that she wished to begin their quest to find his queen straight away. After they had spoken for a while about possible avenues they might take, she'd retreated to a rather enclosed bit of street and took a nap, exhausted after a full night of flying.

He attempted to rest as well, but had only managed an hour or so, which he passed in discomfort, tossing and turning. He couldn't help but feel he was being watched, though of course, he saw no one.

Even when he rolled up a cloak to use as a pillow, the sand still ended up in his freshly washed hair. Finally, he'd given up and decided to throw himself into preparations while they waited for night to return.

He was pacing, lost in thought, when he heard Celesyria's thunderous footsteps padding out from her makeshift nest.

"I did not have nice dreams."

"I didn't sleep well either. I gave up early," he said, gesturing toward the watersacks and leather bags ready to be attached to the deer's saddle. He had removed his gloves, hoping to mend them later, and wrapped his salve-coated hands in strips of cloth.

"You are ready to leave, then?" Celesyria sniffed at one of the bags with her large nose, knocking it over. A few bundles of cactusvine came tumbling out.

"Is this edible for humans?"

Wes laughed, shaking his head. *"Theoretically, maybe. Even I'm not that hungry. But there will be food once we cross into Aridmoor."* He paused, watching as Celesyria let out a loud yawn, stretching her neck toward the sky.

Even after getting to know her better, he hadn't ceased to find her fascinating. Though dragons were a part of his world, until now, they'd been abstract, something he knew existed but couldn't contextualize. He wondered if he would ever stop finding it enchanting to be near her.

"I know of a village that will offer hospitality," he continued. *"Near the Envoy's route."*

Wes listened as Celesyria released a slow breath, the sound enough to compete with the waterfall a hundred yards away.

"We're returning to the route?"

"*I wish to seek a queen, with your help,*" Wes said quickly, his voice hitching in his throat. Though he'd been accustomed since childhood to having a certain authority over others, he couldn't help but feel self-conscious about it here, alone with a creature many times his size and age. "*But I cannot abandon the people of Silverfell.*"

She had ceased moving, staring at him with an intensity that nearly burned.

"*It is not abandonment to seek to bring them the truth, Wes.*"

"*And I will. I will not participate in any more falsehood. But I will not run off and leave the people in doubt in order to seek a queen to rule over them.*"

"*But with a queen as your ally, it will be much easier to cease these false sacrifices,*" Celesyria said. There was an edge to her otherwise calm voice. "*Do you have a better plan?*"

He nodded, feeling sweat beading on his palms. He brushed it away against his pants.

"*If I return with the Claim, I will be able to calm the people who are worried after me. From there, I will speak to the Septemvirate.*"

"*Will they listen?*"

"*I'm not sure,*" Wes admitted, pausing for a moment and listening to the pleasant sound of the river winding through the Dread Ruins. He was pleased that Celesyria had not rejected his reasoning outright. Despite everything, he hoped he still garnered some of her respect. "*Elder Dorold, the head of the Septemvirate, is a good man. I've known him for as long as I can remember. He will at least give me a chance to speak.*"

Celesyria looked off across the city for a moment before answering. The sound of birds calling to one another rose from a nearby pocket of bushes, their song blending prettily with the shushing of the water.

"What you must say will be considered blasphemy, in their eyes."

"According to the law, yes."

"And what is the punishment, according to the law?"

"I must take the chance, Celesyria," Wes said, his voice harsher than he meant it.

He took a breath again, letting the serenity of the scene surrounding them spread calm over him like salve on a wound.

"All my life, I've hated the burden that has been placed upon me. The carrying of the sacrifices, the travel away from home from my earliest years. Those are indeed burdens, burdens that many men would not choose. But they are nothing compared to the true weight that I've been fated to bear. I've watched too many people that I love die in order to preserve the order of things. Now you come along, and you tell me that everything I've lived for is a lie. Does it surprise you that my tolerance for falsehood runs thin?"

"No."

"Then accept that I will do what is right, even if my blood is the price."

"I...I...well—" Celesyria stammered for a moment before starting again. *"I admire your bravery. But you must be careful."*

Wes nodded and began to tie packs to the deer's saddle. *"It's decided. We will leave as soon as the light fades."*

He noticed a sadness in the dragon's eyes as she shuffled over to the side of the river, careful not to trample any of the packs that lay about beneath her huge feet.

Was her worry merely an omen warning of some punishment that was to befall him? Or was there more that she was not telling him? Wes put the speculation from his mind and continued in his preparations.

He had a job to do, and it terrified him.

Chapter Ten

Thick droplets of rain pelted against Celesyria's orange scales as she flew beneath the clouds. The sky that lay before her was uniformly gray, punctuated with occasional flashes of impossibly white shards of lightning. She did not fear being struck—dragon scales were capable of disbursing the energy across her skin without causing her any harm—but she worried for Wes and his deer.

Even with her keen eyesight she could barely see the Envoy and his beast in the darkness, a miserable lump moving across the landscape below, fully visible only when lightning illuminated them.

After traveling all through the night, they were finally nearing the Kingdom of Aridmoor. Neither she nor Wes could see precisely where the border lay, but they had to be very close.

As the leagues rolled on, the red stone and swirling sands had given way to flat plains of brown, dead grass and the occasional patch of hearty spring flowers, sodden with rain.

She watched over her companion with some pity. The riding was much easier here than in Boneshire, and had the rain not come upon them, he would be sitting in a warm tavern by now.

As it was, dawn had finally arrived—though she could see no more than the vague, colorless light that indicated sunshine—and they were still pressing on along the ancient route.

She had considered asking Wes to climb onto her back, and she was sure he'd had the same thought, but neither bothered to voice it. Though she doubted anyone would be outside in such vicious weather, she did not wish to chance anyone seeing her unless it was absolutely necessary.

In any case, even if she could carry Wes for a while, she wouldn't be able to do so when he met up with his men, and it would be unwise to leave him without his newly recovered deer.

She thought of her mother, worrying away in their cavern, and felt a pang of the familiar guilt. *I hate lying. But I am left with no other choice. There is no one else in Umrym who would take up this mission.* She repeated the words she had been telling herself since leaving home. They never completely rid her of her guilt, but it was enough to push it away, at least for a little while at a time.

She kept an eye to the horizon, hoping to catch sight of any new arrivals along the road before they became aware of Wes. The idea made her nervous.

She thought back to what Wes had said when he'd first sent her away, how he had threatened to tell the Septemvirate of her blasphemy. She shivered. Being punished for the crime of blasphemy was something she very much wanted to avoid.

In the early days of Kaveryth, the Elf-Queens were notorious for their torture of prisoners who dared to defy their absolute power. Even to so much as question some aspect of their rule meant facing torment and eventual death. How many thousands of brave men and women had faced the destruction of their bodies in order to do what was right?

The punishments of today were less cruel, at least if she were to face the courts of Umrym or Silverfell, but death was death. She was not eager to meet it.

Celesyria had always been taught that when the race of men returned to the true worship of the Dracodei, they were rewarded with freedom from the elves and their tyranny, but now she didn't know what to believe. The High One was in control, she knew, but it was unclear how His influence had unfolded throughout history. She hoped that He was still here now, watching over them, painting a masterpiece that they were too close to see.

Even so, she was afraid. She was impressed by Wes' conviction, but felt very far from it herself.

I think that he believes me. She squinted down at Wes' tiny figure on the plain below, his hood pulled over his head, useless against the torrent of the rain. *But that doesn't mean that anyone else in Silverfell will. Even if he doesn't betray me to save his own skin, who is to say that the Septemvirate won't punish us both?*

She closed her eyes for a moment, letting the chill of the wind and water wash over her as she pumped her wings.

There was no way to go but forward.

* * *

Wes' stomach growled. Over the last few hours, it had begun to ache, making him want to lay on the ground in a ball and clutch at his insides.

At least I'm not bothered by the rain. He rounded another small bend in the muddy path, only to be faced with yet more of the same gray emptiness. He'd forgotten the chill in the small of his back and the squelching of his socks in his sodden boots.

He'd been preoccupied with urging his deer forward and fighting with the wet and the wind to keep his lamp lit. Even though the path was familiar, many smaller trails led off of it, and if he was not careful, he risked getting lost.

He loved the landscapes of Aridmoor in the summertime, all waving grasses and hills that stretched as far as his eyes could see. The sky was so much bigger there than in the forests of Silverfell, and he remembered many trips where he'd taken a few hours to lay on his back with his companions, staring up at the endless blue.

In the night and the rain, however, the endless sameness was hazardous.

Finally, as murky daylight began to bring some clarity to his route, his prior concerns were devoured by his hunger. His deer—who he now had to walk on a lead, for it was too hazardous to ride him in such unforgiving muck—was rather content to munch at the brown grass along the path, but he was all out of provisions.

He'd begun to find himself jealous of the creature as his hunger deepened, though he was even more jealous of the dragon, who could pluck birds out of the air and swallow them whole.

Ever since he was a child growing up in the palace at Stronghollow, he'd loved to eat. The other children would poke fun at him, telling him that the excess he carried around his middle was more than they got in a month. The Kingdom of Silverfell had been rich in those days, and it was rare for anyone to go hungry, but even so, most of the children Wes knew were the offspring of servants. He felt guilty seeing their slim bellies and spindly legs when he ate more than any boy could need, but still, he never managed to slow himself down.

His older brother was always quick to rush to his defense, reminding the servants' children that it was the royal family who ensured they were able to eat at all, but Wes always got the feeling that even Roven was annoyed with his tendency toward pudginess.

Roven was always the handsome one, always disciplined, always awake with the sun and taking part in some physical activity of his own free accord.

He'd invite his little brother to join the royal hunt for bear meat and ironwolf pelts, but Wes rarely agreed to take part in any more labor than was strictly mandated by their father. He was more at home with his mother in the palace gallery, helping her with her paintings, or following Dorold around on Septemvirate business.

As he trudged forward, watching his boots leave great sticky craters in the mud that covered the path, he thought perhaps that this ordeal might serve as a starting point to yet another failed diet.

"Yep, yep!" he called to his deer, pulling on the lead rope as he rounded another curve in the path that led around a small hill. The animal had found a patch of light blue flowers to eat and was reluctant to leave them behind. The deer finally took a few steps forward, though Wes struggled to stop him from gazing back at the colorful bit of plant life with longing.

Just then, Wes noticed a great feature emerging from the wash of fog before him, on the other side of the hill.

It was a tall round stack, made up of stones piled on top of one another, about as wide around as a large tree trunk. In the twisting paths surrounding Stronghollow, it would be considered unremarkable. But here, on the flat, featureless plain of Aridmoor, it was big enough to warrant being called a proper landmark.

As he drew nearer, he saw the yellow glow of lamplight ahead, individual lights flickering into focus one by one.

Edgecairn. He walked faster, his strength renewed at the side of the village.

It was small, just a single street of shops surrounded by farm holdings, but after the isolation of his travels, Wes felt he was stumbling into a great civilization after years of exile in the wilderlands.

He looked up, noticing that Celesyria was gone, as they'd planned. She had been instructed to fly close only until they reached Aridmoor and relative safety, and from there she would continue to Silverfell, where they would meet up once more.

Wes already missed the sound of her chatter inside his head. She had never been so far from Umrym before, and her enthusiasm for each new place they reached was contagious.

He pressed on, the fog swallowing the great stone cairn behind him as the road wove past it. Wes looked over his shoulder a final time before continuing forward, unable to shake the paranoia that had followed him into the gloom. After what had happened to Lev and Odrigh, he couldn't be too cautious.

He did not have to go very far in search of bodily comforts.

The Heath and Hallow Inn laid at the southernmost edge of the village, and he knew that the barman's daughter excelled in loveliness as well as hospitality.

Wes felt his cheeks go pink at the very thought of pretty Jill in her apron and cap, a little plump in her own right, in the curvy type of way, bringing bread fresh from the oven to his plate. *If only I could marry her.*

He saw the Inn's wooden sign come into focus a few yards ahead, a simple carving of a bear's outline with the name of the establishment scripted in dark red ink. *It's a pity.* He doubted that Jill would be capable of ruling a foreign Kingdom, even if she for some reason agreed to break off her current betrothal with the local blacksmith's apprentice.

Wes continued to daydream as he strode along the path, his feet numb from the wet and cold, as his deer plodded along behind him. Before he could approach the Inn's inviting red door, however, he saw a new orb of light appear on the road, moving toward him, enrobed in mist. A moment later it was joined by another, and then another, each individual glow bobbing about for a moment before coalescing together into a group.

A dozen men on tall horses appeared, each bearing a torch in his hand.

* * *

"Wes Cervos, Envoy of Silverfell," the man in front said with a bow from his saddle, his red curls tumbling out from beneath his helm. "I am Captain Drohma of the King's Protectorate. It is a relief to find you alive."

Wes stepped forward, making up the last bit of distance

between him and the company of men. All of them were wearing light riding armor, and all but two of the men had the red hair, pale eyes, and freckled skin common to the people of Aridmoor. The Protectorate was King Ursa's private watch, he knew, but he had not expected to find them here, so far from the capital of High Keep.

He had several questions, but if he did not eat and drink soon, he feared he would faint. The sun had risen higher in the sky, but still, the rain continued to fall relentlessly. *Surely the Captain would be pleased to speak somewhere comfortable.*

"Much as it is a relief to see you, Captain, I would very much like to get out of this rain," he said, mustering up a formality of speech that he had not had to use since leaving Silverfell. "I'm sure you'll agree that the blazing fireplace at the Heath and Hallow Inn will do."

"Certainly, my good lord," Captain Drohma said cheerily, his smile not reaching his eyes. "The barkeep's daughter will more than merely do, if you get my meaning."

"She is lovely, indeed."

"Yes, it's a shame the tease wears dresses with such an abundance of fabric," Captain Drohma said as several of his companions looked between one another, smirking.

Wes noticed that one of the men did not join in his Captain's joke, instead looking down at his feet and shaking his head. Though he was easily the tallest man in the company, with arms near as big around as Wes' legs, the gesture made him look vulnerable. Wes hoped for his sake that the Captain had not noticed his rebuff.

"Her name is Jill," Wes said, forcing a smile of his own. *Hopefully, she stays well away from you lot.* "She's always been very kind to me."

A lupine grin spread across the captain's face as he and two of his men headed for the Inn. The gentlemanly giant was not included among them.

Wes followed, unsure of any other reasonable course. The tall soldier stopped him, offering his hand for the deer's reins, and Wes obliged after being assured that the animal would get a well-deserved grooming and the best feed they could acquire.

On the inside, the Heath and Hallow looked exactly as it had after the last Feast of Offering, back when the entire Kingdom was shrouded in thick white snow.

Wes drank in the warmth of the candlelight and the smell of hearty bread and meat. The scent of Aridmoor's famous dark stout beer pricked at his nostrils pleasantly as he followed Captain Drohma and his men to a table at the back corner of the room.

They sat on dark wood benches at a red table that had the same bear shape carved into it, all graceful lines and gleaming lacquer. There was a window set into the thick cob wall, looking out into the impermeable fog, with a cheerful vase of the blue flowers he had seen earlier resting on it. There were several other tables, all taken up by dirty farmers in their work clothes, their conversation filling the Inn with lively sound.

He loved the atmosphere of the place. It was so different than the establishments he visited back home in Silverfell, all fussy dishes and staff who pretended to like you. This was an Inn for the common folk, and when he came, he was always treated as one of the same.

Jill knew of his calling and his noble blood, but growing up here in the middle of nowhere, he assumed she never really understood what it meant to other people. He wasn't offended to be treated like a peasant, especially when the peasants here were respected like old friends.

"So, Envoy," the Captain said luxuriously, the last word curling off his tongue like thick smoke. "Did you run into any bandits on your journey?"

"There's been a lot of bad folk about," said one of the other soldiers, raising his hand to call over the barman, who was polishing metal steins at the counter table. "Two villages in the west of Aridmoor. Raided."

"I'm sorry to hear it," Wes said, smiling at the slender barman, thankful for the interruption and for the promise that food was forthcoming. "We live in a dangerous age, indeed."

Wes did not object as Captain Drohma ordered several bear-meat steaks and bowls of saltporridge for the table, along with four mugs of stout.

"Thank you, Captain," Wes said, diving into his food before any further conversation could begin. The fare at the Heath and Hallow was even better than he'd remembered it, and he spent several moments thinking of nothing else but filling his aching stomach.

"I hate to bring sadness to such a marvelous table," the Captain said, his eyes roving across the room even as he ate. Wes saw no sign of Jill the barmaid, to his relief. "But as you say, this is a dangerous age, and growing ever more so. The elves may yet be a threat to us. These bandits to the west did not merely rob us."

"Though they did plenty of that, sir," one of the men said between mouthfuls of saltporridge. The barman swept in without a word, swapping his empty bowl with a full one and plucking the used napkins from around the table with long, thin fingers. He nodded to the Captain and his gaze lingered on Wes, their eyes meeting for a half-second longer than was necessary before he headed back toward the kitchen.

"Yes, they robbed the magistrate blind," The Captain waved his hand as if this was of no consequence. "They also took seven women and over a dozen children. They got away easily, too, having freed most of the horses the night before."

"That's terrible," Wes said, settling back to sip at his stout, his hunger fading to a mere annoying ache that he suspected would not subside for several more days.

"I fear—the King fears—that they have been taken to Nox by way of the Black Beach."

Wes only nodded.

He did not want to discuss Holga and Gohr's capture lest he be forced to answer uncomfortable questions involving a dragon. He did not wish to lie and decided that the Captain had no right to the information he had, at least, not at the moment.

Still, what the Captain said troubled him. Such events were not common in his memory, and now it seemed they were becoming more and more frequent across the Four Kingdoms, especially in Aridmoor and Boneshire, though he'd heard of a couple of presumed slavers operating farther to the north and east, within the borders of Galeharbor.

"Of course, so much of what passes as news is mere speculation," Captain Drohma said, the smile returning to his face as he lapped at his stout. "We know the slavers and bandits take people, but as much as we worry the elves are involved in some darker purpose, it could be that they need slaves for more... mundane ends."

Wes felt heat rising to his face.

"I'd hardly call the abuse of women and children at the hands of these barbarians a mundane end, Captain."

"No, of course not," he said quickly, the other two men

nodding as they watched their leader from over their drinks. "It is a terrible thing, and we will bring justice to those who have committed these crimes, make no mistake about it."

"I trust you will," Wes said with a brief nod, watching the Captain's face for any hint of the man's true feelings. He betrayed nothing, save the dullness of his eyes.

"Anyway. What of your Witness and Deermaster? We received word from Silverfell that you were late in returning, but it surprised me to find you alone and unguarded."

The strange grin returned, reminding Wes of a cat toying with an injured bird. For reasons he couldn't pin down, he did not trust the Captain. Still, there was no other story he could tell but the truth, or at least part of it.

He confessed the fate of Odrigh and Lev, only just managing to keep his emotions in check. Just telling the bare facts of what had happened was enough to flood his mind with memories, pain and sound and terrible sights competing for his recollection.

"Dwarves? Are you sure, Wes?" The captain leaned onto his elbows across the table, letting his rigid back hunch ever so slightly. "Such a thing has not been seen before."

"Never. It's never happened," said one of the other men, who had been silent for most of the meal. Both of them looked even more well-fed than Wes was, though he did not doubt that there was more muscle than flab beneath their uniforms. "Not in the Four Kingdoms."

"I'm sure, Captain. It's not something I want to be true, but so be it."

"Very interesting," Drohma replied, with the same dismissive wave of his hand. Wes caught a glance between him and his men that he could not read. "In any case, we are relieved you are well. Thank the Dracodei."

"I was fortunate." *Odrigh and Lev saved my life.* It was certainly not his own courage that spared him death. Were it not for Odrigh's skill with a bow, he would be with them in the cold mountains now, cold and alone and gone.

"Indeed. Our reasons for being sent to meet you are two-fold." The Captain set down his empty cup, knitting his fingers together. His men looked at their leader, both of them keeping their hands on their drinks, listening. "First, of course, we wanted to make sure that you and your companions were safe. It's a shame that we will not be able to report better news to the Septemvirate."

Did Dorold appeal to King Ursa for help specifically? Or all of the armies of the Four Kingdoms? Wes had lost track of how late he was. Perhaps there had been enough time to seek aid from those as close to Umrym as possible. Aridmoor soldiers were familiar with the wilderlands of Boneshire, and they could reach the Severed Summits much more quickly than Silverfell's men.

"At any rate, King Ursa will also be pleased to know you continue as Envoy. But he has another concern, a matter of some urgency."

"And what might that be?" Wes said, covering the carved horse's eye as he set his cup down on the table. He glanced around the Inn. Several of the farmers had gone, and he could see the barman standing a little closer to them than was necessary, polishing glasses that already appeared perfectly clean.

"Your security is imperative to us, especially taking recent events into account. The King wishes to meet with you. There is an offer he would like to propose for your consideration."

The Captain smiled, signaling for another round of drinks before explaining further. Wes placed a hand over his cup as the barman flitted about. Already, he could feel the pleasant hum of ale deep in his belly. He saw Captain Drohma's brows narrow slightly as the moment of quiet stretched out between them, both men waiting for the other to speak.

I may be young, but I will not be as willfully stupid as you expect.

* * *

"The King wishes to offer me his own Protectorate for the next Feast of Offering?"

"That is correct. The best soldiers that the Kingdom has to offer," Captain Drohma said, flashing his wolfish white smile once more.

The rest of the lunch crowd had filtered out of the Inn, returning to their duties, but Wes could note no change of time by looking through the window. The fog continued to obscure the passing of the sun. "I like to hope that includes myself, but you will have discretion as to your choice of men, of course."

Wes forced a smile.

"That is a generous offer," he began carefully, wanting very much to bolt out of the room. *Surely King Ursa does not think that the dragons will appreciate an army at their borders, let alone that he'll be able to march his Protectorate straight into Whitespire.*

Such a request was insanity, but the look on Captain Drohma's face made it clear that the King's offer was sincere.

"It is Boneshire's turn to provide a Witness for the next Feast, as I'm sure you remember."

"I forget little, Envoy," Captain Drohma said breezily.

"Of course, I would not seek to upend the order of things. Boneshire's Witness should join us."

"But—"

"Surely you know of Boneshire's instability," the Captain said, giving Wes a look that cut him to his marrow. *He cannot possibly know about the children. He's intimidating me, no more.* Wes was not convinced. Rumors of elf-spies in Boneshire had persisted ever since their raid on Silverfell. Surely the Kingdom of Aridmoor could have spies of their own. "It grows worse every year. Who is to say that the squabbling Lesser Houses of Redvale will even be able to produce a Witness next season? And even if they do, why should we trust them?"

"I do not have to trust the people of Boneshire," Wes said. "I trust the Septemvirate. It is they who confirm the selected Witnesses."

"Of course, my lord."

The captain sat up straight in his chair and downed the final dregs of stout.

"I understand your hesitation. It is unorthodox. King Ursa himself will admit as much."

An uncomfortable silence fell over the table. The barman, having run out of glasses to pretend to wipe, returned through a back door to the kitchen. Wes and Captain Drohma looked at each other, until Wes finally spoke, his resistance worn away under the ranking soldier's glare.

"I will have to seek counsel from the Septemvirate. Including Elder Dorold," Wes said pointedly.

"The King will be happy to travel to Stronghollow. We wouldn't want to cause a nuisance. You are welcome to invite anyone you wish to the meeting, of course."

Perhaps the old King's mind is starting to go. The Septemvirate will never agree to this, whatever I say. And I say it's madness.

"Fine. I will send a messenger when I reach Stronghollow to set up the details," Wes said, trying to keep himself from looking at the floor. Roven had always been excellent at official matters, at meetings and debates and at knowing which fork to eat with at diplomatic dinners.

And yet, somehow, it was he who was forced to negotiate with King Ursa's wild ideas. He felt hopelessly unprepared, but what else could he do?

"I'm sure the Septemvirate will clear their schedule for his Majesty."

"Excellent. We also wish to offer you aid in returning to Silverfell. It is not wise for the Envoy to travel alone."

"That won't be necessary, Captain," Wes said, forcing himself to keep his voice smooth. The thought of traveling with these men was unpleasant. His instincts were screaming at him that they were not to be trusted. Furthermore, he couldn't meet with Celesyria unless he was alone.

A spark of an idea flashed into his mind.

"The raids trouble me. I don't wish to take a single man away from the effort to hold these barbarians accountable. Perhaps when the Septemvirate meets with King Ursa, something could be arranged. Our army runs thin these days, but I am sure we could spare some aid." He let the words tumble out. It sounded like something Roven would have said. Perhaps even his father.

After a few moments, the Captain nodded crisply, smiling across the table at Wes.

"You have my thanks, Envoy. It's always, shall we say, preferable to return to the King with news he wishes to hear."

"Right. The King is not like his father, neither. He's got a little fire in 'im," one of the soldiers said, swallowing a belch.

Wes nearly choked on the final sip of his lukewarm ail, a chill rushing over him in the warmth of the Inn.

Captain Drohma glared at his men, daring either one of them to utter another word.

"I should have mentioned that I have some other unhappy news. You would hardly have heard about it in Whitespire, I suppose."

"Oh?"

"There's been a change in this great Kingdom," the Captain said, his mouth curving into an exaggerated frown. "King Radagar Ursa passed to the eternal lands, less than a fortnight past. His eldest son Kylan is now king."

Wes gave his condolences, his mind elsewhere. Radagar had not been a perfect King, but he had been just in his dealings. His son did not have the same reputation, and the rest of his family were no better, especially his wife's other, illegitimate son. Though Wes had not spent much time around either of them since they were boys, he did not find it difficult to believe what he'd heard.

The Inn suddenly felt very hot, and he was relieved when he finally emerged into the chill of the fog. After he bid Captain Drohma and his men farewell, he watched as the men headed east on horseback, their bodies fading into the mist.

The tall man, he noticed, was no longer among them.

He felt the tightness leaving his chest as they went, finding himself surprised it had been so easy to get rid of them.

Almost too easy.

Chapter Eleven

The city of Stronghollow is not what it appears to be.

Celesyria peered out of the tall tower's window, pondering. She could only look with one eye at a time, so she switched between them whenever her neck grew tired, which was rather often. She had become accustomed to the rhythms of the city below, and she watched as the usual man took his cart through the winding, narrow streets, delivering milk as the sun rose.

That was normal. It was afterward that things always seemed strange.

All the rest of the morning, even though the spring weather was pleasant, Celesyria never saw anyone out without a good reason. There were no children playing games, no young girls talking in groups. There were women carrying parcels, or craftsmen carrying tools, but everyone seemed to look over their shoulder as they went, walking as quickly as they could. Though she never saw any crime or even any threat of it, there was a palpable heaviness over the city. It made Celesyria uncomfortable.

It reminded her too much of Whitespire. Of emptiness. Of decay.

Still, at least the sad state of the city gave her something to mull over. It was not as though there was anything better to do.

She and Wes had met in the forests of Silverfell nearly a week earlier, and he'd brought her here three days ago, hidden beneath the cover of darkness.

It was once a guard tower, he'd said, but it had been empty ever since the raid that killed his parents. The roof had been almost entirely blown off by catapult fire, allowing Celesyria to enter from above while staying out of the view of anyone who might pass by on the ground. Having been out of use for several years, little remained in it, and certainly not any books or anything interesting to look at.

He had returned each night to bring her food but hadn't been able to stay long without arousing suspicion.

The hours between were very long, and very boring.

The tower was situated at the edge of Stronghollow's trade district, giving her a good view of the comings and goings of ordinary people.

Here, almost everything but the city walls were made of wood. Many of the peasants lived in simple log houses, often built partway into a hill so that the roof could remain grass or moss, at least, such was common in the area that she could see.

The shopfronts were similar, though they often had wood-shingle roofs. The streets were cobbled in stone, but there were walking paths near the main market square made up of wood planks. Celesyria had a particularly good view of the smith's guild building, which was built around a huge oak tree that grew straight through the roof.

She could only see a glimpse of the strange, wood-paneled palace, hidden behind a great stone wall in the distance. She imagined Wes there, in his childhood home, eating grand food, being met with a hero's welcome as she languished in the abandoned tower. It set her belly into knots. Even if Wes succeeded in speaking to the Septemvirate, she doubted that there would be a hero's welcome waiting for her.

With nothing else to do, she curled up on the floor, thankful that the air was rather warm, and tried to take another nap. She lay like that for a while, wondering whether the rest of Silverfell was in as much decline as Wes had said.

Was the neighboring Kingdom of Galeharbor in the same state? Was there nowhere left in Kaveryth that was truly free?

She thought of home, of the Umrym she had grown up hearing about. A land where dragon and dwarf lived in harmony with one another, where warriors were mighty and revered, and where industry thrived. She smiled to herself, not opening her eyes.

She had believed in that world for so long. Believed that if they simply continued, everyone fulfilling their own little role, things would eventually go back to the way that they were before. Eggs would hatch. Hatchlings would grow. Dragons would stop dying.

Everyone she knew disapproved of her imagination and her desire to learn about things that went beyond the usual purview of dragons or dwarves. And yet, it was they who believed in fantasies. Their whole way of life, the whole culture of Umrym, everything that everyone believed without question... It was all warped, twisted, false.

They could march forward all they wanted, but unless they were willing to face the truth, they would only be walking toward their doom. The High One had a plan. She knew that much, even if the details were hazy and the steps that lay before her were not always obvious.

She hoped that the people of Stronghollow would come to understand it, too, before their own delusions grew roots deep enough to pull them under.

* * *

Wes sat at the head of the table in the palace's great hall, picking at the slice of brown-sugar cake that sat on his plate. He was thankful to have a moment to himself as the Lesser House nobles and members of the Septemvirate went off to join the throng on the dance floor, their fine costumes twirling as they spun and jumped across the expanse.

The people of Stronghollow had been so relieved to find him alive that they threw an even more grand celebration of the Feast of Offering than had initially been planned. He had been home for only three days, and in that time, servants had transformed the city.

The entire interior of the palace was decorated with colorful ribbons and fresh flowers imported from Galeharbor. Along passageways, hundreds of candles glimmered from behind a canopy of artificial leaves that had been painstakingly attached to live tree boughs that had only begun to bud.

Even the streets of Stronghollow had been decorated in

celebration of his return, though he hadn't had a chance to look for himself. He'd been keeping to the shadows and taking the long way around the palace when he brought food to Celesyria, and even then, he feared to stay away for very long.

The weight of their secrets pressed upon his shoulders, and though the atmosphere was one of joy, he struggled to enjoy it.

Earlier that morning, he'd met with Lev's widow and his four children. They were gracious, but no matter how much he thanked them, he could not shake the guilt he felt. Because of him, they'd lost a husband and a father, and the trajectory of their life had been changed forever. His wife, especially, was left with new burdens to carry. Wes hoped that he'd be able to check in on how she was doing, but that, of course, depended on what happened when he set his plans into motion.

He'd mourned the death of his companions since leaving Umrym, but still, he struggled to move forward. Every night as he attempted to sleep, the images of that terrible day replayed in his mind, haunting him. When he had made his way through the familiar forest and followed the familiar curve of the valley toward Stronghollow, he knew that he was bringing tragedy with him. Until then, perhaps, if Captain Drohma had not sent any messengers, Lev's family had been able to hope that somehow he was still alive.

The rest of the city was celebrating him, but for those who had lost the men they loved, Wes returned as a messenger of death.

There was something else that needled at him as he went through the motions of his normal life as Envoy. He noticed the servants in a way that he hadn't before. He found himself taking stock of the peasants who traveled in and out of the palace as well, wondering what kinds of lives they were returning to in the streets of Stronghollow.

Though he had always thought that the Septemvirate ruled fairly and treated their subjects with kindness, Wes wondered if it was enough to compensate for what they took from them to give to the Dracodei.

When his parents had been alive, wealth had been far more abundant. Even if the sacrifices had been false, at least the people had been able to afford their forced participation. Now, he knew, many throughout the Four Kingdoms were becoming destitute, including those within the borders of Silverfell.

And as they struggle to feed their children and set aside a little coin for tomorrow, we ask them to cough up a quarter of what they earn to offer to the Dracodei, Wes thought gloomily, chewing at his cake without tasting it. The food for the celebration was abundant and the decorations were beautiful, and he wanted so badly to get away from it all.

Wes had never considered such things to be unjust. He still thought it reasonable that the King's family should be allowed to live in a manner befitting their state in life, but it was another thing to persist in such extravagance while knowing that his people were being lied to and robbed.

"Envoy Wes?" The voice was so soft that it took Wes a moment to acknowledge he'd heard it at all. It belonged to a flaxen-haired girl in a maid's uniform that was much too large. He recognized her as a servant from the palace's library who had been pressed into service of the kitchen. "Excuse me, my lord."

"Oria," he said, nodding to the child.

"A message came in about an hour ago, I guess it's urgent, as the gateman gave it to Saara, who gave it to me—"

"Thank you," he said quickly, noticing that Elder Jate, the only Boneshire-born member of the Septemvirate, was looking at them from the edge of the dance floor. Some of the Elders did not appreciate Wes' casual acquaintance with the servants, and he feared it would be the child who would be scolded for lingering too long and talking too much.

He plucked an envelope from the girl's hands before she scurried back toward the kitchen, nearly knocking a candle out of one of the tree branches as she went. To Wes' relief, Elder Jate had returned to dancing. He could only hope that the even more crotchety Elder Bram had not witnessed the exchange.

He opened the letter with some interest. A rush of relief washed over him as he read the brief notice. Upon arriving in Stronghollow, he'd immediately asked to see Elder Dorold in order to set up the broader meeting he planned with the Septemvirate, only to be told that the man was away visiting his family in Rivergrasp.

Wes had sent a messenger there to inform him that he had returned alive and well, and according to this note, he was on his way back. Why he'd left right before the celebration of the Feast of Offering in the first place was a mystery. Usually, all of the Elders used the time when the Envoy was traveling to retreat to the temple grounds for prayer.

Now that he knew that Elder Dorold was returning, he grew nervous. He was hardly looking forward to having to tell the Septemvirate the truth about the Dracodei.

At least I'll be able to give Celesyria more of an idea as to when she'll be able to leave the tower. He strained his neck and looked toward the kitchen doors. He wanted to find Oria again and ask her if she could fetch him some books from the library.

He couldn't leave the celebrations without raising eyebrows, and it would be very late by the time he was free to go and see the dragon. He knew he'd get a much warmer reception from her if he brought something to read.

She'd been in a rather foul mood since they'd arrived, not that it was difficult to see why. However strange life in the palace now felt, it was much more pleasant than being curled up in a too-small room and left alone.

Finally, after a couple more hours of feigning merriment, Wes made his way toward his chambers in the north wing of the palace. His legs felt heavy with exhaustion, though he noticed that they looked visibly thinner than when he'd left Silverfell.

He'd eaten far less at dinner than he usually did. There were bigger things on his mind. When he arrived at his locked door, he found a stack of books already waiting for him.

Oria had done what he'd asked without asking any questions, retrieving mostly boring histories that he wouldn't usually touch but perfectly suited to the dragon's tastes. He turned the key in the door, hefted the awkward tomes, and headed inside.

What? Why is she here?

Before he knew how to react to what he saw, his arm slipped, sending one of the largest volumes sailing toward the floor and landing with a thud loud enough to wake the servants. Four more of the books followed, spines bending as they landed on their faces, sending loose sheets of paper flying across the chambers.

"Shhh!" Princess Kessara Manta hissed, yanking Wes into the room and slamming the door behind him.

* * *

Wes stood stupidly by as Kessara bolted the lock to his chambers.

He'd been expecting to head out to see Celesyria and then to go to bed as early as possible after such a tiring day. Instead, his dead brother's betrothed had appeared in his sitting room. He ran a hand through his curls, remembering too late the pomade that one of the lesser noblewomen had smeared in it. His hand now smelled like spoiled fruit.

"What are you doing here?"

"Sorry to startle you, Wes. How are you?"

She strode over to one of the chairs that were sitting near the large parlor fireplace, beckoning him to follow. He did so, looking the Princess of Galeharbor up and down as she sat.

She was as pretty as ever, with bright blonde hair and pale gray eyes that contrasted with her tanned skin. For some reason, however, she was dressed as a soldier, in light armor and a hooded cloak suitable for travel. *She's dressed like Odrigh*, Wes thought with a pang in his heart.

He could imagine the man in happier times, singing around the campfire on the way to Whitespire, his blue eyes dancing. Though Kessara shared his coloring, they were from very different worlds. His hands were rough, accustomed to tying knots and hauling fish baskets.

Kessara looked more like a child playing dress-up, her delicate fingers and spotless skin incongruent with her Kingdom's practical military garb.

"Glad to be home, I guess," he said, settling into his chair. The fire crackled merrily behind its grate, driving away the slight draft of chilly spring air that always seeped into his rooms.

"We're all glad to see you safe," she said, pausing for a moment and meeting his eyes, saying nothing more.

"May I ask the reason for all of this cloak and dagger?"

"All the what?"

"Nevermind." Wes shook his head. "Is everything okay?"

"My father would not have sent me if it was," she said, fidgeting with the edge of her cloak. "There have been reports of dwarf boats off of the north coast. Multiple reports. From credible men. Men that we trust."

"How?" Wes felt his pulse begin to quicken. The dwarves of Umrym hated water. He couldn't picture them setting foot in a boat. And even if they could, where would they launch it from?

"The Black Beach?" He asked.

"We don't know, but I doubt it," Kessara said. Wes agreed.

The dwarves were hemmed in by mountains to the west and north of Umrym, mountains that ended in sheer cliff faces. They could mine their way through if they wished, but it would be almost impossible to reach the base of the valley that led toward the Black Beach, let alone reach the ocean itself.

"Even if they managed to forge a path, how would they have brought their boats through?"

"They must have traveled inland, through the Severed Summits and into Boneshire," Wes said. He recounted as quickly as he could what he'd experienced in the fallen Kingdom, omitting the part about the dragon. He breathed a sigh of relief when Kessara did not pick away any further at the details.

"Even if dwarves are moving freely within Boneshire and they made it to the Black Beach, why would the elves allow them to pass so near to Nox's shores on the other side?"

"I have no idea," Wes said, imagining the continent in his mind, trying to get a grasp on where the short race may have traveled. "The only other possibility is that they went all the way to the southern sea and headed north once they reached the western shores of Galeharbor."

"The Farplace lies to the south," Kessara reminded him, shaking her head. "No one who has attempted to go beyond the shallows has returned alive, and traveling near the shores of Boneshire poses its own risks."

"Fair point. They would be traveling through the territory of several criminal factions. Who could they broker an alliance with? The Magistrate of Redvale?"

"Exactly," Kessara nodded, her blonde hair bobbing at her shoulders. "No matter how we look at it, if the reports are indeed accurate, the dwarves must have made some alliance in order to reach my Kingdom. Whoever those allies are, it does not bode well for any of us."

Wes nodded as he glanced out of the window at the night sky, wishing that he could send a message to Celesyria to tell her that he'd been held up. He had tried to speak to her in his mind, but the old guard tower was too far from the palace. He hoped that eventually he'd learn to project his thoughts farther, or would at least be able to hear her at greater distances.

"My father wishes to seek the advice of the Septemvirate before this news reaches the other Kingdoms."

"Especially now that Radagar Ursa is dead."

"More like murdered," Kessara muttered. Wes waited for her to say more.

Instead, she stood up from her chair and headed toward the window, keeping far enough back that no one would be able to see her on the small chance that someone was looking in from the ground, three stories below.

"Anyway, that doesn't matter now. Kylan Ursa is King, and we must deal with it. Aridmoor is Aridmoor. They're our allies as long as it suits them, and right now, it seems the wind is shifting. It's down to us, now. There is no one else we can trust."

Wes joined Kessara at the window, looking out into the night. She stood with the posture of a future queen, her chin held aloft, her shoulders sloping only slightly. He stood taller, trying to coax his neck straight. He could not deny her words.

"I fear you're right, my lady," he ventured. "The dragons have become very quiet. They no longer strike fear into the hearts of our enemies as they once did."

He expected her to look at him, wide-eyed, perhaps chide him for impiety. Instead, she nodded briskly, continuing to stare out the window, her face revealing no emotion.

"Can you help me to hide in your palace until I can arrange a meeting?"

He nodded, thinking about where he might find for her to stay and who might be able to assist her once she was safely hidden away. Palaces had a way of attracting spies to come work as servants. It seemed he would need to place his trust in young Oria once again.

"I have my own meeting to call," he said. "When Dorold returns. But I will see to it that you can remain here in privacy if that is what His Majesty deems necessary."

"Thank you," she said, turning away from the window to face him with apparent effort. "It is true that I came here to call this meeting on behalf of my father, but there is more I need to tell you."

Wes chuckled, uncomfortable beneath her intense gray gaze. "Please tell me that there is nothing worse going on than mysterious dwarven ships to the north."

"That depends on your definition of worse," she said, looking at her feet. She had worked a thread free from the bottom of her cloak and was twisting it around her pinky finger.

"Just tell me already. You're acting strange."

"Fine," Kessara said, sucking in a breath. Wes' smile faltered.

"I'm here to broker a marriage, at the request of King and Queen Manta. Happy?"

Surely, no. Not that. Not possible.

"Yes. They want the two of us to get married, for the sake of our Kingdoms."

Chapter Twelve

Wes woke up but did not open his eyes right away, allowing himself a few moments to think before he faced the day that lay ahead.

Every time he carried the sacrifices to Whitespire, he returned to Silverfell with a lingering appreciation for his bed. He rarely missed the attention of servants or the beauty of the palace when he traveled, but sleeping on the ground was something he never managed to get used to.

He could feel the gentle warmth of the fire and smell the hint of flowers budding outside of his window. All around the palace courtyard, the gardeners would be preparing for spring to arrive in force, the green leaves and flowers making the city's buildings blend into the forest. Wes could feel the soft sunlight beaming against his eyelids.

Perhaps I've overslept. The Caravan of the Claim will not be heading out until later this morning...

He sat upright, squinting in the harsh ray of light streaming in from his window. There was something else, something much more urgent tugging at his mind. The Caravan was the least of his concerns. Kessara's visit the night before came flooding into his memory.

He hadn't been at his most gentlemanly. As a matter of fact, he had offered her little more than mumbled promises to discuss it later as he nearly threw her out of his chambers.

He had laid in bed for several hours, but eventually sleep had claimed him, and with it, blissful ignorance.

Now, though, he had a day of Feast celebrations to attend, and he'd promised to talk to Kessara more about what she'd proposed after getting some rest.

She nearly did propose, didn't she? He strode over to the washbasin and splashed cold water on his face. He struggled to stop himself from laughing maniacally at his reflection in the ornate mirror hung on the wall.

He settled instead on a poor impression of Queen Manta, his voice rising in pitch until it neared hysteria. "Now, Kessara, I know you loved Roven Cervos. Yes, dear, I know he was handsome, brave, and a gentleman. But you have your people to think about. Roven is dead. Instead, you must marry his fat little pork of a brother. It won't be so terrible, dear! He's a nice boy."

Wes, failing to amuse himself, pulled on his trousers. Yes, he needed to find a queen if he wanted to ensure the survival of Silverfell, but this was hardly what he'd had in mind when he had agreed to Celesyria's plan. Kessara was beautiful and had a good heart, but she was also Roven's betrothed.

He could imagine his brother's face, peering through the veil that separated the Eternal Lands from the living world, his jaw tight with fury at his little brother for stealing his wife. Roven was virtuous, but even he had limits to his selflessness. Then again, if it really were a matter of saving all Kaveryth from destruction, perhaps he would understand.

Or perhaps not.

Wes shook his head, pushing his worries from his mind. Fully dressed, he headed out to face the more immediate demands of the day. After a rushed breakfast and a dreadfully boring meeting with a few members of the Septemvirate about the Witness selection for the next Feast, it was nearly time for the Caravan to depart.

* * *

Wes was seated near the back, riding a tall stag whose antlers were decorated with bits of colored ribbon. Surrounding him were a company of soldiers, who, like him, were dressed in deep green riding cloaks and black felt caps.

Unlike him, they were allowed to wear their proper swords at their belts. The women in charge of costuming had confiscated his remaining curved knife, despite his protests, and in return, he was expected to carry a fussy silver pillow with the Claim sitting in the center beneath a piece of protective lace.

Seeing that they had a fair way to travel before meeting any spectators, Wes stuffed a corner of the pillow beneath the front of his saddle so he could keep both of his hands on the reins. He hoped that he would find his knife safe and sound afterward, and wondered if anyone had yet found the other half of the pair, left behind in the wilderlands of Boneshire.

"I'd be careful with that," said a soldier called Moorn, whose deer stood next to Wes' own. "I'm told Elder Bram is on the warpath this morning."

"Why?" Wes asked, rolling his eyes as he returned the pillow to his hands, letting the reins fall gently against his deer's neck. They were moving slowly, but still, riding with only his legs to balance him was tiring.

"Someone filled the band's horns with sawdust," he said, smirking. "Elder Bram was supervising the rehearsal back at the barracks. He didn't seem to like the great crescendo."

Wes stifled a laugh as the Caravan reached the edge of the palace grounds. Moorn was forced to ride ahead of him as the column narrowed to fit through the gate. His calves burned as he guided the deer down the cobbled path, avoiding the branches that formed a living tunnel overhead.

Up ahead, he could see the seven members of the Septemvirate—with the notable exception of Elder Dorold—riding in a neat row, each one on a pale gray doe. They wore long gray robes, similar to those they donned for normal meetings, but these had detailed embroidery and beadwork along the sleeves and across the neck.

From farther ahead, Wes heard the army band striking up. Crowds cheered along the streets of Stronghollow as the head of the Caravan passed by. Wes couldn't help but smile as he heard the rising sound of horns, followed by the pounding of drums. The music brought back happy memories of his childhood, when coming home meant seeing those he loved as well as enjoying the festivities.

After a few minutes, he settled into the flurry of activity around him, smiling as little children waved to him. The Caravan was not so much for him personally as it was for the office of Envoy and the Claim itself, but still, he found it difficult not to get caught up in the attention.

Attention I never asked for. He held the pillow carefully with one hand, returning the wave of a particularly zealous young boy in a butcher's apron.

The moonscar fell to me by chance. It could just as easily have been one of you. I wish it had been, believe me.

Finally, after what felt like a very long time holding the Claim aloft on its silly little pillow, they began to make their way back into the palace grounds. Before Wes could get his deer through the gate, however, he saw someone wave to him from a window in the old armory.

Kessara. He did not wave back, instead pretending that he had not seen her. He was sure that she was just being friendly, but the thought of so much as looking at her at the moment made him feel rather nauseous.

Surely, this was a terrible sign for the potential of their marriage.

He was relieved when Moorn fell in beside him. Soon, the two men were chatting away happily, distracted from the bustle until they reached the stables several minutes later.

"I think I'm going to visit my parents," Wes said after talking for a little while longer, desperate to get away from the crush of bodies that still milled around the palace grounds, enjoying the last hours of festivity until the next Feast came. The cemetery on the edge of Stronghollow would be peaceful, and he had not brought bread to their graves since returning from Whitespire.

"See you later?"

Moorn slapped him on the back and headed off, joining several of the other soldiers who were heading over to the courtyard, probably to find some visiting maidens who had not yet endured their charms.

Wes stripped off his cloak and hat, laying them carefully near his deer's saddle before heading off behind the stables. The mausoleum was not far, and there, at least, he could get a quiet moment to think. He knew he had promised to speak to Kessara, but he couldn't face her, not now.

With any luck, he could hide out until it was time to go and see Celesyria. He hoped that she would have some wise advice, because he had no idea what he was doing.

* * *

As Wes entered the old guard tower, Celesyria's eyes fell immediately on the book-shaped bundle wrapped in oilcloth that he held in his hands.

A rainstorm had begun a little while before, and every few minutes she heard the crash of thunder as lightning lit the sky. She was about to comment on the treasures he had brought when she noticed the look on his face.

Wes stood there in the dim candlelight, his hair sopping wet, his skin sallow.

"I brought you some books," he said, with no hint of a smile. He undid the bits of string that held the oilcloth closed and laid four dusty-looking volumes on a table near the door.

She allowed herself to glance at their titles for a couple of seconds. *A Complete History of Auranthian Armor Techniques. Vavoren Archive, Volume III. The Calamity of Graveheim.* The fourth title was too small to read. She attempted to conceal her excitement as she turned back to her friend. There would be time to read, too much of it, soon enough.

"You look ill," Celesyria said, failing to think of a more tactful

way to ask him why he looked so awful.

"In case you missed it, it's raining. I was outside in the cemetery when the clouds rolled in. I feel like a drowned ditch rat."

Celesyria was relieved to see a slight smile tugging at his mouth, but still, she was troubled. He had never come to see her the night before, and now he looked as though he'd seen death.

"How was the Caravan?"

"It was nice. Happy. Like old times, except for the small fact that it's all a lie."

"I saw the women dancers with their ribbons on sticks. It was beautiful," she said sincerely, thinking back to the frantic twirl of color and the pounding of drums as the parade passed near the edge of Stronghollow. She had watched from start to finish.

However bitter Wes was, she could see the value in celebration, in giving the struggling people something to look forward to beyond the daily struggle of trying to keep their families fed. She suspected that, like the Envoy himself, there was some level of truth to the tradition of the Claim, a deeper meaning to the High One that had been lost to memory.

"They're called the Springdaughters. They are trained in the palace from a young age. Some of them can dance on the tips of their toes."

"The dragons have a troupe that dances in the sky, though it's grown rather small, since..."

Wes was not meeting her eyes. He leaned against the wall, looking down at his soaked boots. Silence hung between them until it began to grow uncomfortable. She picked at a bit of stone with a claw, wishing that she could fully stretch out. She had never had much interest in joining the Caela dancers, but the thought of swirling about in open air had never been more inviting.

"There is something I have not told you," Wes said aloud, his words falling on top of one another. "There is another person who hides in Stronghollow."

"What do you mean?"

As though remembering who he was speaking to, Wes resumed talking within his mind, recounting how Princess Kessara had been sent to Silverfell by King and Queen Manta. Celesyria was troubled by the news. She had only ever known the dwarves as allies. Now, it seemed, groups of dwarven traitors were wreaking havoc across Kaveryth.

"Do you trust her?" She asked.

"What choice do I have? I have to trust her parents, as well. We have no true allies left but Galeharbor."

"So why do you look so miserable?"

"Because the noble family wishes for us to marry."

Celesyria started to chuckle, a tension that she did not know she was feeling rippling out of her body and leaving her calm. *The High One was still in control of His creation, even when it seemed impossible that things will come together in time.*

Wes' frown only deepened, and she stopped laughing, trying to read the look in his dark brown eyes.

"I repeat," she said finally. *"Why do you look so miserable? Did we not recently establish that finding a queen is the only way to save your Kingdom?"*

"I told you. She was my brother's betrothed. In any case, I didn't think that a Princess would fall on my doorstep before I even got a chance to reason with the Septemvirate. I am nowhere near ready for this. I'm only seventeen!"

Celesyria cringed inwardly. She'd forgotten that Roven had been betrothed to the Princess of Galeharbor before his death.

Still, Wes had to see that the issue at hand was bigger than he and his brother.

"Such things do not happen by mere chance. We weren't expecting it. Does that not indicate to you that perhaps this sudden arrival of a suitable future queen may be the work of the High One?"

Wes did not look convinced. *"Perhaps."*

"You speak often of Roven's righteousness," she continued, trying to keep the excitement from her voice. The Princess's arrival did seem to be a miracle, the more that she thought about it. So many events had fallen into place for such an event to occur. It could not be a mere coincidence.

"He would understand. He would want what's best for his people. You already trust Kessara Manta, you said so yourself. Together, you could free the people of Silverfell from these burdensome sacrifices."

Wes paced back and forth against the tower wall as thunder hammered behind him, making the glass windowpanes rattle against the old wood.

"The House of Manta has its own reasons for wishing to negoti-ate a marriage. Even in these dark days, the army of Silverfell is the best trained in the Four Kingdoms. Aridmoor's army is larger, but ours is superior." Wes paused for a moment, though he did not stop pacing, his feet marking out the same small space, over and over.

"With the sighting of dwarf boats off of their coast, it makes sense that he would want to ensure access to our overland trade routes."

"It seems it would be a wise alliance."

"It would be."

"But?"

Wes let his eyes fall to his feet once more. *"I don't love her,*

Celesyria.”

She looked at him then, noticing for the first time how very young he was. Responsibility had been placed upon him since a young age, and losing his family at twelve must have caused him to mature even faster.

But he was still seventeen.

She was nearly two hundred years old. There were some things that could be learned only by experience, by time spent living. She could not possibly expect him to understand what she saw if she did not teach him.

“Marriage goes beyond love, Wes. It always has.”

“You think I don’t know that? My parents were betrothed when they were younger than I am now. They barely knew each other until they had already pledged to marry.”

“As were mine. Such arrangements are common in Umrym, especially among the Guardians. So far, no one has approached my father about taking me as a mate,” she said, unsure whether or not the thought made her smile. She may have understood the ways of love a little better than Wes did, but that didn’t mean she envied his position. She wanted to marry when the time was right, and she wanted it to be her choice, just as he did.

“They’re missing out,” Wes said, letting a small smile reach his eyes. *“You’re quite the catch.”*

“So is Kessara, it would seem,” Celesyria dodged the compliment, thankful that she could not blush.

“She is. She’s beautiful, smart, and kind. Even more importantly, she knows how to manage a Kingdom. She’s been preparing to take the crown practically since she learned how to walk.”

“But that’s not the problem either, is it?”

“No, you’re right. It’s not a her problem, it’s a me problem. I just don’t know what it is,” Wes said, sighing as he ran a hand

across his still-damp hair. *"Maybe you're right. Silverfell needs a queen, and one has appeared as if by magic. But I'm not the one she wanted to marry. She loved my brother. How can I take his place?"*

"How does she feel about this potential marriage?"

"I have no idea. I've been avoiding her," Wes admitted.

Celesyria rolled her eyes. *"Perhaps actually asking her that would be a good place to begin."*

"I suppose you're right. But I guess I just—I want to see how she responds to the meeting first. She may not still be willing to marry me after I tell her I plan to burn our entire faith to the ground. That's not even accounting for the King and Queen's opinion."

Celesyria nodded. This was true enough. Even if they chose to trust her, it was another thing entirely to know that she'd be a willing participant in their plans. She knew that well enough thanks to her friendship with Gramnok.

For several moments neither of them spoke, both lost in thought as they listened to the sound of rain pattering on the roof.

"Celesyria," Wes said finally. *"There is something else that weighs heavily on my mind. What does the High One want of us? He does not want the coins we sacrifice, but surely there is something He desires of His people."*

"Well," she said, struggling to find the right words. *"I have only read portions of the Codex. There is still so much that I don't know."*

"But what do you think? What is your intuition?"

There was a pain in his eyes that she couldn't place. It made her heart clench in her chest.

She thought about the knowledge that she had gained. It had been enough to drive her away from her family and across

Kaveryth. It had been enough to convince her to commit the crime of blasphemy and to be seen as a traitor against her race.

And yet, there were so many questions that she could not answer. So many things that she had to simply brush aside, in hope that one day the truth would be made known to her. She only hoped that Wes would accept the uncertainty, at least for now. She didn't know of anything better that she could offer.

"There is a portion of the Codex Veritatis that I have memorized," she said softly. When Wes didn't respond, she began to repeat the familiar words to him, her own buried pain rising to the surface.

"...A soul is necessary for all who belong here, and a soul that race will never possess," she finished.

"So dragons do not possess souls? The Farplace is their only possible destination when they die?"

"That's what the High One says."

"And you still wish to follow Him?"

"It's hard for me to explain," she started, lowering her head so that his eyes met hers. *"But yes. I will follow Him. The High One has made it clear that He wishes to use me, even if it's hard to understand how."*

"Perhaps that is what He asks for," Wes said, biting a fingernail between his teeth. *"Could a true God have need of money? It seems so silly to me now. He wants more than what we give. He wants us. All of us. Everything we would hold back."*

He was silent for a long while. Celesyria thought he looked angry, his dark eyes narrowing beneath his pale, still-damp forehead.

In so short a time, she'd spoken more of her secrets to him than she'd ever entrusted to any other. And yet, there was so much she did not yet know about him. Behind his intense gaze was something more. There was a grace in him. There was a nobility that went beyond an accident of birth, beyond a glimmering old scar in the shape of a crescent moon.

* * *

Two days later, the weather had not improved, nor had Wes found the courage to speak to Kessara.

He paced around in the back of the Septemvirate's meeting hall, looking down at the mud from the courtyard which hung stubbornly to the legs of his formal trousers. They hung visibly looser than they had the last time he'd worn them, though he still found the cut too tight to be comfortable. He was trying to look serious and capable, but instead, he feared he looked like a child going to a grown-up party.

Wes coughed, the sound reverberating off of the walls of the huge room, all made of slick stone and wood polished to gleaming. Even during the time of celebration that always followed the Feast of Offering—when the rest of the palace was covered in greenery, flowers, ribbons, and other decorations—the hall was left untouched.

Wes felt strange calling such a meeting. He couldn't help but feel intimidated, waiting for the seven Elders to arrive and take their seats on the great wooden thrones that formed a circle in the center of the room.

According to the laws of Silverfell, only the king or queen could call an official meeting of the Septemvirate, however, the Envoy was permitted to summon the Elders for reasons of counsel, and he hoped that they would permit this slight variation from the plain letter of the law.

Wes snapped to attention as the great wooden doors at the

far end of the room shuddered open. He strode toward the Elders, his back uncomfortably straight as he tried to ignore the pounding of his heart. He was sure that the smile on his face looked fake, but he held it there, cheeks aching.

Someone else should be here. Anyone else would be an improvement. Anyone. But Roven would be my first choice.

"Wesley, my boy," Elder Dorold was the first to speak, taking the last few steps toward the ring of thrones with an agility that belied his age. *If he hasn't started calling me Wes by now, he never will.*

He looked even older than the last time Wes had seen him, shortly before setting out for his last journey. His back seemed to stoop lower, and his ears had sprouted more white hair.

He grinned and clapped Wes on the arm, letting his Head Elder's staff rest in the crook of his bony elbow.

"Goodness, you look so handsome. Congratulations on another successful Feast of Offering!"

"Thank you, Dorold." Wes was indeed happy to see the head of the Septemvirate, but it bothered him that he did not mention the death of Lev, or of Odrigh straight away. *As long as the coins reach the tower, that's what matters.* His smile faltered.

"What's this about?" Elder Bram asked, crossing his arms against his hollow chest. Like the rest of the Septemvirate, his formal gray robe touched the floor and hid his feet. Unlike the others, however, his clothing bore no mark of the thick mud that surrounded the palace after the heavy rain that had stubbornly persisted since the day of the caravan.

Probably got some poor servants to lay out their coats for him to trod upon.

Wes swallowed his annoyance and waited as Elder Dorold strode to the center of the thrones.

"Elders of the Septemvirate, I thank you for your presence here," he said, his voice echoing throughout the meeting hall. "Please, sit."

The elders took their seats, but Wes, having none, stood awkwardly to the side of Elder Qofi's throne as the head Elder continued.

"Our Envoy has told me that there is a matter he must discuss with the entire Septemvirate." He took two steps back, gesturing toward the center of the ring of thrones. There was an awkward pause. Wes could hear Elder Bram and Elder Jate tittering in their own thrones.

"Take the floor, son."

Cheeks burning, Wes did so, forcing himself to look toward the door lest he stare at his feet.

"Good Elders, I thank you in advance for your counsel. I have never sought to call such a meeting since the death of my father and mother, the King and Queen of Silverfell."

He caught Dorold's eye, and the man gave him a brief nod of approval. *So far, so good.* He drew another breath before continuing on.

"The law clearly states that an Envoy—"

"Yes, we know the law, else I would not be here wasting my time," Elder Bram cut in, leaning forward in his throne, the ancient wood creaking. "I want to know why we have been summoned. Surely, we can dispense with the formalities."

"I had planned to be in Briarcroft by now," Elder Gunnan added. "My daughter is marrying a Lesser House noble from Aridmoor. With this hideous weather, I fear I will be late if I don't ensure that I have extra travel time."

Elder Bram glared at his fellow member as Wes cleared his throat.

"I understand that your great service to our Kingdom leaves you with little time for frivolity," he said, stumbling slightly on the final few words.

"But it is this very commitment to serve that compels me to share with you what I have learned."

"I always have time to hear the needs of my people," Elder Qofi said.

"It goes without saying."

"Indeed. Are you implying otherwise, Envoy?"

"Let's get on with it," Elder Bram snapped at the bearded Elder. The men went silent, looking toward their leader.

"Tell us, my boy," Dorold said, rubbing at his temples with the tips of his fingers.

"Right," Wes said, trying to think of how he wanted to begin, the moment of quiet setting his heart racing once again.

He rather agreed with Elder Bram—the whole thing would be much easier if he could dispense with the formalities—but he knew that if he spoke casually, the man would find another way to condemn him.

"As you have no doubt heard by now, my Deermaster and my Witness were killed. What you probably did not hear was that Lev and Odrigh were slaughtered by dwarves."

A gasp sounded out throughout the room.

"I heard such a rumor from one of Aridmoor's soldiers in recent days, but never did I imagine it was true," Elder Gunnan said.

"Are you certain, boy?" Elder Dorold asked.

Wes assured him that he was.

"The soldier that Elder Gunnan spoke to was correct. On my return journey, I spoke to Captain Drohma of King Ursa's Protectorate and told him what had happened. He told me that slavers had raided two villages in Aridmoor. He suspects that the prisoners were taken to Nox."

He paused a moment, letting the gravity of the situation settle in.

"Furthermore, when I was traveling through Boneshire, I was able to free two children who had been captured by slavers." He hoped that the Elders would not ask too closely after Holga and Gohr, who were certainly guilty of the same blasphemy he was. "Those slavers were dwarves, or at least, close enough to them to be carrying provisions of dwarf-make."

"This is dark news, very dark..." Elder Rahma, the oldest in the Septemvirate, said in his whisper-soft voice. "Dorold, what do you make of this?"

"I wish to hear more of what the boy has to say before I offer an opinion." Dorold nodded to Wes, bidding that he continue.

Now for the difficult part.

He was struck with a strange urge to pray to the High One for help but brushed it aside. Even if Celesyria was right on that point, what good could it do now? It was too late for some intervention from the Eternal Lands. As usual, he was on his own.

* * *

"I met another on my travels," Wes began, trying to keep his voice from quavering. Everything he said in the large room echoed as the Septemvirate sat waiting. "Before my encounter with the children. A dragon."

The Elders glanced at each other as Dorold beckoned him to continue.

"She is a scholar of history," he ventured. *Of the amateur sort.* "She has visited many dwarven libraries in the far-flung corners of—"

"Very interesting. What does this have to do with the dwarves?" Elder Bram interrupted once again, tapping at the edge of his throne with his fingernails.

"I'm not entirely sure," he admitted, wishing very badly that the unpleasant old man had not come. "It speaks to the shifting of the foundation that the Four Kingdoms rest upon. I am hopeful you will be able to make sense of it."

"Please continue," Elder Dorold said, raising his eyebrows at Elder Bram until he let his fingers lay still on the polished oak.

Wes nodded and plunged forward. Stalling wouldn't save him, and it might lose him some allies.

"In these libraries, she found several fragments of the Codex Veritatis."

Wes expected a gasp, or perhaps a few indignant shouts, but they never came. Instead, several of the men laughed.

"The Codex is a myth," Elder Bram said, sneering. "Surely, the good Envoy did not call us here to seek our counsel on some children's bedtime story."

"That's quite enough, Elder Bram," Dorold snapped. "Let him finish."

"This dragon sought me out because she believed her race would not listen to her. She told me of a prophecy, referring to a thousand years wherein the people of Kaveryth would be allowed to persist in error. At the end of this time," he paused, not wanting to use the High One's name until he had a chance to explain. "The creator and ruler of all Kaveryth would begin to punish those who have usurped the worship due to Him."

There was no laughter now. Wes waited for a beat, but no one said anything.

"Surely the Septemvirate would concede that the behavior of the dragons has become strange in recent years? I've noticed it on my travels. I suspect our soldiers and merchants have observed the same. The skies are quieter than they've ever been, and we've been given no explanation as to why."

"We have seen less of them since the King and Queen were killed, I suppose," Elder Derden conceded finally. "What of it?"

For a moment, Wes felt unable to answer.

All of the Elders were staring at him. Elder Bram looked murderous, and even Dorold looked displeased. *What if Celesyria is interpreting the Codex Veritatis wrong?* Panic gripped his chest, and he had to force himself to continue to breathe. He was about to make a huge accusation based on writings he had not even seen for himself. An accusation that was itself a serious crime under the laws of Silverfell.

"Wes," Dorold prompted.

He thought of Holga and Gohr, and the words they'd shared with him, safeguarded by their people for centuries. He was beginning to believe that he had felt the hand of the High One rather than the mindless touch of coincidence, but it was another thing to assert as much when his reputation with the most powerful men in the Four Kingdoms was on the line.

Furthermore, he could not risk their safety by sharing that prophecy. He would have to find a way to convince the Septemvirate without it, at least for now.

"Some of the dwarves seem to be allying themselves with elves. The dragons no longer patrol the skies over Kaveryth. I could go on. Our world is in peril. On top of that, my own

House hangs by a thread."

"A weak thread," Elder Jate muttered, loud enough for Wes to hear from where he stood.

"The world is not as it was before," he continued. "This prophecy makes sense of—"

"That is hardly enough evidence to believe such tales," Elder Rahma said, the fierceness in his eyes betraying the softness of his speech.

"I agree." Wes paused for a moment, allowing his concession to sink in before continuing.

"In and of itself, these calamities are not enough to be sure. But the dragon is from Whitespire, from a legacy family of Guardians. The dragons have not been commanded to step aside by the Dracodei. Nor have they chosen to neglect their duties on their own."

"What, then?" Elder Bram asked.

"We see few dragons because they are dying, my good Elder," Wes said, standing up to his full height and taking a step toward the man's throne.

"I understand that you have always disliked me", he continued, anger thrumming in his chest. "But I have never doubted that you care about the people of Silverfell and all the Four Kingdoms. Please, for a few more minutes, listen to what I have to say."

Elder Bram sat firmly against the back of his throne, his cheeks flushed.

"Other than the Dracodei, dragons are not immortal. I fail to see how—"

"At the time when the House of Noctua fell, their numbers had fallen to only four thousand. Now, there are half that number. More are dying every day," Wes said, surprised at the authority in his voice. He had no other choice. He could not allow the men to downplay what was happening as some quirk of nature.

"They have hidden this from us, but the dwarves of Umrym know. That is why, I suspect, some within their midst are defecting to their former enemies in Nox."

"That doesn't make sense," Elder Gunnan chimed in. "Even if there are fewer dragons than there once were, the dwarves must know that all of Nox is helpless against the power of the Dracodei."

Wes looked at his feet. He focused on the tiny cracks in the stone floor as he listened to the final echo of Elder Gunnan's words. He'd been given a perfect segue into the real reason that he'd come.

There is no turning back. I must try to do what is right, whatever the cost.

"Those dwarves may have read the same texts from the Codex as my friend has," he said carefully. "Or perhaps the elves of Nox have read them and convinced these dwarves of their truth. In any case, the meaning cannot be avoided. The Dracodei—"

Before he could continue, Elder Dorold rose to his feet, rapping his staff against the edge of his throne.

"Much has been said this day. I am calling a recess."

"But—"

"Effective immediately!" Elder Dorold nearly yelled. Wes shrank back as each of the Elders rose from their thrones in unison and began walking wordlessly toward the door at the far wall, their robes swishing against the stone as they went.

"Elder Dorold—"

"Not now," he whispered to Wes, so low that the others did

not hear. "Keep your mouth shut until they leave."

Wes obeyed as the rest of the Septemvirate filed past him. His heart was racing, and he could feel sweat beading upon his brow, but he bit back the harsh words that rose to his tongue. He'd finally worked up the courage to speak, only to be silenced before he could say a single word.

The whole situation angered him.

He was the final person keeping the House of Cervos alive, the chosen Envoy of all the Four Kingdoms, and yet he was, in actuality, completely powerless.

He thought of Celesyria, alone in a tower, waiting for him. Trusting him so much that she was willing to risk her future and perhaps even her life on the slim chance that he could bring the truth to Kaveryth. He couldn't let her down.

Chapter Thirteen

After what seemed like a long while, the great door to the meeting hall slammed closed a final time. The Septemvirate Elders would go to their lounge where they could discuss him in private and find new ways to pick apart what he had to say. It would be doubly difficult to get them to listen when the meeting continued.

Wes waited, listening as the echoes faded into silence before speaking.

"You made me look like a fool, Dorold," he said, forcing himself to keep his tone calm.

Dorold's voice betrayed no hint of his usual gentle demeanor. "What you are saying is not merely foolish. It is madness."

"I—"

"Wes Cervos, I have cared for you like a son all these years,"

Dorold snapped. "You will not speak over me as though you are my equal."

Wes let his hands rest behind his back, pressing his fingertips into his palms until they burned.

"Our Kingdom is suffering, son."

"That's precisely what I'm trying to explain. I'm trying to tell you all why it's happening."

"The destruction is beyond even what you see," Dorold said, more calmly. "All across this Kingdom, there are reports of strange maladies. Water that has been lifegiving for hundreds of years that is suddenly unfit for drink, as though it has been cursed."

Wes thought back to the river that ran through the Dread Ruins as Dorold continued.

"Your mother lamented that families in Silverfell were becoming smaller," Dorold said. Wes nodded. She had always hoped for more children herself, but she had never been able to become pregnant after Wes was born. "Since her death, the rates of birth have completely collapsed. We are not even replacing our population.

"And the problems do not end at our borders! We know that Galeharbor's crops have been nearly decimated by strange flying insects that have begun to arrive every summer. Both of our Kingdoms now rely heavily on grain imports from Aridmoor. King Radagar Ursa was fair. We now must hope that his son is as magnanimous, or we will risk famine."

Dorold finally paused for breath. The anger seemed to have left him entirely, his head hanging on his neck like a sail bereft of wind as he reached out to clasp Wes' shoulder.

"If we lose the protection of the Dracodei, we will have nothing left to ensure our survival. You must understand.

Things are already growing dire. We cannot risk making things worse. To even speak these blasphemies imperils the entire Kingdom."

"But what if it is these offerings to the Dracodei that are bringing down evil upon us?"

"What are you suggesting?" Dorold asked.

Somewhere across the palace, the tower bells chimed the noon hour, their tolling muffled by layers of wood and stone. Despite the stress of the meeting, he was hungry, and longing for a few minutes alone to think.

"I am suggesting that we cease the offerings."

Dorold opened his mouth to speak, but Wes took a step closer and held up a hand.

"For a start. From there, I plan to find the Codex Veritatis, in full if I can, and figure out how to restore worship to the true God. To the High One."

Until that moment, the plan had been murky, some far-off shore that had yet to come into focus. Having a greater sense of the path he was to tread filled him with determination. *One step at a time.*

"Wes, you are not thinking clearly," Dorold said, glancing about the room as though the sparrows resting in the rafters were spies, ready to report every word to the Dracodei.

"And besides, on what authority can you presume to make such decisions?"

"I am the Envoy. Without me, there can be no sacrifice made."

Dorold said nothing. His eyebrows drew down over his eyes as his cheeks began to grow red.

"You will not be the last Envoy this Kingdom sees, boy."

"Is that a threat, Dorold?" Wes asked, unable to stop his

voice from going shrill.

He felt the strange, stupid bravery he found only in moments of anger. He let it in, knowing that if he stopped now, he would fail.

"You head the Septemvirate. You could get rid of me. Blasphemy is a crime. But if you invoke the law, I hope that you have the courage to oversee the requisite punishment."

"Surely you don't think I wish you harm. You're like a son to me," Dorold said, pleading, his hand aloft as though undecided whether to strike Wes across the face or to embrace him.

No, I don't think that. But your guilt and your loyalty are the only leverage I have.

"And you are a father to me. But I cannot follow you into folly. You cannot pretend there is no risk in continuing on our present course. We have faithfully offered more than our people can bear, and for what? The skies are empty. Our Kingdom is alone."

"You remind me so much of your father when he was young," Dorold said, letting his hands fall to his sides as he stared up at Wes. "So bright and full of lofty ideals. But it is the stooping back of age that brings us to wisdom."

"I do not claim wisdom. Only truth."

"That may be, but even truth can be wielded by fools," Dorold said, reaching for his staff and pulling his long robe tight around his thin body. "You cannot put your hope in the word of this dragon. We have dedicated our lives to serving the Four Kingdoms. You have to trust your Septemvirate, or the House of Cervos is already dead."

How badly I wish that I could, Wes thought, noticing for the first time how old his mentor really was. When Dorold died, he would be more alone than ever before.

Can I bear to stand opposed to him in the final years of his life?

Wes began to speak, but before he could, the door of the meeting hall flew open.

His friend Moorn strode into the room, his boots clattering against the stone. "Forgive the interruption, Elder Dorold—" he stammered, noticing Wes standing in the center of the seven thrones. "—and Wes. Er, lord Envoy. I was ordered to inform you at once that King Ursa and his Protectorate have arrived at the palace gates."

* * *

The next few minutes passed in a blur. Wes stood in the center of the thrones as the rest of the Septemvirate filed back into the room, chattering under their breaths like village girls on market day.

Dorold would no longer meet his eyes, taking his place on his throne as he beckoned for the other Elders to follow. He had planned to tell them of Captain Drohma's strange request from King Ursa, but there had not yet been a chance.

Has someone invited the new King of Aridmoor here under some other pretext? He wondered. *Or has he simply decided to make good on his promise to visit without an explicit invitation?*

Before he could consider the matter further, the sound of Elder Dorold's staff striking stone rang out across the meeting hall, silencing the remaining conversation. Wes willed his body to still. He was the only one standing, and fidgeting would make him look even weaker than he was.

"Our meeting continues," Dorold said. "I attempted to convince our Envoy to take another path. He refused. Is that a fair assessment?"

Seven pairs of eyes turned to him. His stomach quivered. Wes wondered if it would be worse to cry or to throw up on the floor in front of them. Swallowing, he managed a nod, his eyes meeting Dorold's for a fleeting second before he looked away.

"Good. In any case, if he will not accept my merciful protection, he leaves me with no choice but to allow the full charges he brings to be heard by all. Soldiers!"

At his call, two mid-ranking soldiers that Wes did not recognize began to pull open the wooden doors. They bowed to their waists as a man robed in red strode toward Wes, a sly smile playing across his lips.

It took Wes a moment to recognize him.

He had met Kylan Ursa many times as a boy, but as a man, Wes had only seen him in passing. As a King he was almost unrecognizable. He was easily a full head taller than Wes, with broad shoulders and forearms corded with hard muscle.

Instead of trousers, he wore his legs bare beneath his long red tunic, typical of Aridmoor custom. Even his calves looked powerful. *Well, Kessara, if you want to marry a handsome and powerful King, I have a better idea...*

"Thank you for your hospitality on such short notice, my good Elders," the King said, bowing his head as he reached the edge of the circle until the older men reciprocated. He turned to Wes, raising his chiseled chin slightly toward the ceiling. His smile did not touch his eyes. "It is good to see you again, my old friend."

"Likewise," Wes managed a weak smile. The sickly feeling in his stomach had only grown worse. Kylan Ursa now ruled over a Kingdom that his people relied on for their very survival. If what Dorold said was true, Silverfell could not afford to lose their alliance. He felt the possibility of avoiding indictment on charges of blasphemy slipping away.

"May I ask what brings you to Stronghollow so soon?"

"I will conduct this meeting," Dorold said mildly, tapping his staff against the floor once again. "The Four Kingdoms of Kaveryth have always relied upon one another. King Ursa comes on his own business. But, seeing that he is already here, I have decided that the Envoy's accusations may benefit from a broader hearing."

A chill wormed its way down Wes' back. Dorold rarely called him by his title, even in more formal settings. Until that very moment, he had not believed that his mentor would really carry through with his threats. But there was no mistaking the hardness in his dark green eyes.

The Dorold that he had grown up knowing seemed far away, buried beneath competing loyalties he could not grasp.

"I agree," Elder Bram said. The other men craned their necks as they listened to the man speaking from his throne. "Despite what blasphemies our dear Envoy may or may not believe, I would say that the providence of the Dracodei smiles upon us this day. As I have already discussed with you, Elder Dorold, there is another person who deserves to be present. Is there any objection from my brother Elders? My King?"

Dorold called for the soldiers once more. The whispered chatter resumed between the Elders as Wes glared at Bram. He had gone far beyond his usual orneriness and distaste for Wes. But would he do anything to jeopardize the people of the Kingdom?

The Elders began to shout their votes into the room, unanimous in favor of Bram's proposal. King Ursa merely nodded, resting his hand against the side of Dorold's throne.

"Order," Dorold slammed the staff down again, more forcefully, as the great doors swung open a second time. The Elders fell silent at once, each one leaning nearly out of his seat to get a better view of who the unexpected visitor was.

This time, there was no mystery.

* * *

Princess Kessara Manta walked slowly across the meeting hall, a guard holding onto each of her elbows tightly enough that Wes knew she was not free to come and go as she pleased.

She wore a plain cotton dress in blue fabric, the bottom edge soaked through with mud. It left a swishing trail of muck in her wake as she drew nearer, meeting Wes' eyes, her expression unreadable. Her hair was sopping wet, sending dark patches blooming across the back and front of her clothes.

"Are you alright?" Wes exclaimed, taking a few steps toward her. She nodded. There was a warning in her eyes that he couldn't place.

Dorold raised a hand, and the soldiers released her. Wes' mouth fell open as he observed the pale white marks left on her forearms from where the soldiers gripped her.

"How dare you handle a Princess this way. Release her!"

"I will not warn you again, Envoy," Dorold snapped, gripping his staff with white knuckles. "You may have called the meeting for reasons of counsel, but the proceedings remain mine to command."

"Dorold, please," Wes said, fighting to keep his voice calm. He took a few steps toward his throne, trying his best to avoid King Ursa's eye. "How did you find her?"

"My lord, if I may," Elder Bram droned from his seat, looking bored. "For the benefit of the others present."

Dorold waved a hand. Wes stood firmly in place near his throne. Compared to King Ursa, he looked like a child, sneaking in to watch his father govern. But rage had overcome his earlier embarrassment. *Why was Kessara being treated like a common prisoner rather than the daughter of an allied King?*

"The princess will assure you that she meets with us today of her own free will," Bram said, drawing his robe around himself as if to stave off the nonexistent chill. "The soldiers are merely a formal escort."

Wes looked up at Kessara. Indeed, the marks on her arms had already faded.

"It is true, my lord Elder," She said, clearing her throat. She would not meet Wes' eyes. She looked toward the center of the thrones as Dorold waved her forward. She gave a bow of her head before doing so, taking graceful strides until she was in the exact center of the proceedings. "I came to Silverfell at the behest of King Errol Manta of Galeharbor, in order to meet with the Septemvirate."

Bram stared at Wes triumphantly as the other Elders began to chatter amongst themselves once more. Before Dorold could call order, she continued.

"But there is more," she glanced at Wes, the faintest shadow of a grin on her pink lips. *Please, please, not a public proposal.* He would have no choice but to give her an answer. Which, he supposed, was probably her plan. *I should have talked to her while I had the chance. Why am I always so weak?*

"I had intended to meet privately with the Septemvirate, seeking their counsel about a sensitive matter before my father brought it to the attention of the other Kingdoms and their rulers," she continued. Wes released a breath. Perhaps she would not say anything. "But first, I approached Wes Cervos,

Envoy of Silverfell, for aid."

Elder Bram looked murderous but kept his mouth shut.

"Why would you trust him over the men you claim to seek as counsel?" Elder Jate asked.

"A good question, my lord Elder," Elder Qofi added.

Dorold raised his staff in warning as the chatter began briefly before falling flat once more. "Princess?"

"As many of you will no doubt recall, his elder brother Prince Roven and I were betrothed to be married before he died," she looked around the room, her head held high, allowing her words a moment to sink in. "Is it so strange to you that I would put trust in the last surviving member of a family I almost became a part of?"

Wes could only stare in admiration. *Celesyria is right about one thing. Kessara would make an excellent queen.*

"Be that as it may," Elder Rahma said. "You must concede that your decision to hide within the palace allows for a certain level of suspicion to be warranted."

Bram placed a hand across his heart.

"A servant loyal to me informed me of the Princess's presence for that very reason, my lord Elder. I meant no harm."

Wes could barely suppress the colorful words that sprang to his lips. Trusting young Oria had been a mistake. No one else but Celesyria knew that Kessara was in Stronghollow. *It was not on account of any loyalty to Elder Bram, that much is certain. He probably threatened her.*

"I readily offer forgiveness, my lord," Kessara said, bowing to Bram from the waist. Wes caught a smile that she had not completely managed to hide as Bram's face went even redder. "You only wished to ensure the safety of your Kingdom. Your loyalty to your people is admirable."

"Of course," Bram stammered. "Thank you, my Princess."

"I'm glad that is settled," Dorold said, gesturing to Kessara to step out of the circle. "The Princess will have her hearing as soon as I can arrange it, privately, if she wishes." He glanced at King Ursa, who only looked bored.

"Is there any other secrets the Envoy wishes to tell us before we proceed?"

Wes forced himself to meet Dorold's eyes. He could see disappointment within them, and it made his heart hurt. Despite everything, he longed for the man's approval. Perhaps there was still a chance.

"No, my lord Elder," he answered somewhat truthfully, thinking of the dragon in her tower.

I do not want to tell you until the time is right. Until there is a chance that you will listen.

* * *

Although no sunlight reached the meeting hall, the gnawing feeling in Wes' stomach made it clear that his usual lunch hour had long since passed.

He had done as Dorold requested, giving a full account of what Celesyria had told him, once again omitting the details of Holga and Gohr's prophecy. He would use it as proof of the Codex's veracity only if strictly necessary. The last thing he wanted was for the Septemvirate to assume he sought some higher power for himself.

He expected chatter to start up as he finished, but none came. Instead, the Elders were glancing at each other, uncertainty plain on their faces. Only Elder Dorold and Elder Bram remained impassive. King Ursa looked furious, and Princess

Kessara was trying without success to catch Wes' eye.

I wish I'd told you everything. I don't know who else I can trust. His stomach growled beneath the padding of his belly. Finally, Elder Jate spoke.

"I agree with Elder Dorold," he began. "This is a scandalous suggestion. We suffer even now. Without the protection of the Dracodei..." He did not finish. He shook his head, sending his silvery hair falling across his cheeks.

"Do you forget the greatness of this Kingdom?" Elder Rahma choked out. He was so thin that his robe seemed to drown him as he turned to Wes, one finger raised. "The greatness of your own House, before the elves came with their destruction?"

"No."

"It was not by chance or human might that we reached such glory. It was by the aid of the Dracodei—"

"You could be wrong. It's happened before."

"Who saved Silverfell, in the end? When our King and Queen were killed, and we had no one else to aid us?" Elder Derden asked, his voice filled with venom. Everyone fell silent for a moment, staring. Wes rarely heard the man speak at all, and when he did, his voice was always as soft as new grass.

"Elder Derden," he started, noticing the eyes of the room falling upon him once more, making him squirm. *How can I defend a truth that I am not yet sure of myself? Can I have faith while holding to doubt?*

"Though the hour was late, the Guardians came to aid us, in the end. They drove the elves back to Nox."

"Had the dragons not intervened," Elder Derden continued, his voice returning to its normal gentle pitch, so quiet that Wes strained to hear him. "You would be dead, too. The House of Cervos would have followed on the path of Noctua."

Before Wes could formulate a response, Kessara took a couple of steps toward the center of the circle, ignoring Dorold's hand, raised in warning.

"If the House of Noctua was allowed to fall, what makes you assume that the rest of our Houses will be spared?" She asked, looking at each of the men in turn. Her blue eyes burned. "Did Boneshire refuse to offer their fair share to the Dracodei?"

"Princess, they—" Elder Gunnan started.

"They gave of their wealth to the gods, as the other Kingdoms did. And it was not sufficient to spare them. I do not claim to know whether Wes Cervos is telling the truth, or if the Codex Veritatis even exists," she continued, ignoring raised hands and muttered retorts. She glanced at her feet. "However, I think Wes' doubts are reasonable. In fact, I share them."

The entire room gasped, including Wes himself.

Kessara had heard nothing save what he told the Septemvirate, and yet, she was ready to risk charges of blasphemy to follow the truth he'd been entrusted with. Once again, he found himself staring at his feet, turmoil roiling deep within his chest. *I am not the person meant to deliver Your message, High One. The fact that I want to believe isn't enough.*

Dorold banged his staff against the floor in an attempt to restore order. The chattering continued for another moment until Wes cleared his throat, stepping into the circle and resting a hand on the Princess's arm. His fingers shook, but she stood still, even statue-like, beneath the withering gazes of the men surrounding them.

"Thank you," she whispered, low enough that only he could hear.

"My lord Elders," he began, drawing himself up to his full height. Kessara stayed next to him, unmoving. He drew a breath, hoping to draw some of her courage to himself. "The Princess is right. We do not know for certain that our sacrifices have been blessed by the Dracodei."

"What, then, is the purpose of the Claim?" Elder Bram asked, chewing on the flesh of his cheek. Wes could see that Dorold was giving him a warning glance from his throne.

"The Claim is made of metal," he looked at the Elders, trying to avoid Bram's narrowed eyes. "We rely on it because that is the way things have always been done. I remove it from the sacred cave each time I leave the offerings, but that doesn't mean we know how it gets there, let alone how it is made or by whom."

Elder Derden was looking across the room, his stormy eyes focused on nothing, stroking his beard between two fingers. Elder Dorold was shaking his head, his cheeks flushed beneath a shadow of stubble.

"There are things we cannot know. It does not follow that we know nothing."

"I never said we did," Wes said. "But these questions are important. If I am right, the people of our Four Kingdoms are offering wealth they cannot spare to imposters. Please, my lord Elders, I ask that you at least investigate the possibility."

"You do not know what you are saying!" Elder Jate bellowed. "This is not something we can commission the Academy at Vaevar to study. If this alleged message from the Codex Veritatis reaches beyond these walls, the people will spread it across Kaveryth whether it is true or false. The Septemvirate will lose the confidence of the people. How will we govern them if they no longer trust us?"

Before anyone could attempt to respond, King Ursa stormed into the center of the thrones where Wes and Kessara stood.

They shrunk back, noticing that his hands were balled into fists, his eyes full of steel.

"There is another detail. My Captain, Drohma, told the Envoy that I wished to consider sending my own Protectorate to safeguard him on each Feast of Offering. I had intended to speak to my lord Elders about this matter. Now, I arrive in Stronghollow to find the Envoy seeking to bring distrust of my rule to all of my subjects," he said, his deep voice thrumming with barely-contained fury. "Never did I imagine such a thing would be said openly in the meeting hall of the Septemvirate. Never. And by a son of such a noble—"

"Your Majesty," Dorold said quickly. He glanced at Wes, a mix of pity and anger on his face before he returned his gaze to the young King. "Be assured that the charge of blasphemy remains in the canons of the law. It is not without potential consequence that the Envoy speaks."

Wes took a step in front of Kessara and faced the head Elder. "False accusations, too, are proscribed in our laws."

"So you deny it?" King Ursa spat.

"Yes. I seek only the truth. My people deserve to know it."

"The blood of Cervos may yet run in your veins," King Ursa spat, looking down at Wes as though he was a bug venturing too near to his boot. "But the people do not belong to you."

He paused, lifting a finger to Wes' face and brushing his cheek.

"You bear the moonscar. You are not allowed to rule Silver-fell. It seems our good Elders have allowed you to forget that fact. No longer. I will see to it that blasphemy charges are brought. You will serve as Envoy between stints in a prison cell."

He turned aside from Wes, looking instead to Kessara. Wes

clutched his hands against his sides, trying to still their shaking. *Not even the most serious charges in the Four Kingdoms can free me from my burden. They can condemn me only to a living death.*

He thought of meeting Celesyria for the first time. It seemed so long ago, in a life that did not belong to him. The fact that he had been willing to listen to her was madness. Now, he was about to lose everything, and there was nothing he could do.

"I must remind our dear Princess that it was not by a lack of obedience to the sacrifices that Boneshire lost her ruling House. They fell because their Envoy sought to assume the crown. You speak blasphemies based on your ignorance, all to protect the very person who will bring down your Kingdom."

Wes caught Kessara's eye. All hints of her teasing, knowing smile had vanished from her face. Beneath tendrils of blonde hair, he could see the fear in her eyes. Even a Princess was not immune to charges of blasphemy.

This is not an argument you can win, he wanted to say to her. *You've said too much already. You fall upon the mercy of the Elders now. But there is another path that we may yet take.*

He let the Elders continue to squabble for a moment, gathering his thoughts. He felt the plan of what he would say come together within moments, but the courage he needed was more difficult to find. Once more, he thought of Roven. He thought of his mother and father, so willing to risk themselves for the sake of another. Did their blood truly run within his veins?

He raised a hand and stepped in front of the King, heart pounding. He was a member of the House of Cervos. That had to be enough. *I have courage, High One. Help me to find it in time.*

Chapter Fourteen

Without looking, Wes' hand found Kessara's.

For a moment, he just held it, feeling the softness of her tanned skin beneath his thumb. She was so warm. Above the din of raised voices and the stamping of Dorold's staff, he swore that he could hear the pounding of his own heart. He dared a glance at her.

There's no time for anything more.

He looked into her scared eyes, willing her to understand what he was about to do. There would not be a second chance.

He turned to face King Ursa and began to fall to the floor as though bowing. A look of surprise crossed his face, followed by fury.

Wes felt his right knee hit the stone as he tugged on the Princess's hand. Kessara stepped forward at once. She stood still as the rest of the room went silent, but there was no hint of surprise on her face.

Her chin was held high, her expression unreadable. Even in her humble attire, she looked every bit a queen.

"Kessara Manta, Princess of the Kingdom of Galeharbor, I ask you to be my bride," Wes choked out, unsure whether to continue holding her soft hand with his own sweaty one. "I have no ring, but I offer you a Kingdom, to rule as your own."

King Ursa stood there, slack-jawed, as Kessara finally smiled, nodding her head and dipping into a curtsy. Relief flooded over Wes in a torrent. Perhaps things would work out after all.

"Dorold, this is simply—"

"He doesn't even have a ring!"

"We cannot allow—"

"You know what he is doing!" Elder Bram howled before being cut off by the repeated slamming of Dorold's staff against the floor.

"It would be an honor to marry into your noble House," Kessara said, pausing to give Wes a gentle kiss upon the back of his knuckles. He blushed to his toes. The feeling of terror, it seemed, had faded away, though he still wasn't sure how exactly he felt.

"I accept your proposal."

She said each word carefully, loud enough that the whole Septemvirate as well as King Ursa could hear her.

"Well, that's it, then," Elder Dorold said, striking the floor once more as some of the Elders began to whisper. "I will remind you all that a king or queen can only be charged with crimes of religion by the consensus of the monarchs."

"There has been no wedding, let alone a coronation." Elder Qofi objected.

Dorold held up a hand. "The canons are clear, and the subject was put to the Academy in 1586. Princess Kessara is, as of this public engagement, to be treated as any reigning monarch in the Four Kingdoms."

"I will have this matter studied by my personal scholars."

"I have no reason to deceive you, but you are free to soothe your doubts, Elder Jate."

"But what of Aridmoor—"

"Surely there has been a more recent precedent—"

"My lord Elders!" King Ursa boomed, raising a hand.

Kessara and Wes shrank away, their hands still clasped together. Wes was certain that Elder Dorold was correct, but still, paranoia nibbled at him. Wes had asked Oria to find a volume of the ancient canons, and Celesyria helped him to confirm that mere engagement to Kessara would keep her safe from certain charges, at least for the time being.

"I doubt that the King and Queen of Galeharbor have much interest in bringing a case against their own daughter. I also know for a fact that royal immunity does not extend to matters of treason," Kylan Ursa glanced at Kessara, a sarcastic grin on his lips. "In any case, it does not matter. The good Princess has been deceived by the Envoy as well. It is he that the eye of justice should look upon."

Without another word, he strode toward the doors of the meeting hall.

Wes and Kessara glanced at each other as Dorold attempted to regain order. Just before he met the threshold, King Ursa looked back over his shoulder, the same mocking smile clouding his otherwise handsome features.

"Aren't you coming, lovebirds?"

"For what?" Wes asked, squeezing Kessara's hand protectively.

King Ursa rolled his eyes.

"You already proposed to the poor girl without a ring. Would it be too much for you to conduct the rest of your engagement in the traditional manner?"

"I—"

Without further explanation, the new King headed out into the hall, his red cloak fluttering behind him.

* * *

Glimmering orange scales fell to the ground as the iron manacles bit into Celesyria's legs. She groaned at the pain, the sounds of her agony rumbling from deep within her chest as the red-cloaked soldiers dragged her forward.

She guessed there had to be at least twenty of the men, many of them taller and broader than the Silverfell soldiers she'd seen from the window of the old tower. Even with so many, they would have struggled to overpower her had she not cooperated. *Stupid.*

"Please, listen to me," she cried out with her mind, desperate to make contact, any contact, with one of the people surrounding her. The faces of the soldiers betrayed nothing indicating that they'd heard her speak.

She searched the eyes of the men walking closest to her, hoping for some flash of recognition, some hint of empathy, but there was nothing. They continued to drag her into the center of Stronghollow with chains so large that they could clasp their hands around each of the links.

"Let me go!" She called aloud as they passed by a market, arching her neck and shouting as loudly as she could. Peasants and artisans stared up at her with wide eyes before looking down at their feet and pretending to return to their business. One of the soldiers at her side brandished a spear. She felt the bite of sharp metal lodging between scales as he pressed the tip against her throat.

"Silence, dragon."

She looked up at the sky as she spoke from within, calling out to Wes. The sudden storm clouds that had swept into Stronghollow a couple of days before had not left, though for the moment, the rain had ceased.

A raging storm would be fitting. Such a day belongs to fog and thunder.

As they reached the next turn of the street, she stumbled against one of the wooden buildings, wrenching the joint of her foot. She howled in pain and anger as the men continued to force her forward.

"I said be quiet!" One of the other soldiers yelled, raising his spear in warning. Her entire body ached, but the pain in her ankle was growing worse by the second. She bit back the groan that threatened to burst forth from her throat.

"*Please, listen to what they say,*" Someone said within her skull. The voice sounded like it belonged to someone female, and young. *A child.*

"*Who are they? Who are you?*" She asked. She glanced around as best she could as the soldiers continued to drag her along, unable to get her bearings. The street they were on— comprised of a smattering of tents, trees, and wooden structures—was so narrow that she could not see where it headed, nor could she turn her head to figure out where she'd come from.

"*Soldiers of Aridmoor's army,*" the little girl said. "*It is strange.*

They are not supposed to be in Stronghollow. Please, be careful."

Before she could say more, they reached their apparent destination.

Stretching out before her was a courtyard like none she had ever seen. The ground was made up of huge slabs of wood in every color and type of grain, all cut to perfectly interlocking angles.

Every dragon-length or so, there were trees growing out of dark green ceramic pots that were big enough for several humans to take a bath in. Though it was too cold for them to have grown leaves, the trees were decorated with ribbons in a myriad of colors, dancing in the slight spring breeze. Despite the gloom, it gave the space a festive air.

Beyond a tall stone wall that lay across the courtyard, she could see more of the towering trees, as well as the peaks of wooden structures that seemed to reach the clouds. *The palace at Stronghollow.* She forgot her wounds for a moment as she marveled. *How is it possible that someone like Wes could have grown up somewhere so grand?* Even the Guardian's quarters could not compare to it.

"Where are you? Please, I need to see a friendly face," she asked the unseen child.

"Move!" One of the soldiers yanked at the chain that bound her injured leg. She bit back flames. Ever since she was a child, her parents had warned her of the ancient oaths the dragons had made when they were summoned to Kaveryth, which certainly forbade lighting agents of the crown on fire.

The dragons could never attack the Four Kingdoms under pain of exile back to the Farplace, and though the terms of the agreement were not entirely clear to Celesyria, she tended to assume that using fire as a weapon was always verboten. Even in the great battle for Boneshire, the Guardians had relied on other means to fight the elves.

"Near the pine." Celesyria strained her neck as she shuffled across the courtyard, her claws leaving thin marks on the wooden shapes. Finally, she spotted her ally. She was a small girl in a plain green work dress, her cropped hair covered by a gray kerchief. Their eyes met for only a moment before the little girl shied away, staring at her scuffed brown boots. *"I don't want to get into trouble."*

Before Celesyria could say any more, the sound of horns filled the courtyard. The music was, like the ribbons, altogether too cheerful, continuing as two doors set into the palace walls creaked open. She blinked twice, trying to make certain of what she was seeing. They were made of wood, painted so perfectly to match the stone that she had not known they were there at all.

Before she could examine it further, a crush of red-clad soldiers and citizens in ordinary clothing piled into the space in front of her, blocking her view. More horns joined the first ones, their happy song culminating in a loud crescendo followed by a sudden silence.

Celesyria turned, looking for the little girl, but she had disappeared. She attempted to speak to her, but there was no response.

"I announce with great joy, to the citizens of Stronghollow and all Silverfell, the happy engagement of Envoy Wes Cervos and Princess Kessara Manta of Galeharbor!" A voice boomed from somewhere at the front of the throng.

The great mass of citizens burst into wild cheering, clapping, and shouting. She saw men lift their daughters onto their shoulders, plucking ribbons from the trunks of the great potted trees and waving them as they yelled.

The soldiers charged with her guard were not cheering. Instead, they looked puzzled, letting the chains go slack as they stood staring out toward the palace gate.

A moment later, Celesyria realized why.

Standing there, with a tidy line of green-clad horn musicians standing at each side, was an important-looking man clothed in fine red garb. *The new King of Aridmoor.* She did not have time to react further to his presence.

Behind him stood Wes, and the girl she assumed was Kessara. *His betrothed.*

* * *

"*Wes!*" She cried, charging forward, forgetting her chains. The soldiers were caught off guard as she stepped toward the gate. She felt her bonds tighten and then go slack, heard the sound of bodies being dragged across the wood, but she did not stop.

The sea of people parted as she approached, falling backward into one another, their cheers turned to screams. She felt the sting of a sword blade, no more than an annoyance, as it slashed across her left flank.

"*Wes, what's happening?*"

"*Celesyria?*" Wes stared dumbfounded toward her as he was ushered out through the palace gate and into the courtyard.

"Stop!" One of the soldiers screamed from her side.

Everything seemed to be moving in slow motion. She continued forward, but her ankle burned more than ever, and the confused cries of the crowd muddled her ability to listen for Wes. More soldiers found their way to her sides, attempting to get new chains around her legs and wings as she flailed around, disoriented, trying to reach her friend.

"This is hardly tradition, my King," a graying man in a long robe was saying, his hand clamped firmly around Wes' forearm as they trailed off after the man Celesyria could only assume was King Ursa.

"It is the task of the Septemvirate to—to—" he stammered as the man in red swirled around to look at him. Celesyria could not see his expression, but the fear reflected on the face of the old man spoke clearly.

"P—p—perhaps it would calm the crowd if I were to explain, my lord."

"Perhaps."

"Watch out!" Wes' voice shouted aloud, moments too late. The membrane of her wing caught in a tangle of branches on one of the courtyard trees. As she tried to tug herself free, one of the pointed wooden ends pierced straight through the sensitive flesh.

She screeched with pain, distracted long enough that one of the soldiers managed to get another chain around the base of her left wing.

She stumbled backward, feeling the sickening crunch of bone as her back foot crushed the leg of one of the red soldiers. His scream pierced her ears as she tried desperately to get free, her wing bleeding more profusely each time she shifted her weight.

Finally, she felt the tension release as a strip of the membrane tore straight off of her wing. She cried out again, so blinded with pain that she stumbled on her injured ankle, sending all of her body weight straight into the trunk of the tree.

"No!"

"Move!"

"My lord—"

Voices of soldiers and peasants mingled into nonsensical cacophony. She tried to use her bulk to stop the huge tree from falling, but the blood pooling at her feet made her slip, her feet skidding on the wooden slabs as the weight pressed upon her. The tumult of the crowd below faded into silence as she twisted out of the way.

The gnarled tree began to fall through the air.

For a second, the entire crowd seemed to hold its breath, suspended in a place outside of time until a great crash sounded. Pieces of wood splintered off, flying into the crowd. The top of the tree hit the palace wall, sending chunks of stone skittering across the courtyard. The ceramic pot shattered into a million pieces, sending bits of mud and shattered debris flying into the faces of the crowd.

"Don't struggle," Wes said, sounding far away. *"Please, be still. It'll be alright."*

Celesyria took a breath, feeling the relief of cold air rushing toward her lungs. Her heart was thumping so loudly that she could scarcely hear the sound of the soldiers as they swarmed her, laden with fresh chains.

She clamped her jaw shut, certain that if she allowed a single tooth to show, she would end up burning the army alive before she could stop herself.

The crowd murmured to one another, milling around the courtyard with no clear direction. Celesyria caught several furious glances cast her way, but many looked at their feet rather than allowing her to catch their eyes. The princess was talking to Wes, her hand resting on his shoulder. His face looked calm, but she could see the hint of red around his eyes.

She hoped for the sake of his pride that he could choke back his tears.

She managed to lift her ankle, relieving some of the pressure from the manacle as the soldiers finished setting her new bindings.

She couldn't bear to gaze at her torn wing. Dragons lived long lives and healed quickly from wounds that would kill almost any other creature, but they were not impervious to injury, let alone were they immortal.

She was confident she would be able to fly again, in time, but for the moment, it was little comfort. She was trapped, being treated hardly better than a forest rabbit caught up in a hunter's snare.

Even if they let me go, my parents will know everything. Will they even admit me back to Whitespire after what I have done?

* * *

"Please, everyone! Be calm. No one appears to be hurt," the man in the gray robe said finally from his place near the palace wall. He tapped the wooden staff he held several times until the lingering chatter abated.

"Now," he continued. "I'm sure that King Ursa wishes to explain for himself why there is a dragon in the courtyard."

"Yes, my lord Elder," the King said with a wolfish grin, striding past the older man and beckoning the musicians to form their ranks beside him once more.

"Though there has been a recent engagement—" he nodded to Wes and Kessara "—there is something else that the people of Stronghollow should know."

He paused. She watched as the crowd leaned ever so slightly

toward him, waiting.

He turned to Kessara, poking a finger against the bottom of her chin. The girl did not even flinch. *Every bit a queen.* Celesyria admired the girl's pretty features, but she could tell that her true beauty lay deeper within. It was a rare woman who could carry herself with such natural grace.

"The man that this Princess agreed to marry told the Septemvirate that portions of the legendary Codex Veritatis had been found." He paused again, failing to conceal a smile as a wave of speculation and gossip flooded across the crowd.

"According to the Envoy, this book tells us to cease offerings to the Dracodei. Your Envoy dares accuse his divine rulers of being false usurpers!"

Celesyria listened in horror as King Ursa told the crowd nearly everything she had told Wes. *It's exactly as I'd feared. Had Wes secured the alliance of Manta before speaking to the Septemvirate, perhaps this could have been avoided.*

The crowd erupted as everyone tried to speak at once.

"What are we going to do?" She asked Wes, trying in vain to stand in a way that was comfortable amid her bonds. Part of her wanted to tell him how wrong he'd been, tell him the cost of his stubbornness, but she knew it would be cruel. She was sure that he already bore the weight of his own regrets.

"I was hoping you knew."

"I didn't exactly plan this. They told me that you summoned me!"

"What?"

"They told me the chains were a precaution," she choked out. *"For the comfort of the Elders and the peasants. They told me that I would frighten the city folk if I were to walk up to the palace without any bonds. It's the only reason they were able to capture*

me."

There was a pause before Wes answered. She couldn't blame him for being at a loss for words. They had been subjected to unthinkable behavior.

"They lied."

Before he could say more, the King turned back toward the Princess, standing so close to her that she could surely smell his breath against her nostrils.

A chill breeze rippled across the courtyard as the clouds grew darker, threatening yet another downpouring of rain. Celesyria watched as the Princess shivered in her thin cotton dress, leaning into Wes for warmth. Despite everything else, she couldn't help but think of the two of them together, wondering if the awkwardness she could sense between them would pass if given enough time.

"The dragon that told your worthless heir about the Codex is not some idealist seeking truth," King Ursa's voice boomed. Celesyria watched as Kessara's eyes went wide, but her mouth remained in a firm line. *How much had Wes kept from her?*

"She's a traitor to the land of Umrym. She seeks to destroy her race, the noblest creatures in all Kaveryth."

Shocked murmurs sounded throughout the crowd. Faces all around her wore expressions of shock and even grief. She found it hard to blame them. For the people of the Four Kingdoms, the Dracodei were the driving force behind everything they did.

Their worship, their culture, their myths, all of it was related to the dragon gods. In their minds, there was nothing that had come before. Any affront to them was an affront to their very souls.

Even though the other dragons of Umrym were not seen as

divine themselves, they were still viewed with great reverence. After all, it was by the teeth and claws of the Guardians that the Dracodei kept the elves of Nox at bay.

For any dragon to go against their own race was an act of impiety worse than any crime of religion that a mere human could commit.

"He does not speak the truth!" Celesyria cried out, her voice so deafening that even King Ursa fell silent for a moment before regaining his composure.

"Are you not a candidate for the Guardians?"

"Yes," she admitted, trying to lower her voice. Speaking out loud always felt unnatural, and the last thing she wanted was to remind the crowd of her size and power.

Still, the crowd drew back from her, perhaps fearful that she would lose her temper and send another tree crashing toward them.

Parents drew little children near to themselves, looking up at Celesyria with wide eyes. The girl who had spoken to her earlier was nowhere in sight.

"You come from a legacy family of Guardians, correct? Your parents have both offered their noble service?"

How do they know of my family? The panic she had pushed aside was rising within her chest once more. She glanced at the older man in the robe, who had been joined by six other men in similar dress. *The Septemvirate, in the flesh.*

Their mouths bore no expressions, but she could tell by the slight lift of their brows that this information was new to them as well.

Did Wes tell Captain Drohma about me?

"Yes," she cleared her throat. She wanted desperately to lie, but what good would it do? If King Ursa knew her family, it was too late for her to protect them.

"And do your parents approve of your expedition to Silver-fell?"

"No. They have nothing to do with any of this. They know nothing."

"We will be the judge of that," King Ursa said, looking toward the seven older men. The Elders nodded toward the King as he continued speaking.

"Is it true that you have always envied the wealth of the Dracodei?"

"No, your majesty." *What?* The question surprised her. Despite her less than sterling reputation, she was not known as someone who cared very much about possessions. She had few personal belongings, and most of those were old books that had long since been discarded by others.

"Interesting. So you deny questioning why the Dracodei require sacrifices of coin and other treasures?"

A memory of her last conversation with Gramnok flashed in her mind, filling her with dread. *Someone was listening, just as he had feared.* She swallowed, unsure how to answer.

"Yes. I mean, no, I did say—"

"You hear it from her own mouth!" King Ursa crowed, pointing a ring-laden index finger toward her. The crowd, including the children, joined him as he jeered.

"Her accusations and blasphemies are too wicked to repeat aloud," he continued, his voice rising and falling, pausing and rushing forward, working the crowd into a frenzy. They moved closer to her, apparently satisfied that the volume of chains that encircled her would keep them safe.

And they're right. I wouldn't dare risk exile by breathing fire.

"But her reasons for spreading these falsehoods are even

more scandalous. The Dracodei have called upon all of the dragons, including the Guardians, to take on a more modest quality of life to better serve the people of the Four Kingdoms. This dragon had grown accustomed to the wealth typical of a legacy family of Guardians. Now that a small fraction of that wealth has been set aside for greater uses, she dares to accuse the Dracodei of theft! Of greed!"

He paused for effect as the mob of peasants, artisans, housewives, and children heckled her even more, a few of the young men grasping for bits of the broken tree pot and throwing them at her.

The soldiers in red moved in more closely around her, raising their hands in warning to the youths as they pulled the chains more tightly about her torn wing. She winced as her weight was forced back onto her injured ankle, but she clamped her jaw shut, unwilling to let the savage crowd witness any more of her pain.

"The dwarf Gramnok has affirmed that this dragon is known for her fantastical stories throughout Whitespire. She speaks of a being she calls the High One. She attempts to draw others away from the proper worship of the Dracodei."

Gramnok? Her heart felt like it would burst. The dwarf had never been adventurous, but never had she dreamed that he would betray her. *This cannot be true. It can't be.*

"The King has been told only a partial truth," she said, finally, her voice quavering as she looked out across the crowd. The eyes she met reflected only hardness and hatred. "I admit I've questioned why gods would need money. But I've never wanted your gold for myself. I only wish to spread the truth. That is all I have asked of this Kingdom or any other."

"Enlighten us, dragon," King Ursa drawled. "If you have

such knowledge of the truth, why have you continued to live in service of a lie? Gramnok tells us that you have held these traitorous opinions for some years, and yet, you were prepared to join the Guardians. You allowed your righteous parents to think that you were loyal to your race, when in fact, you were plotting to betray them. How can you expect anyone to trust you?"

Celesyria clamped her jaw against the pain once more as the soldiers began to urge her away from the courtyard. King Ursa was ordering his men to bring her to the dungeon.

Wes was yelling at him, protesting her innocence, but she couldn't bring herself to focus on the words. Did any of it matter now? King Ursa was right. She had lied to her parents. She had been a coward. But in the end, she had come to Silverfell to tell the truth, and that much, at least, she had finally managed to do.

The rest was up to the High One.

Someday, I will fly again. Even if they keep me here for the rest of my life, the end will come, one way or another, and they will have no hold over me.

She closed her eyes as she continued forward, the dark gates of Stronghollow's dungeon rising up before them. She savored the breeze against her face, wishing more than anything that she could fly one last time. She missed looking at the stars. Most of all, she missed the joy of knowing that as long as you kept moving, nothing bad in the world could touch you.

Maybe the Farplace was like that.

Maybe there, she would never have to land.

Chapter Fifteen

Wes fought to keep his footing as several of King Ursa's soldiers rushed past him, following the men who had dragged Celesyria away. The city folk followed behind them in turn, shouting and jostling for position amongst themselves.

"Are you alright?" Kessara asked, patting uselessly at the droplets of muck that the stampede of soldiers had splattered across her arms.

"I'm fine. It's Celesyria I'm worried about," he replied, looking off to where she had stood only minutes before.

Surely Dorold will demand that she receive treatment from our healers. He shuddered to think of the injury to her wing. Before she'd been dragged into the depths of the dungeons, she'd assured him that it would heal.

But he had a better view of the injury than she did.

"I know," Kessara said, her expression unreadable.

Will her loyalties follow my own?

Before he could consider the matter further, the Princess pointed toward the open gate. "Look!"

From behind the palace walls, they watched as several companies of the Silverfell army emerged. Hope rose within his chest as he watched Dorold and Elder Gunnan speak to one of the captains. King Ursa stood with his arms folded across his brawny chest, watching the strange parade head toward the dungeon.

Silverfell's soldiers were loyal to the House of Cervos, but with no monarch on the throne, they took orders from the Septemvirate. The tension of the scene simmered into a quiet distrust as the local army regained control in the chaos. Dozens of peasants and shopkeepers returned to their homes, leaving bits of torn ribbon and other detritus in the mud behind them.

Outside of Wes' hearing, the Elders began to talk amongst themselves. Every few minutes, one would gesture toward him and Kessara.

Finally, as the last of his soldiers marched out of sight, the King left his post at the edge of the courtyard and strode toward Wes and Kessara.

"Now that we have a moment, I wish to speak to the Princess in confidence," King Ursa said, glancing over his shoulder at Dorold, who nodded.

"I have nothing to say," Kessara said sweetly, giving him a half bow. Wes watched as he balled his fist against his side, the tips of his fingers going nearly as red as his tunic.

Lay a hand on her, and you will answer to me. The confidence he felt confused him. Even without dozens of soldiers at his beck and call, Kylan Ursa was a foot taller than Wes and strong enough to fight a stag and win. The idea that he was in a position to defend the Princess's honor was laughable.

"Don't be so sure of that, my Princess," King Ursa said, oil dripping from his words. "Come along. It will only be a minute."

Wes snorted. "I always knew you were jealous when she chose Roven, but this is pathetic, even for you."

"Wes, don't!" Kessara snapped. King Ursa closed the distance between himself and Wes in a single pace, his fist raised. Wes pressed his eyes closed, awaiting pain and blood.

"My King," came Dorold's calm voice from somewhere behind Kylan. "Surely violence will not be necessary. Wes meant no insult to your Majesty."

The Elder glowered at Wes as he laid an arm across his shoulders and half-dragged him toward one of the great trees, deftly avoiding getting his feet wet in the large pool of water at its base. He maneuvered Wes with surprising force, leaving the King where he stood.

"Let me go. He'll hurt her," he pleaded, trying to shake himself free. He didn't want to injure the old man, either.

"Wes, stop this," Dorold chided him in the same way he might have told him to keep out of the desserts before supper a decade previous. "She's fine."

He finally managed to look back toward where he and the Princess had stood, but she was already gone.

"She'd better be."

Dorold laughed. "I never knew you to have such a flair for the dramatic. It reminds me of your mother."

"Discovering age-old secrets has a way of changing a person," he muttered, sitting down on the edge of the ceramic pot and resting his back against the great oak planted in it. The trunk was so huge that his tired back could perceive no curve in it, and though his stomach still ached from hunger, it was a relief to rest.

"I did hope you would change your mind," Dorold said, sitting down next to him. He gave Wes a weak smile that didn't reach his eyes. "I really thought that you would."

Wes only shook his head, staring at his lap. Before he could think of anything to say, the rain began once again, pooling on the larger branches above before rolling onto their heads.

The crowd was nearly gone already, and in the Western sky, he could see a hint of the sun behind the clouds as it dipped toward the horizon.

The excitement is over. A piece of the ribbon from the celebration landed on his shoulder. His return, Kessara's appearance, the caravan—it all felt like it had happened a lifetime ago, to someone else. He had not been entirely hopeful that meeting with the Septemvirate would be easy, but never in his wildest imaginings had he thought that it would end with Celesyria in prison and him close to it.

It is not only Celesyria and I who await this dark night. Silverfell cannot carry on this way. My people cannot bear the weight of this tyranny forever. They will break. And when they do, everything will fall apart. What is it that the Elders do not understand?

"King Ursa is a little high-handed, perhaps," Dorold continued without preamble. "But we will not allow justice to give way to barbarity. The Septemvirate will contact the Guardians as well as the dwarves in Umrym before the dragon's fate is sealed."

He lifted a hand as though about to pat Wes' knee, but decided against it at the last moment, letting it rest instead on the damp edge of the planter pot.

"What of my fate, Dorold?" Wes asked, his throat catching.

Before he could answer, the horns rang out once more, their insistent melody mingling with the percussion of rainfall.

* * *

Wes allowed himself to be led by Dorold toward the palace wall.

Even if I could run away, where would I go? He eyed the soldiers that filled most of the courtyard. Many of Silverfell's soldiers had returned to ranks, but still, King Ursa's red-clad men were just as numerous.

Now that the chaos had faded, some of the more curious peasants had returned to observe the proceedings. They watched Wes, eyes filled with unspoken questions. *I know even less than you do.* He wished that they could understand that he was not against them.

It was hard to blame them.

They had grown up in the same world he had, the same cultural norms influencing everyone from their earliest years. He had at least had the opportunity for deeper study. If he hadn't figured out the truth of the Dracodei, he could hardly expect a peasant farmer from Brechin to know the truth without being told.

He watched King Ursa and Kessara return, walking side by side.

The rest of the Septemvirate stood behind them, assembled in a half-circle, facing the courtyard. Without a word, Dorold moved to join them, leaving Wes next to a group of serious-looking Aridmoor soldiers.

Servants had lashed a white canopy to the palace wall and two of the nearest trees with astonishing speed, sheltering the

Elders from the driving rain.

Night was coming. At the edge of his vision, Wes watched boy servants hefting ladders against the trees, clambering up and lighting dozens of candles that were hidden between the branches. Usually, Wes found the sparkling yellow lights dancing in the trees to be beautiful. In the backdrop of gloom and gray, however, they only increased his longing for sunshine.

Kessara caught Wes' eye and gave him a fraction of a nod. He returned it, puzzled, as she raised a hand and called for attention. Both parties of soldiers stood statue-still, their swords resting against their red or green-clad shoulders.

"People of Silverfell." She clapped her hands together loudly, to little effect. Many of the civilians had already gone home, and those who remained were unlikely to be sympathetic. Public meetings that took place after dark always seemed to attract drunks looking for novelty and those who were criminals themselves, more eager to see someone punished than justice done.

"Can we not retreat to the hall of meeting, Princess?" Elder Rahma cut in, shivering beneath his robes.

"We will not be long, my lord Elder," King Ursa said, giving Elder Rahma a scathing look as the man took a couple of clumsy steps back to his place. "This matter concerns the whole of the Four Kingdoms."

Wes tried to catch Kessara's eyes again as the King spoke, but she was staring out toward the newly-lit trees, her damp cheeks gleaming with droplets of rain.

"I have taken counsel from the Septemvirate, and they have advised me that it would be wise for me to postpone my engagement to Wes Cervos until an investigation of his claims, as well as a proper trial for the crime of blasphemy, can be conducted. I love him very much," her voice caught in her throat and she paused for a moment. Wes realized with surprise that her cheeks were covered not in rain, but tears.

She thinks of Roven. Kessara swallowed, wiping away the tears with the sleeve of her dress before continuing on.

"But I do not wish to accept the crown under the weight of such doubts. I believe that the King and Queen of Galeharbor will share in my concerns."

She glanced toward Wes for a half-second, visibly pained.

Fear and relief rippled through him in equal measure. *She must have made a deal. She'll be safe.* Kylan Ursa placed a hand on her shoulder and patted her stiffly, an impersonation of empathy that made him want to punch him square on the nose.

But what of my House?

What of Silverfell?

The soldiers of his Kingdom whispered to one another, shifting in their positions as water and muck pooled at their boots. Within a matter of moments, it seemed, gossip had spread beyond the courtyard and out into the streets.

More people of the respectable sort gathered anywhere that they could find a place to stand, having returned with broad hats and umbrellas to shelter them from the rain.

"I speak for all of my soldiers, as well as my subjects back in Aridmoor, when I say that it pains my Kingdom to see our old allies living through such tumultuous days," King Ursa started, taking a few steps forward until he was scarcely covered beneath the canopy of oilcloth.

"We see how the common folk suffer. We know that the burdens you bear are great."

For just a moment, Wes could see shadows of Kylan Ursa's

father, Radagar, in his son's face. Radagar had been a rather aloof man and a demanding husband and father, he knew, but he always treated every citizen, no matter how lowly, with respect.

He was gifted that way. Able to make people fight for him, to be loyal to the plains Kingdom of Aridmoor, straight through to their bones. Kylan had no hope of matching his father's skill, but Wes feared that his emulation would be convincing enough for those who already feared the reprisal of the elves if the Dracodei were to be displeased.

"But it is not the time for you to grumble against your duties," he continued, gesturing across the expanse of bodies before him, unconcerned with the rain and the chill.

"With the support of Galeharbor and the blessing of the Septemvirate, I wish to help you to restore Silverfell to her former glory."

Even King Ursa's soldiers broke attention, gossiping to one another, the buzz of hundreds of whispered voices filling the air. The peasants and merchants who had returned to the scene wore looks of confusion as they chatted with their neighbors. Somehow, in a matter of minutes, the edges of the crowd had swelled outward.

Beyond the courtyard, he could see lights in the upper floors of houses beginning to come on as darkness fell. He hoped that most of the Kingdom's subjects were sitting down to dinner with their families, enjoying a good meal before a warm fire rather than standing about to witness this travesty.

It was humiliating to know just how many people who had once respected him would now see him as a criminal, even a traitor.

Wes tried desperately to speak to Celesyria, to no avail.

Kessara looked toward the Septemvirate. *What is he talking about?* Wes bobbed his head back and forth, searching for Dorold's face as he got up from the tree pot and strode toward the half-circle of men.

"What is going on?" he called out, his voice hushed by the pounding of rain against the smooth wood of the courtyard. Dorold shook his head as he turned away. Wes felt soldiers move in on either side of his body, their thick arms pressed against his own.

A moment later, he watched in horror as the Elders approached King Ursa one by one, bowed, and kissed his ring. After Kessara had followed suit, the head of the Septemvirate walked to the edge of the canopy, a few stray droplets of rain landing on top of his white head as he began to speak.

"As soon as it can be planned, there will be a formal ceremony inaugurating King Kylan Ursa as temporary Steward of Silverfell."

Dorold raised his staff, but he did not need to sound it. The audience had already gone deathly quiet. Wes was certain that his face bore the same look of shock he saw all around them.

A steward from another Kingdom? Has such a thing ever been done? How dare they make such a decision here, in the shadow of night.

"Through this formal alliance of our Kingdoms, Aridmoor's army will join our own soldiers in defending Silverfell. Trade will flourish. As you all know, we rely heavily on Aridmoor's farmlands for many of our necessities. We will all enjoy the benefit of lower prices and abundant supply.

"Of course, our new Steward will continue to defer to our counsel when he can," Dorold glanced at King Ursa, but he moved too quickly for Wes to discern what was meant by the smile on his wizened face.

"Needless to say, we will not heed this disastrous advice our Envoy has put forth. In Galeharbor, in Aridmoor, and in Silverfell, worship of the Dracodei will continue. As a matter of fact, it will increase, as never seen before!"

The crowd applauded as the Elder raised both of his hands to the dark sky.

Wes felt like he would burn beneath the gaze of hundreds of eyes staring at him.

I told you, Celesyria. An Envoy has no power. This was a fool's errand.

"These uncertain days are not a time for doubt, but greater faith!"

Elder Dorold crowed as the cheers swelled, mingling with the hammering of the rain. The other members of the Septemvirate were shouting their approval even as they pulled their robes in tightly against the night chill.

Wes couldn't even feel it. He could only watch in horror as the legacy of his father, mother, and brother was cast aside like kitchen scraps. Dorold was unrecognizable. His smile seemed warped somehow, revealing an undercurrent of cruelty that Wes had never witnessed before in all of the years that he had known the head Elder.

He had thought that Dorold might be the one person in Stronghollow who would listen. Instead, Wes was now watching as he dismantled his Kingdom, piece by piece.

"My good citizens, I will not keep you any longer. The night grows cold, and tomorrow will bring much planning and labor. Let us return to our houses."

The crowd cheered again. Wes watched as mothers bundled little children close to them beneath their umbrellas, tying hats over loose curls and gathering belongings that had fallen to the ground. Friends reunited. The soldiers waited on the edge of stillness as rain soaked their already wet clothes.

"A final thing," Dorold raised a hand. The crowd quieted.

"As the Princess said, we will pursue a fair investigation and trial of our Envoy and his dragon friend. Our new Steward is in full agreement that this is a matter of justice."

Wes held his breath, waiting. He had not been surprised to see the rest of the Septemvirate go along with such a plan. Even Kessara, he was sure, had her reasons. But to see Dorold so willing to kiss the ring of a foreign sovereign was something he'd never imagined he would witness.

"Regrettably, for the time being, Wes Cervos is a threat to the peace and security of Silverfell. He may attempt to conspire with the dragon if he is allowed to go free before trial date. Soldiers, please convey our Envoy to the Stronghollow penitentiary."

* * *

The two nearest soldiers gripped Wes' arms like twin vices. Wes stood rooted to the spot, openmouthed, as he watched Dorold and the rest of the Elders weaving toward the palace gates. They were chatting to one another as though they had concluded a routine meeting about land allotments with the Lesser Nobles. He could even hear the occasional polite chuckle, probably in response to one of Elder Gunnan's infamously terrible jokes.

Dorold did not so much as look back at Wes before he was out of sight.

"Don't worry, lad," the nearest soldier to Wes' right said,

loosening his grip. "Stronghollow penitentiary is known even among Aridmoor criminals as being soft. You will be treated well."

Wes craned his neck to look for Kessara.

She was standing alone under the canopy, and he could see several servants waiting to take it down, their faces betraying poorly-disguised annoyance at her aimless presence. To his relief, she turned to face him, her eyes going wide at the sight of the number of red-clad soldiers that surrounded him.

She began to mouth words, but before she could finish, King Ursa appeared and snaked an arm across her shoulders, leading her toward the gate and into the candlelit palace grounds. He could see the stiffness in her neck and back as she walked, as though she was ready to slip out from beneath his heavy grip and run away into the night.

Wes swore under his breath.

"I'd be thankful, son," the soldier continued, apparently not having noticed Wes trying to get the Princess's attention. "Before I joined the army, I worked as a guard at the prison in High Keep. Now there's a place that makes even the hardest men falter. Bread and water, and you was lucky if the maggots were already dead when you started eating."

"Good to know," Wes said with ill-concealed disgust, noticing for the first time the silvery-pink scar that marked the man's eyebrow. He did not doubt that the prisoners did not take kindly to being locked up, nor would they hesitate to blame a lowly grunt for the fact of their captivity.

The soldier nodded to his companion, and the two men began leading Wes the same way that Celesyria had been taken. This time, though, they would not be heading for the dungeon. Wes had never been to the penitentiary, but he knew that it lay beyond the city's eastern walls, not far from the road to Briarcroft.

Wes followed without protest, thankful that King Ursa's soldiers had not felt the need for manacles. Celesyria had not been given the same consideration.

He watched as the rest of the courtyard began to clear out for the second time. Unlike on an ordinary night where violent crime was a constant threat, the city folk who bore umbrellas walked home at a slow, even leisurely pace, talking amongst themselves.

None of them paid Wes any attention as the soldiers ushered him past.

Mere days ago, you were cheering me on as I rode through the city. Now, you don't even see me. It's like I don't even exist, now that I've fallen from some arbitrary grace.

Somehow, that felt even worse than his people hating him.

The sky had long since grown completely dark, the rain clouds left little hope for any moon or starlight.

Silverfell soldiers broke from their neat ranks and fanned out in several directions, some heading for the barracks, others for the stables, and several of the higher-ranking men heading for whatever merriment may be found within the palace walls after night fell.

Wes saw Moorn there, a blank stare on his face as his friends jested with one another. When he caught Wes' eye, however, he looked away as though he had been burned.

As he and the soldiers stepped from the wood of the court-yard and into an even muddier side street, he saw another group of soldiers he had known since childhood rush past.

They nodded to the Aridmoor men, but their eyes bore looks of pity.

Will none of them oppose this madness? He tried to keep pace with the long strides of his captors, the water in his boots squelching between his toes with each step. *How can they trust that the Stewardship will be temporary when our ruling House has all but fallen? Have they simply given up and accepted outside rule?*

He cringed as the full meaning of his own words sunk in. He had accepted the rule of the Septemvirate, ever since his family had been slaughtered. He knew it was not ideal, but there had been no other choice. Perhaps this was the same thing. Was there any point in trying to escape their inevitable fate?

Before he could ponder the matter further, however, he caught a glimpse of a familiar face, hidden in the doorway of a dark bookshop. Oria was pressed against the building to avoid the rain, almost hidden in the shadows by her ragged gray cloak, but her pale blonde hair and sharp eyes were unmistakable.

To his astonishment, she stepped off of the stoop and into the muddy street as the soldiers passed by, letting her hood fall uselessly at her back.

"I'm sorry," she cried to him, tears mingling with rain on her pale cheeks. "I had to tell them about the Princess. They threatened me. My family is near starving as it is. Forgive me."

She gestured to the run-down store, her skinny arms jutting out from beneath her cloak.

He opened his mouth to speak, but one of the soldiers raised a hand, silencing him.

"Mind your business, child, and I will let this pass."

"This is my business. Elder Bram—"

Wes watched helplessly as the soldier lashed out at the child, striking her across the face with a hand that looked nearly as large as her head.

"I don't wish to arrest you. Sh—sh—shut up," the soldier stammered, looking at his hand as though it had been someone else that had hit the girl.

"It's okay," Wes said to Oria, his voice shaking with rage as he watched redness rising across her slapped cheek. She did not cry immediately, but he could see the quaking of her lip and the tears rising behind her eyes. "Do as he says."

The other soldiers looked at each other as yellow eyes raced back toward the shop door, a sob escaping her as she turned the knob and burst inside, leaving her wet cloak in a pile on the stoop.

"We will not speak of it, the poor child," the one at his right said, with a pointed look at his companion who had hit her. "She's had a bad turn as it is."

The man who slapped her fell behind the rest of the soldiers, saying nothing. Wes noticed that no one moved to take his place in restraining him. He walked more easily with only one arm encumbered.

They continued their march forward, walking by clusters of remaining passersby and several groups of Silverfell soldiers. The mood was somber. The colorful ribbons and glowing lights were fading away as they reached a shabbier quarter of the city, and he could see several beggars hiding in alleyways and on doorsteps, threadbare blankets pulled tightly around their shoulders.

Elder Bram has always been a snake. I thought the Septemvirate was better than this. I thought Dorold cared for our people.

Nearly everyone he passed looked through him as though he were invisible. A few gave him frowns of pity, shaking their heads. One emotion was plain on every face, no matter how impassive.

Fear.

Since my parents died, they have all ruled the Kingdom not by virtue and servitude, but with fear. Everything they have done has been twisted. They have used the misfortune of this Kingdom to keep our people poor and docile for the sake of their own power.

They were only a couple of streets away from the wall now. Watchtowers were manned by Silverfell guards night and day, lest the city be breached by thieves, slavers, or worse.

He knew these men. Such a task was not appointed to those with the highest ranks, nor to the lowest tier of the army. Only a loyal soldier with experience, yet expendable if the worst came, could be trusted to watch over the gates by night.

He continued forward, stepping just quickly enough to avoid drawing the ire of his captors.

I am not as alone as it seems. He craned his neck upwards, trying to read the faces of the Silverfell guards standing atop the towers. *My isolation is an illusion, just as the Dracodei are an illusion. Their power relies on our willingness to submit to it. Everyone fears crossing the line on their own.*

He fought back the surge of hope and terror that filled his heart as he continued walking. He knew he was running out of time to craft a plan, but he struggled to focus as despair tempted him to accept his fate.

Celesyria said that the Envoy has a genuine purpose. But even if I do, the High One has given me no way to know what that purpose is, or how to fulfill it. He stared up at the starless sky. It was cold, but the rain had slowed to a gentle patter, and the wind had calmed somewhat. The great city gate was drawing nearer. Beyond the wall, he would be alone with the red soldiers.

There was no other choice left but to pray.

He thought of his prayers to the Dracodei.

Like most everyone in the Four Kingdoms, he'd been raised to petition the dragon gods for everything he needed, even everything he wanted. He remembered Roven as a young child, begging their parents to bring him to the temple so that he could offer a basket of spring berries in hope of acquiring a deer of his own.

He'd gotten one a few days later, a beautiful cream-colored stag that he'd named Griffin. Wes had always taken it for granted that it had been the Dracodei who had given him what he asked, through whatever mysterious means that they saw fit. He was not always as bold in his requests as his elder brother was, but still, he almost always received what he prayed for.

He thought back to Oria, and the beggars, struggling for their very survival. He thought of tradesmen who had boarded up their shops and merchants who had left their stalls empty, unable to make a profit on their goods. These people worshiped the Dracodei too. And yet, when they prayed, the gods were silent. The help that they'd begged for never came.

Maybe You won't answer me either, High One. I'm always asking for things. I'm always selfish. But, perhaps You miss the old days when people sought Your help. At least, I hope that's how You feel... Does God feel? Anyway, I would appreciate some guidance. A sign. Something. Respectfully yours, Wes Cervos.

He shook his head, feeling like an idiot. If the High One created the world, he knew what Wes needed anyway. But it felt right to ask.

For several moments they walked in silence.

Wes watched as the local soldiers nodded to their new brothers in arms. His heart hammered against his ribcage. Something would happen. It had to. The last time he had appealed to the High One, however clumsily, he'd been saved from being eaten by ironwolves.

Unless it was a coincidence. Unless I was right to doubt. He and the soldiers drew up to the city gates. There would be no allies on the road to the penitentiary. Time had run out.

Chapter Sixteen

The door that led out of Stronghollow was different than the one leading into the palace. It was not hidden within the stone, rather, it was huge and imposing, all sleek dark wood with huge metal fittings. Wes had always thought it conveyed security. Now, it reminded him how difficult it would be to return to the city, even if he could get away.

One of the Aridmoor soldiers called out to the men in the gatehouse, bidding them to draw the huge door up on its chains so that they could make their passage through.

Torches burned all along the thick stone wall on either side, great lines of them leading out of sight, into the darkness of a city nearing sleep.

One of the soldiers in the gatehouse rushed to his end of the massive winch, grasping the handle. The other man, however, rushed to the ladder leading down. He wore his light brown hair long beneath his helmet, and though there was something familiar about his face, Wes did not recognize him.

Despite the shout of protest from his partner, he continued toward the red-clad men until he was standing in the middle of the road. The Aridmoor soldiers stared at him, and the other Silverfell men who stood against the city walls shifted from foot to foot.

"Gentlemen," he said, nodding to the other local soldiers near the door, his voice loud enough to catch the attention of men standing farther off.

"We're not going to go along with this."

Silence fell. No one moved for several heartbeats.

"This Envoy—" he gestured to Wes, finger pointed accusingly "—has always been loyal to this Kingdom and her people. Now, we are going to allow another monarch to send him to prison, and to march his army into our capital, unopposed? Really, lads, is this what you are willing to give your lives for?"

Wes forced himself to remain still as the remaining soldier tightened his grip upon his arm for a moment, his face going red. He glanced toward the local soldiers and back at his own men, waiting. The other Silverfell soldiers were still standing, staring, as though waiting for someone to give orders.

"Look," the friendlier of the Aridmoor soldiers said finally, taking a step toward the long-haired man. "I don't want trouble here."

"Neither do I, hence the problem."

"Be smart," he pleaded, letting go of Wes and marching up to the soldier, his boots sticking in the muddy street as he went. "We will not be drawn into any games. We're here to feed our families. I know you and all of these men wish to do the very same."

Murmurs of agreement sounded among King Ursa's soldiers, but to Wes' astonishment, the Silverfell men did not join in.

They stood alongside their torches, eyes shifting from one man to another. Wes bit back a curse. They were men trained to take orders, he knew. If King Ursa was the only one willing to give them, he would be the person who they followed.

"It is our duty to obey, not to question our betters," the red-clad soldier continued.

"I advise that you ensure your fellow soldier learns it, or I'll be forced to offer him an education myself." He still sounded pleasant. He did not seem to relish the idea of violence.

Two of the Silverfell men standing near the door rushed forward, grabbing the man who had spoken by the tops of his arms and half-dragging him back toward the wall. They had no difficulty moving him. He was not very tall, nor very muscular. He was younger than Wes had initially thought, still a boy rather than a grown man.

The Aridmoor soldiers waited until the rebel was out of the road, looking back and forth between the soldiers on the line and those that remained in the gatehouse.

Calculating how many of us there are. How many of us there would be if we chose to stand against them and their King.

Before the soldier could grab hold of Wes once more, the restrained boy shot him a look. There was no sadness in his eyes, no look of desperation.

It was something more, something Wes found himself able to read without really understanding why. Somehow, the message was clearer than words on parchment.

This is your sign. Take courage.

Without knowing what he was doing, Wes lunged for the

sword at his captor's belt, ripping it from its sheath before the man had a chance to react. He darted backward toward the Silverfell men, brandishing the weapon with both arms, trying to avoid stumbling and landing on his rear end.

"Wrong," he said, his voice deepening into a near growl as he faced King Ursa's astonished soldiers. *If the men behind me choose to slit my throat, it's over.* He did not dare take even a glance over his shoulder.

"Your oath was not merely to obey and to follow orders. You took an oath to defend Silverfell from her enemies, within and without. You took an oath to serve the House of Cervos, so long as the royal line endures. I am forbidden from commanding you, but your duty to protect me stands."

The Aridmoor soldiers drew their swords, walking forward slowly, amused looks on their faces.

Wes watched, shaking, as a sliver of moonlight broke through the heavy cover of cloud, gleaming upon the edges of their sharpened blades. His own borrowed sword, made for a man much bigger than he was, was so heavy that he struggled to hold it aloft.

There is no way I can fight anyone with this. The clarity he had felt moments before was fading away like a dream upon waking. He'd seen only one soldier willing to stand against King Ursa. One. And yet, he was gambling everything on the idea that more would fight. It was madness.

"You think you're brave?" One of the red-clad soldiers said, an ugly sneer sliding across his mouth.

No. My parents were brave. Roven was brave. I can't even take care of myself, let alone protect my people.

Before he could stop it, the sword slipped, the point nearly touching the muck of the road before he regained his grip. He longed for his own knife. He was not a great warrior, but he would have stood a chance, however slight.

"There's being brave, and then there's being stupid," the soldier continued, taking a few more steps toward him, swinging his sword as though it carried no weight at all. Wes stepped backward, nearly stumbling, certain he was about to run into the end of one of his own men's swords. "I'd say that starting a one-man army right before battle counts as stupid."

"Two," came a voice behind Wes, followed by the sound of a sword being drawn. "You mean a two-man army."

* * *

"Three."

"Four."

"Five."

Wes stumbled forward, nearly dropping his sword for a second time as the Silverfell soldiers rushed past him. The long-haired man had been freed, and he rushed toward the soldier who had insulted him, swinging his sword with apparent ease.

A few of the others shouted their own numbers, and several of the men fled toward the streets of Stronghollow, either to report their comrades or to avoid the conflict altogether. *It doesn't matter.* Wes was unable to suppress the smile that rushed to his face.

There are enough who are loyal to Silverfell.

We will oust King Ursa and the Septemvirate, I will make Kessara queen, and we will be free.

He shook those thoughts aside as he exchanged his Aridmoor longsword for a dagger that one of the other soldiers passed to him.

It was better, but still, the lack of practice was written in his stiff muscles. Even after losing some weight on his journey home, he did not move quickly, and he struggled to break through the clusters of fighting men to find a target.

Adrenaline drove him on, pushing through the press of men. More men on both sides had joined the fray, and he could see women leaning out of their windows in houses near the wall, eager to catch a glimpse at yet more excitement.

He watched as one young-looking Silverfell soldier cut down two of Ursa's men with one stroke, sending their third companion rushing toward the door at the city gate. To his relief, other soldiers had raised it, allowing any who wished to flee to do so. He did not wish to see a bloodbath, however angry he was at Kylan Ursa's men.

Several more red-clad men followed the first deserter, rushing out onto the road and running as fast as their legs would take them.

"Ha!" One of the Silverfell men clapped Wes on the back, sweat pouring down across his brow as he stood for a moment, watching all directions for action before diving back into the fight.

Wes gripped the dagger more tightly, unsure where to go. He felt he was in the way. Everywhere he looked were men locked in violent embraces, the sound of clashing steel ringing out across the city.

Suddenly, he locked eyes with one of the Aridmoor soldiers.

For a split second, there was a clear path between them. Three Silverfell men were fighting off seven of King Ursa's soldiers nearby. Another lone ally lay against the wall of a house, bleeding from a chest wound. Many of the others had fought their way further back into the city and were now several streets beyond the radius of Wes' cry for aid.

He stood still, his stomach curdling as the man strode toward him, a look of resignation on his rather handsome face.

Wes couldn't decide how to hold the dagger properly. The small blade shook in his hand, the gold handle slick with his sweat. It was clear to him that it was more of a decorative ornament than a knife meant for fighting and killing.

His mind flashed back to his childhood. He'd spent many, many hours training with the sword, but he'd never been good enough, always falling behind the other boys his age. Eventually, his mother had the idea to train him to use a bow for ranged combat, and knives rather than a sword for fighting in closer quarters. It had helped, but still, he'd never mastered the skills of a warrior.

Roven was so much better than him that he found it hard to believe they shared parents. *And yet, I live, and he is dead.*

He let the dagger rest at his side as the opposing soldier advanced, the urge to give up filling him once more as he witnessed the destruction that surrounded him. *More death. More loss. My fault, all of it.*

He glanced around wildly, considering a second attempt with one of the huge longswords that King Ursa's soldiers carried. *No.* He raised the dagger as the soldier ahead stepped over one of his dead companions. *It would be more suicidal than this child's blade.*

Besides, every sword of the right length and weight that he saw was currently in the hand of a living Silverfell soldier. This was good on the whole, he supposed, if it meant they were winning.

It certainly seemed they were. More and more Silverfell soldiers had poured in from the direct streets leading to the palace. The Aridmoor men were still coming, swarming along back alleys and pouring out of taverns, but their numbers were visibly shrinking.

There's only one problem. If I die, none of it will matter. The Septemvirate and King Ursa will get their way, and the old Silverfell will be lost forever.

There was no time left to think.

The approaching soldier was familiar, Wes realized, but he couldn't seem to place him. He was close enough now that Wes could see the tangle of wet red curls sticking out from beneath the edges of his cap. His tunic had an intricate pattern running along the bottom edge that was different than the other soldiers around him.

Some kind of rank insignia?

Wes' thoughts spun as he braced for the first blow.

He heard the hiss of displaced air as the man's stroke fell, followed by a jolting ache in his arm. Somehow, he had blocked the sword.

The man pulled back a few steps, curses pouring forth as he moved to make a second strike. Wes met his long blade once again, though this time, the impact was enough to send the dagger sailing out of his hand.

Wes lunged to the ground, grappling for the blade, as the soldier raised his sword once more for what was sure to be a killing blow. He was suddenly aware of his neck, his chest, his arms, even the feeling of his curls brushing against his ears. Unlike the soldiers, his entire body was exposed and unprotected.

His fingers closed around the handle of the blade, slick with mud and rain and sweat. He lurched backward, his feet sliding on the muck in the road, desperate to find purchase.

He watched as if in slow motion as the sword sliced into the ground where his head had been mere seconds before.

He was on his feet.

The soldier yelled as he tripped over a fallen Silverfell soldier, managing to hold onto his blade, but losing his footing and falling onto his rear. Wes surged forward, his chest heaving. The two men had ground up the already muddy street into a mire beneath their boots, and every step forward threatened a fall.

Before Wes reached the soldier, he was intercepted by one of the Silverfell guards. The man turned to the Aridmoor soldier on the ground, raising his sword above his head as the man scrabbled backward, his heels kicking up clods of mud that splashed against the opposing soldier's green cloak.

Before his sword could fall, Wes shrunk back in horror as an arrow narrowly missed his head, sticking neatly into the soldier's back.

The man tensed for a moment, his arms stiffening as his hand lost its grip on the sword.

He fell impossibly slowly toward the red-clad soldier, his knees buckling as his face smacked into the muck.

"Pity," the Aridmoor soldier said flatly, touching the man's helmet with the tip of his boot.

"He could have been my brother," he continued, looking up at Wes. "But instead, you chose death for your men. Is your life so much more valuable than theirs?"

Wes took a step back. The adrenaline rush lay behind him, and he felt sapped of energy. Guilt rushed in to fill its place. He knew that the soldier was trying to weaken his resolve, but understanding the tactic did not lessen the sting of his accusation.

Why must my life be surrounded by such endless death?

The makeshift battlefield, which had been so full mere minutes before, had largely emptied out. Dead bodies dotted the road, and in several places, the mud was mingled with thick red blood.

No one else was coming to save him. He had gotten lucky once but knew it would not be repeated.

It was over.

The Aridmoor soldier took a few steps forward, his face a mask of pity.

"Surrender, and I will put in a good word with the King," he said, taking a few slow steps forward. Wes heard the telltale crunch of bone as the man stepped on the tips of the fallen soldier's fingers.

"He wouldn't kill you, anyway. I doubt he wants to wait for a new Envoy to be born. Better to imprison you, as he planned before."

Wes kept his eyes on the soldier, taking his own careful steps forward. The remaining sounds of battle faded away, replaced by the rushing sound of blood in his ears.

There was only one chance.

He watched as the soldier raised his sword, giving it a turn with a flourish of his wrist. Wes noticed that there were darker patches on the detailed edge of his red tunic. *Blood.*

"See, I have no such qualms," he continued, the barest hint of a smile showing on his otherwise impassive face. "My half-brother is ambitious. He thinks always of power. I'm a simpler man."

He leaned toward Wes, resting a companionable hand on his shoulder, as though he was about to whisper a secret in his ear.

"I'm more interested in vengeance, myself. I'm not a cruel

man, but I do have a strong sense of justice. You brought death, and now you must die."

One chance.

Before he could move, Wes yanked the dead Silverfell soldier's sword from where it had fallen.

He stepped backward before the other man could react, holding the sword in both hands. To his surprise, they were no longer shaking.

He did not waver as the man rushed toward him, raising his blade, ready to strike.

Time stopped.

Wes did not risk breathing.

There.

The soldier's feet slipped in the muck, just as Wes had foreseen. His boots stuck. He couldn't right himself. He did not have time even to cry out as he fell forward, his sword falling as he flailed his arms, fingers grasping at nothing but air.

The razor-sharp blade slid through his chest as Wes pulled his hands away.

The Aridmoor soldier fell neatly on top of the man that his companions had killed, their blood mingling on the ground, a bitter brotherhood forged only by death.

Zanek. Waves of nausea flowed through him as the memories fell into place. He forced himself to take deep breaths, letting the bracing air fill his lungs.

He'd met him before. As a boy, on a diplomatic trip with his parents to High Keep.

Zanek had looked so much like Kylan's late mother. She had not been a good Queen, but Wes would not have wished her illness on anybody.

Now, he was responsible for the death of her son, whom Radagar Ursa had raised as his own.

Of course. Kylan Ursa only let him live because he was illegitimate. If he'd been a candidate for the throne... He did not need to finish the thought. He no longer underestimated King Kylan Ursa's ruthlessness.

He dared to take a moment to glance up at the sky. A shaft of moonlight cut through the clouds once more, illuminating the droplets of blood that dotted his fingers, discoloring the edges of his fingernails.

"There are worse things than death," he whispered to the darkness, stepping over bodies as he strode toward the center of Stronghollow.

"Yes, I think you're right about that."

Wes turned in time to see Dorold frowning at him before he felt an excruciating pain blooming across the back of his head. He fell to the ground, his last thought clear in his mind before everything went dark.

You were wrong to hope in me, Celesyria.

You should have found someone else.

* * *

When Celesyria closed her eyes, she could imagine that she was home in Whitespire, still a child.

The ceiling of the cavern would glow with orb light, casting everything in shades of blue. Her parents would be sleeping nearby, getting their rest before the new day dawned. She would be sleeping peacefully, or resting as she was now, eyes closed, thinking about all of the adventures that awaited her.

Somewhere above, the sky would be wide open, the expectations of Guardian life were years away.

Instead, she lay in almost total darkness, curled into a ball against the dampness that seeped out of the dungeon walls. The soldiers who had imprisoned her had permitted her a few candles, and she could produce brief flashes of illumination by carefully breathing fire, but it was not nearly enough to cut through the oppressive and constant gloom.

The guards changed shifts twice a day, but beyond that, she struggled to keep track of how many days or even hours had passed. Some of the guards would speak to her briefly when they brought her meals, but none had an answer as to how long she would remain a prisoner.

She wasn't sure if she wanted to know her fate anyway. She knew that if she was to be convicted of blasphemy, she could face execution. She couldn't imagine the horror of sitting there in the dungeon, counting the shift changes until the day and hour she was to be killed—if they even gave her a warning at all. Perhaps they would just come and lead her to a killing field...

No. She pressed her eyes more tightly together, shivering at the thought and the cold. *The common laws of all Kaveryth are clear. All creatures, even the elves, are entitled to a proper trial before they face justice in any of the Four Kingdoms, or in the land of Umrym.*

She thought of her parents. Would they have yet received word of her fate? Would the leaders of the Guardians demand a trial to take place in her homeland, or would they permit the Septemvirate and the King of Aridmoor to try her on their own authority?

Though she had read more on the topic than most, there were far too many questions about the canons that she could not answer.

Worse, she was not the only creature she had to worry about.

From what little she had seen of the Septemvirate's deliberations, Wes had been in deep trouble himself. *Trouble that he would never have been in had I not dragged him into it.* However essential he was to the plan of the High One, she could not help but feel guilty for her own involvement in bringing him to such danger. And what of the Princess? Would she bear any guilt?

She opened her eyes for a moment and turned around in the too-small space, trying to get comfortable. She was never successful at this, but she experimented with her position just the same. She had nothing better to do.

The soldiers, seeing that her behavior was subdued and trusting in the strength of the thick metal bars, had freed her of the chains that had tied her to the walls when she first entered the dungeon. However, she continued to wear the manacles on her legs, and they bit into her skin no matter which way she tried to lie down.

Perhaps the people of the Four Kingdoms will be content to accept my punishment as sufficient for both of our crimes.

It was a small hope, but a hope just the same, and she tried to focus on it. Fear pounded in her skull.

I am not necessary. If the High One has chosen Wes as the one who will lead all Kaveryth to the truth, He will not let him be killed. Wes will be okay.

She breathed in and out, trying to acclimatize herself to the fear that threatened to break her.

If it came to it, would she have the strength to accept death for what she believed in? If that day came when she faced her end at the mercy of an executioner's blade, would she be able to confess her belief in the High One, or would she deny Him?

She felt tears stinging her eyes. It wasn't fair. She knew that dragons did not have souls. She would not die awaiting life in the eternal lands, reward from the High One, or the comfort of those who had journeyed into death before her.

She could only hope that the Farplace was better than this world, better than this life.

But there was little foundation to place that hope upon.

"Why does it have to be Wes who You have chosen?"

She cried out to the High One, stunned by the rage that lay behind her words. *"You have brought me to Your truth, Your very messages to Your creation, and yet, You deny me a soul, something given to even the lowest of men?"*

She began to cry, unable to stop the tears from flowing. She curled her head beneath her wounded wing, the sudden flash of pain making her groan into the nothingness. She did not hear the movement of the guards. At night, it seemed, they kept watch at an unknown location farther from her cell. At that moment, she was thankful for the relative privacy as she began to cry.

She knew that her words were faithless, the wicked prayers of someone deserving of the Wrathlands, but she could not seem to stop them.

"I thought You were guiding everything that happened. I thought You were able to bring good even out of evil. So where are You? Where are You when I need You the most?"

Chapter Seventeen

Wes was awake, he was sure, but he couldn't seem to open his eyes. Every shift of his muscles sent waves of agony coursing through his limbs.

Even though the wound was located somewhere on his head, it felt as though every nerve in his body was burning. His mind watched in morbid fascination as blooms of color danced on the back of his eyelids, lighting up like signal fires.

Some indeterminate amount of time later, he awoke again. The pain had dulled only slightly, enough to make room for some rudimentary thoughts about where he was and how he'd gotten there. He could hear the sound of metal clanking and men talking, but the words did not carry far enough to reach him.

For several minutes he lay there, listening, trying to make

sense of the jumble of nonsense that floated around him like an aura.

The third time he awoke, it was as though his eyes opened a few seconds before his brain turned on, leaving him breathless.

He sat upright before he could consider the consequences of doing so, sending waves of misery radiating down toward his toes. He bit his tongue, but avoided screaming. It was bearable now, but only just.

"Wes," A voice said, a male one, closer now. "Drink."

He blinked a few times, trying to find the edges of reality. He was in a cell, clearly, with stone on three sides and a wall of metal bars on the other. The floor was stone as well, but beneath a layer of dust he could see a green-painted wooden inlay that had once been beautiful.

There were several oil lamps suspended far above his reach which gave the room a warm look despite the chilly night air that poured in through the one small barred window at the top edge of the back wall.

Stronghollow penitentiary. He felt reassured to be there as opposed to somewhere else, but he couldn't remember why. Though the pain had lessened, he couldn't shake the unpleasant sensation that his ears were stuffed full of cotton. The man said something else, but he couldn't quite hear it. It sounded far away.

He could see the water, though, held in a small glass cup behind thick metal bars. Suddenly, it was the only thing he saw, as though the rest of the cell had disappeared behind a thick black fog.

Ignoring the pain behind his eyes, he stretched his hand through the bars, grasping for it. "Careful!" The man hissed, waiting for Wes to stop moving before pressing it gently into his palm. He was dressed in a thick gray cloak, the hood drawn, obscuring his face in shadow.

"If you break it, they'll assume you're using the glass to make a shank. It'll be my head for bringing it."

Wes gulped at the water, gripping the glass carefully this time, not stopping for air until the vessel was empty. His stomach clenched at the onslaught of the cold water, but the pain in his head began to abate immediately.

In a rush, the prior night's events came flooding back.

He felt the back of his head, remembering the initial blow, the look of disappointment on Dorold's face. To his surprise, he could feel that someone had carefully cut away his hair and placed a bandage over the wound.

"I can't stay long," the man said under his breath, leaning back from the bars and looking behind him, where Wes could see a short set of wooden stairs leading upwards and around a corner. "Much has happened in just three days."

"Three days," Wes said, trying to get a look at who was speaking. The voice was familiar, but he was in too much pain and too exhausted to place it. He hoped that someone would bring him food when morning came.

I've been unconscious for three days? What has happened to Celesyria? And Kessara? The more complicated thoughts made his head begin to pound once more, but he couldn't help it.

Last he remembered, the soldiers of Silverfell had been driving King Ursa's men out of Stronghollow. Now he feared that things had taken another turn.

"Don't comment," the man said, tilting his head toward the stairs, listening.

"What—"

Before he could say more, the man threw back the hood of

the cloak to reveal the red cap of an Aridmoor soldier. Wes closed his mouth before some curse could pour forth, taking a couple of involuntary steps back from the bars.

Moorn was standing before him, the usual spark of playfulness absent from his eyes.

"What are you doing?" Wes asked slowly, noticing that each movement of his jaw caused a fresh prick of pain in his head.

"Like I said," Moorn slipped the thick cloak back over his head. "Much has happened."

* * *

Wes pressed his head against his fingertips, listening as Moorn filled him in on what he'd missed. Every minute or so, his friend raised a finger to his lips, listening and watching the stairs for signs of company.

Somewhere above, Wes could hear the stamping of boots, punctuated by the occasional barked command. So far, though, no one else had entered the otherwise empty cellblock where they kept him.

"You can appreciate my predicament," Moorn said, his voice hushed. "Right after you were taken, a good five hundred Aridmoor reinforcements poured into the city. They must have been camped out somewhere close, though where they could have gone that they avoided detection, I've no idea. At any rate, the remaining Silverfell soldiers were given the option of surrender or death."

"They chose surrender, I'm guessing."

"To a man."

Wes rubbed at his aching temples. For a moment, he thought he'd found allies. So many had picked up their swords and fought for him. How could it be that the survivors had been so quick to bow to a usurper?

Moorn cut in quickly. "It's not a sign of betrayal, if that's what you're thinking. Those who were willing to stand up to Aridmoor already did."

He gave Wes a pointed look from beneath his cloak before going on. *Of course. They already chose death.*

"So that leaves those like me who never got involved in the first place."

"Where do you stand, then?"

Moorn pulled back the cloak a little, revealing a flash of his red tunic. "I never said I wasn't a coward, only that I didn't directly betray you."

I led them to their death for nothing. His chest felt tight, the discomfort of anxiety competing with the aching within his skull. *All the while, King Ursa was bringing in enough men to crush us anyway, along with uniforms for those who chose to move to the winning team.*

"So why are you here?"

"The soldiers charged with guarding you will be back in the morning with food and water. You'll be treated well enough here." Moorn shrugged.

Wes said nothing. When he was a child, he always rushed to speak, asking every question that he could. As he'd grown older, he learned that sometimes silence was the best way to get answers.

"I came to offer hope," he said finally, his voice small in the depth of the prison.

Beneath the cloak, Wes could see the pallor of his face and the dark hollows beneath his eyes. "I wanted to tell you that your dragon friend is alive and that the Princess is safe in

Stronghollow for now, though I hear she has been claiming sickness and avoiding all social functions. The investigation of your claims and the trial you are entitled to is being planned."

Wes wanted to yell at him. *You come to offer me hope, dressed in the standard of our enemy? The standard of the army that slaughtered dozens of your fellow soldiers?*

Instead, he nodded. Though Moorn was indeed a coward, it was hard to place much of the blame upon his shoulders.

The Septemvirate was the only recognizable authority in Silverfell, especially with the sole representative of the noble House in prison. If the Elders allied with King Ursa, and there were not enough local soldiers to institute military law and order themselves, there was little that the remaining soldiers could do. Especially if the royal family of Galeharbor was willing to go along with their plans as well.

"Thank you for coming here," Wes said, surprised at the catch in his throat as emotions threatened to overtake him. It was a small gesture, but he was truly thankful for it, all the same. At least he knew that his friends were alright for the time being.

"I'm sure it was a risk to you."

Before Moorn could say more, however, there was a sound of scuffling footsteps approaching from above. The man's face went white, and he nodded to Wes, pulling his cloak tight and heading for the exit without another word.

Moorn rushed up the staircase, taking the steps two at a time. Within a few seconds, Wes was alone once more.

He did not hear any sound from above that Moorn had been captured, nor did anyone else come down the stairs. He waited for a while, the pain in his head returning somewhat, with nothing to distract him from feeling it. He was sure he had a concussion, but at least he'd have time to recover.

A brief flash of hope filled him as he attempted to speak to Celesyria, only to be crushed a moment later when she did not say anything back.

Of course she could not hear him. His captors were smart enough to know that dragons could at least sometimes communicate with men and took no chances. The palace dungeon was too far away.

Wes stepped back from the bars, balling his hands up into white-knuckled fists for a moment before sitting down on the small cot he'd been given, defeated.

There was nothing in the room that would help him to escape, and even if he did, he had nowhere to go. He could attempt to get close to Celesyria, but that would require her to escape, too. He'd be caught immediately. Without a way to communicate beforehand, even a brilliant escape plan would prove pointless.

Of course, he had no such plan anyway.

At least Celesyria's alive. His relief over Kessara's safety was more complex. Had she been truly reluctant to accept King Ursa's allegiance, or had she been pretending all along, helping King and Queen Manta to broker a deal with Aridmoor whether or not Silverfell assented?

Then again, if she was really on the King's side, why hadn't she told the people that she would never marry Wes at all, regardless of the outcome of his case? He kicked himself for failing to communicate with her while he was still free.

What difference would it have made? I couldn't have gone through with marrying the woman my brother loved, even to save the Kingdom. Even if we managed to secure her rule, how did we intend to produce a legitimate heir? That part of things certainly can't be feigned.

Standing up from the bed, he strode over to the barred window. Placing his hands against the sill, he looked up, the rush of cold air refreshing against his skin. He could not see the moon from where he stood, but after a moment, his eyes settled on something familiar.

Cervos. He used a fingertip to trace the stars that formed the deer-shaped constellation. *A House nearly as old as Kaveryth itself, cut off, fruitless. At least Noctua fell by the sword. I doom my Kingdom even as I yet live.*

He touched his cheeks, surprised to find tears there.

Somehow, he had thought that if he at least tried to live up to his family's name, he would be free to stop hating himself, stop blaming himself for the ghost of death that followed him everywhere he turned.

Dorold always used to tell me that time heals every wound. He wiped his eyes with the ends of his sleeves, the mad urge to laugh rising within him. He was so tired of crying. So tired of how weak he was.

He's wrong. Those who believe in the Dracodei and those who believe in the High One agree on one thing: those who die live forever. And if my life is any indication, I will not escape this pain when I die.

I'll endure it in the Wrathlands, for all eternity.

* * *

Days turned into weeks, and weeks turned into months.

Moorn never returned alone, but Wes saw him several times, always with Aridmoor soldiers. Which made sense, Wes supposed, if Silverfell's army no longer properly existed.

It seemed that the foreign army was beginning to trust

Moorn, which had the opposite effect on Wes.

He always tried to catch Moorn's eye with some telltale glance, in hopes of some assurance that he remained even a little on his side, but he always looked away, a warning in his eyes.

The penitentiary was not so bad.

His concussed head had taken three weeks to heal, but after that, he began to grow strangely comfortable with the routines of his new life. He was always kept in solitary confinement, which was by far the worst aspect of his stay, but for the last week or so they had begun to allow him a couple of hours outside on the prison grounds, late at night when no one else was present but his guards.

Since Moorn's first visit, none of the other guards had been willing to tell him anything about his trial or the current political affairs in Silverfell. However, with the aid of time, some became willing to make small talk. They would tell Wes about their wives, their children, and life back home in Aridmoor. Some of the very same men he had seen on the makeshift battlefield, cutting down his childhood friends, had become the only companions he had.

At first, he barely spoke himself, content simply to listen to the ordinary tales of other lives, but over time, he found himself willing to speak a little.

He couldn't talk about the death of his family, let alone more recent tragedies, but he found himself able to share happy memories.

King Ursa's soldiers enjoyed learning more about life in Silverfell. More than one of them confessed to Wes that they never wanted to be sent here, and that they deeply missed the wide open plains of their homeland. Many said that they felt suffocated by the endless trees and prevalence of shadow.

Wes never lacked food or water—even before Moorn's visit, the guards assured him that they tried every few hours to restore him to alertness—but he never got more than the minimum ration needed for health.

For the first time in his life, Wes was no longer what he would consider chubby.

His stomach was flat, and his thighs no longer squished so tightly together when he walked. His clothes still fit with some minor adjustments, but even the guards noticed a marked difference in his appearance.

Of course, next to the native Aridmoor soldiers, he still looked far more boyish than his seventeen years would suggest. His face was thinner, but it was still his. He'd never been particularly handsome, and losing weight hadn't changed that.

After his first month passed, he began to notice a distinct change taking place in the demography of the guards.

At first, they had always been Aridmoor men, all red hair and freckled skin and legs like trees. Soon after that, he saw men he recognized as former Silverfell soldiers in red uniforms keeping watch on his cell, always escorted by King Ursa's own men.

As he reached the day that marked the end of his second month in prison, he was shocked to see two soldiers he had known from childhood keeping guard over him.

Alone.

He did not dare attempt to speak to them or even get their attention, fearing both his punishment and their own, but it was an interesting development nonetheless. The new Steward and the Septemvirate were beginning to truly consolidate their forces, putting greater and greater trust in the men who had formerly fought under the standard of Silverfell.

This should have encouraged Wes, and yet, he couldn't bring himself to think too much about it. He had grown weary of watching every one of his hopes being dashed before his eyes. Instead, he tried to focus on staying as sane as he could, even as the isolation began to rip into him more and more.

I doubt the trial will happen at all, whatever Moorn said. He sat on his cot one evening, listening to the bells that signaled the change of guard shifts. The thought troubled him.

Never before had he imagined that Elder Dorold would have been willing to lock away a member of the royal House without ensuring justice was first done. And yet, he was willing to turn over his own people to a usurper. *I would be wise not to put too much stock in Dorold's integrity.*

He stood up and began to pace, in hopes that using his muscles would help him to push the worries out of his mind.

He had to accept that this cell—this life—were what his plans had finally led to. He doubted he would regain real freedom, but the summer Feast of Offering would be coming up soon, and that, at least, he could look forward to.

If they weren't going to kill him, they would have to allow him to bear the sacrifices to Umrym. They had no choice.

At least he would get a chance to see the world outside the prison walls again, even if he was under lock and key. He doubted that the guards would bring him on a route close enough to speak to Celesyria as he left Stronghollow, but he reserved some small hope that they'd forgotten to keep them apart.

A half grin rose to his face as he thought back to his conversation with Captain Drohma.

It seemed that he would be marching into Whitespire with

an army at his side, after all. Whether or not the Guardians were in on King Ursa's plot or not, though, he had no way of knowing. In any case, even the dragons couldn't kill him, for the same reasons that the Four Kingdoms had to keep him alive.

Before he could consider the implications further, he heard the telltale rhythm of boots on the staircase and strode over to the bars, wondering who would have the night watch.

For the last week straight, he'd been guarded by Aridmoor men, twin brothers who looked far too young to be in the army. Clearly, the men in charge did not see him as posing much of a threat.

He was surprised to see Moorn heading down the stairs, his sword hanging neatly on his belt, his bare legs looking somewhat reedy beneath the red tunic of Aridmoor.

For the second time, he was alone.

* * *

Wes could hardly believe his luck. As more days went by, and the Feast of Offering drew ever nearer, Moorn was given guard of his cell more and more often.

He usually had another soldier with him, but it wasn't always an Aridmoor native, and there were hours here and there when he was left alone. Wes hoped that Moorn was simply reluctant to do anything that might indicate to his new brothers-in-arms that he had a prior relationship with the prisoner.

The alternative possibility—that Moorn had changed sides entirely, leaving him with no allies at all—was too depressing to bear.

In some ways, Wes found his imprisonment more lonely on

days that Moorn was on duty.

They spoke little, and when they did, neither dared to discuss anything more personal than the weather or the latest palace scandal. Wes did learn, however, that King Ursa's stewardship of Silverfell was becoming rather highly approved by the citizens of Stronghollow, and even some in the rural villages spread throughout the Kingdom.

The thought that perhaps his people were better off with him gone was never far from his mind as the long days passed before him.

At times, he would feel a flicker of hope, and for a few hours, he would tell himself that the reports he heard did not mean anything.

His mother had always said that to die by the truth was better than to live by a lie, and her wisdom had stuck.

Perhaps King Ursa and the Septemvirate could crack down on thieves, execute slavers, and improve the trade of goods. But as long as the people continued to be robbed of their wealth to fund the worship of mortals, they would never be free, no matter what their opinion was on the matter.

In his darker moments, however, doubt continued to creep in.

It grew stronger and stronger as time went on, with no news of his ultimate fate forthcoming.

In the daytime, Wes could look out of his single window, watch the clouds pass overhead, feel the rush of the early summer breeze upon his skin. Some nights, he watched the stars. The comforting stag's head was ever-present, but over time, he found himself forming constellations of his own and making up tales of their heroic deeds.

But not every night brought stars.

There was nothing Wes hated more than being unable to sleep, without even the stars or moon for company. Sometimes, it was even worse. Wes would huddle beneath his thin blanket as rain slipped in through the window, bringing a damp chill that didn't pass until the sun had been up for a few hours.

The guards were expected to stay awake for their night watches, of course, but rarely did, and it wasn't as though he was about to tell tales about one to another.

On one such miserable night, a mere two weeks before the summer Feast, Moorn was keeping watch alone, passed out sitting on his stool even as lightning split the sky outside and thunder hammered against the roof so loudly that Wes nearly felt it shake.

He sat tucked into the corner of his cot, his blanket wrapped around himself so that he could avoid touching the frigid wall. Though summer had come to Silverfell, the season's warmth never seemed to last very long once the sun went down.

It had not been a good day, even by the usual Stronghollow penitentiary standards. The pear he'd been given for breakfast had gone moldy, which Wes noticed after taking an enthusiastic bite, eager for fresh food.

He had not been able to go for a short walk outdoors in over a week, and no one seemed able or willing to tell him why. The former Silverfell soldiers seemed on edge, treating Wes with a sudden harshness that he couldn't explain and didn't dare ask about.

So it was that Wes lay awake that night, trying and failing to find something hopeful or noble to think about as the storm raged outside. He thought of Celesyria, who could always find some positive work of the High One even in the worst situation, but the thought brought annoyance rather than comfort.

Looking up at the wooden slats of the ceiling, he spoke aloud, careful not to wake the nearly catatonic Moorn, who looked as though he was about to fall to the ground at any moment. "I could use a pair of wings right now, Celesyria," he whispered, smiling at the memory of the Dread Ruins, of Holga and Gohr, and of a time when he still believed he might be able to make a difference in the world.

"What in Kaveryth are you talking about?"

A female voice sounded from the darkness outside of his cell. Wes sat bolt upright, uncomfortably close to the edge of the bed, only just managing to stop himself from falling off.

"Moorn! Moorn!" The woman hissed, her voice insistent. He could hear the soldier grunting in response. Wes squinted, the single candle near the staircase useless against the heavy black shadows.

"Sorry to wake you, but I need a favor."

The woman shook Moorn gently, putting out an arm as though she could stop him from tumbling out of his chair with surprise when he awoke. Wes stared, open-mouthed, noticing the tail of a blonde braid peeking out from the woman's hood.

She may not have had wings, and Wes feared yet another disappointment, but he allowed the tiny spark of hope to warm him just the same.

Even if it would only last long enough to get him through this one cold, dark night.

Chapter Eighteen

Every night, when she was left alone, Celesyria prayed to the High One.

Often, she complained.

Life in the palace dungeon was almost unbearable, and it grew more so each day as the loneliness threatened to consume her completely.

As she had no window to the outside world and most of the guards made no attempt to speak to her, it was the change of temperature that marked the passing of the days. It was cold at night and sweltering in the daylight hours, and she used this knowledge to scratch a record of time passing into the wall at the corner of her cell.

At first, she hadn't minded the loneliness. She'd never been particularly social, and she enjoyed her own company. She would close her eyes, trying to imagine that she was in some library deep in the mines of Umrym, with no company but the occasional dwarf-woman passing through on her rounds.

There were, of course, no books, and the guards were not so friendly as the dwarves, but it served as a distraction. She would make up stories about the men who kept her captive, thinking of what their lives must consist of when they left the depths of her prison.

Sometimes, snatches of conversation gave her clues.

At first, she'd been terrified of all of the red-clad soldiers, certain that they'd enter her cell and stab her with hot pokers if the mood struck them, but soon she came to see that things were not so clear.

She could not excuse the way that they had treated her, but over time, she found that she could empathize with them. She knew as well as anyone how difficult it was to go against what your society—and your position within it—dictated that you do.

Prayer helped, as well.

When she sat there at night, reaching out to the High One within her heart, she realized how lowly she was. As she sought to draw nearer to the creator of all things, she began to understand that He was infinite, and she was finite. There was a distance between them that could never be resolved.

The thought of being so small frightened her, at first. As a dragon, she was used to the security of her size and her physical power. The realization that she was not in control of anything was a lot to take in. But she could sense that her heart was being shaped, transformed into something new.

Over time, she hoped that she would be able to peacefully recognize the truth for what it was. It was a good thing to be humble. It was a good thing to put your trust in someone who was perfect, because she was not and never could be.

Eventually, she decided that she may as well dedicate some of her time to praying for the men, and for her own peace despite her circumstances. She prayed for Wes, too, wondering if he had managed to secure his freedom. Perhaps she was already bearing the punishment for both of them.

The Feast of Offering drew near, and she prayed that amid the commotion that would mark his departure to Whitespire, she would be able to receive some news of his fate.

Though she had been promised a trial of her own, no word of it had reached her ears, and many nights she could scarcely bring herself to pray with the heavy weight of despair upon her heart.

She would wake up some days with a renewed hope that seemed to spring forth from within, only for it to be withdrawn again later, no matter how she tried to cling to it. Though nothing external ever changed at all, her heart felt constantly adrift.

That was the hardest part.

But still, she pressed on. Somewhere, deep down, far beyond the doubt and the fear that she felt, there was a deeper hope, a hope that she simply knew.

If she was faithful in her prayer to the High One, He would answer. Even when she could not feel His love, or understand why He was allowing events in Kaveryth to unfold the way that they were, she trusted that He knew the way forward.

She only had to hold on.

* * *

Celesyria awoke to the burning smell of lightning as thunder crashed overhead.

Her eyes felt heavy, and there was a chill that radiated across the membrane of her wings that indicated night had fallen hours before. She stood up, blinking away sleep, as she attempted to itch at her ankle with the opposite claw. The heavy iron manacle was, as always, in the way, but she was pleased to notice as she stretched out that the rip in her wing was almost entirely healed.

"That was close," one of the guards said, smiling a little as he glanced up at the stone ceiling. Celesyria looked over at him, peeking out from the wing she'd been examining.

A few of the soldiers spoke to her on occasion, usually to remind her of something to do with her food or the call of nature, but she had not heard anything resembling small talk directed at her since she had arrived.

This soldier in particular looked rather intimidating, even to a dragon. He was far and away the tallest soldier she'd seen in her life. His arms and legs were thick with bulging muscles, and his bright green eyes flashed with a clear intelligence.

"The building is strong. I don't think we have anything to worry about," she said, trying in vain to keep her voice at a whisper. Her throat felt as though it was thick with cobwebs. She had rarely spoken aloud since leaving home, and it was surprisingly easy to fall out of practice.

"*Any chance you can talk this way?*" She asked in her mind, but the soldier clearly did not hear her, continuing to speak before she had finished her thought.

"I'm more worried about flooding," he said, looking up at the ceiling again as though a leak may burst at any moment. "It's happened before."

She looked up.

"Not here," he chuckled to himself. "Back home."

Back home in Aridmoor. She was curious about what else the man might tell her about his homeland. Her imaginings about the plains Kingdom had grown more and more elaborate, and she wondered how closely the nation's culture resembled her musings.

She doubted that dragon-sized bears actually roamed the meadows, devouring those who dared wander too far into the wilderlands, but it was amusing to think about nevertheless.

"Oh."

"I lost my father to a flood. He was in the lowest level of High Keep's dungeon when the Waymere River dam burst a few years back."

"I'm sorry."

"I'm sorry that he was a violent drunk," the soldier said, looking at his feet for a moment before continuing.

"I don't miss him. But I do wonder about him. Where did he end up? He never made any attempt to get his life in order. But when he died, everyone spoke of him like he was bound for the Eternal Lands. It was hard to hear someone who had hurt me and my mother being canonized after his death."

Celesyria hesitated before speaking, not wanting to offend the man. Even though she was still rather intimidated, it made her happy to know that he felt like he could confide in her, even as a stranger. She resolved to pray for the man's father, just the same.

"I know you have no reason to care about this," the soldier continued, waving a hand in her general direction. "I don't talk about him much, though, and sometimes his death gets to me. Funny, isn't it?"

"I understand. Sometimes you can love someone you don't like very much, if love means wishing the best for them," Celesyria ventured.

There was something earnest in the way that he spoke that made her want to trust him. It had been so long since she'd been able to confide in anyone. He walked closer to the edge of her cell, leaning against the bars, close enough that she could bite his hand off if she chose to.

He lowered his voice to a conspiratorial whisper.

"Since my father died, I realized how many questions I had about the way things are. But I've never been allowed to really talk about my doubts. For a little while, I wish I could be free to just..." he trailed off, looking at his feet for several seconds before drawing a breath and continuing.

"Anyway, I have no one else to talk to about these things. So thank you for listening."

"And I'm already known as a blasphemer and a traitor, so I have nothing to gain by tattling to the other guards," she prompted, giving him a wink with her gigantic eye.

"This is true."

"What do you want to know?"

A smile spread across his face, so bright and genuine that it almost made her forget where they were.

"Everything. I mean, I know that's not possible, and it's probably not humble to want that, but I can't help it. The world is so huge. I don't understand why people feel like keeping their own perspective so small."

"Exactly!" Celesyria said, sounding more exuberant than she'd meant to. The soldier's enthusiasm was contagious. She thought back to her many talks with Gramnok about discoveries she'd made or intellectual trails she wished to follow. There had been so many times that she had tried to explain the very same feelings to him, but he could never seem to understand.

Even so, to his credit, he'd always been willing to hear her out. He'd always tried to see things from her angle, even if he didn't agree. She still couldn't believe he'd betrayed her, after all of their years as friends. After everything she'd trusted him with. It still brought fresh pangs to her heart every time she thought of it.

She'd always thought he'd be loyal to the end.

It hurt so much to know, too late, that she was wrong.

"Everyone's talking about you and the Envoy. Apparently he killed twenty Aridmoor soldiers singlehandedly and has a secret brother he plans to install on the throne of Silverfell. And you were the one responsible for the cows being slaughtered outside of Rigan."

Celesyria shook her head. It felt so good to laugh, even a little. "That's completely ridiculous."

"Trust me, even out there, it's hard to get a straight answer about anything that's going on." He gestured in the general direction of where the sky lay, above several layers of rock and dirt. "I feel like the scandal of it all kind of overshadowed the most important thing."

"The assertions that were made about the High One," Celesyria said after a brief pause.

"Yes. It's been strange. I don't know. I shouldn't be saying this, but..."

The soldier trailed off for a minute, looking over his shoulder, though the room was empty save the two of them.

"I won't say a word," Celesyria assured him.

"It's not that. I guess I worry that you'll think I'm crazy, but here goes. Sometimes I dream about Him. At least, I think it's Him, even though I have no idea what he looks like. It's like He's speaking to me, sharing things that I couldn't possibly know. You've at least read parts of the Codex Veritatis. I have so little to go on."

He ran a hand through his straight red hair. Celesyria thought he looked a little older than Wes, perhaps old enough to have a young wife and a first baby back home in Aridmoor.

"Despite all of that, I still have doubts. Like, how do I know any of this is true? Maybe it's just wishful thinking."

"Seeing the Codex wouldn't necessarily change that," she said finally, letting her head rest on the ground near where he stood. For the first time in a long while, she ignored the bite of the manacles cutting into the raw skin of her ankles where the scales had been rubbed away.

"I'm not an expert or anything—" She paused until he nodded in agreement. "But it seems to me that the High One has different ways of reaching people. For some of us, it's the logic of it, the reason, the fact that His existence brings together so many things and makes them make sense. But I don't think that's the only way."

"Especially now. How can anyone come to him by way of reason when all Kaveryth has conspired to silence mere mention of the High One?"

She nodded approvingly, realizing that she did not even know His name. Maybe he had more than one. Maybe she would discover new, mysterious titles that would explain more about Him.

"I think you're right. In these dark days, I think He focuses more on touching our hearts. He doesn't lie in wait. We're already so lost, all of us. Instead, He runs to us. Whether it's fulfilling a prophecy, or speaking in a dream, or leading unlikely messengers to His written words, He... He fights for each of us that he chooses."

She felt a swell of emotion rising in her chest. A month ago, she wouldn't have been able to offer many words of comfort, but after so many hours spent in prayer, she found it much easier to know what to say.

"But why would He choose me?" The soldier asked, his voice barely above a whisper. "Ever since King Radagar's passing, I've been living a lie. I earn my coin by being part of an army that I no longer believe in. And now, this mysterious High One shows up in my dreams? It makes no sense."

"I understand. I've had the same thoughts. I don't know why He would choose me, either. And yet, I know that he has. All that I can do is to try and walk the path He has laid ahead for me."

A tear slipped from Celesyria's eye as another great roar of thunder sounded overhead. Like the soldier, she had spent so much of her life misunderstood, seeing the world in a way that didn't make sense to anyone else.

Some deep-down part of her had hoped that bringing the truth about the Dracodei to the people of Kaveryth would fix things. She wanted to make people see that she had something to offer.

And yet, following the truth had only made things worse for everyone. She feared that her parents would never speak to her again. She didn't even have a soul for the High One to bring to the Eternal Lands.

And yet, despite it all, she was sure, now more than ever, that He had a plan for her. That He cared about her.

It wasn't over, not even in a dungeon, not even in the storm and the dark.

"I have some idea why," the soldier said softly, taking hold of the keys that hung on a hook near the entrance to the dungeon.

"I believe the High One is real. And He brought me to you."

She sucked in a breath.

Before she could protest the risk he was taking, he unlocked the gate to her cell and stood waiting. She took a couple of steps forward, the sudden possibility of freedom so intoxicating that she nearly ran through, forgetting to be cautious, forgetting everything.

There would be leaves on the trees outside. The sky would soon be blue again. The forests of Silverfell would be filled with fresh meat in abundance. Clouds would float by, and she would fly above them, watching the world shrink away as she ascended.

"I release you on one condition," he added, raising an arm to bar her way.

"You take me with you, and show me the Codex so that I can read it for myself."

* * *

"You want me to let you into his cell?"

"Yes."

"You must know that I can't possibly allow it, my Princess."

"Not long enough for him to leave. Let me in, and you can lock it straight back up afterward."

"I could get in trouble. They've only just begun to trust me to keep guard by myself down here."

Wes' eyes began to adjust to the darkness.

Moorn was awake, rubbing at his eyes as he got up from his

chair and paced, glancing up at the stairs every few seconds. Kessara was dressed in a rather ornate black dress covered in shimmering beadwork, with a turquoise cloak thrown over top.

Wes blinked, trying to force the tiredness from his body. *Isn't it the middle of the night? Is there some midnight ball going on up at the palace?*

"Come on, Moorn," Kessara said, giving the soldier a pleading look.

Wes was not aware that they knew each other but supposed it made sense. Roven and Moorn had been friends as children, and perhaps they had remained closer than Wes realized.

"I agreed to let this sham trial play out, but I'm tired of waiting. I want to see my betrothed."

"You can see him," Moorn said, pointing at the bars of his cell. "He's right there."

"Hi," Wes put in.

The light was too dim to be sure, but Wes thought he saw Kessara roll her eyes. "The Feast of Offering is two days away."

"Right, that's a good point," Moorn said. "I'm sure you'll get a chance to see him off."

"Yeah, in public. With a crowd of people around."

"So?"

Kessara marched over to where Moorn stood and looked up at him with raised eyebrows. "I don't want to stand in a crowd and throw cherry blooms at him. I want to say goodbye properly!"

"I doubt the Septemvirate or the Steward will mind if you wish to say goodbye, crowd or no crowd."

The Steward. The use of King Ursa's new title made his stomach roil. Still, Moorn was probably right. When the Envoy left Stronghollow there was usually a huge celebration the night before, followed by a parade that led the departing party toward the Aridmoor border.

Though he was no longer in his Kingdom's good graces, he doubted they'd miss an opportunity to remind the people of how important the sacrifices were, especially those who lived out in the countryside and did not take part in the city's celebrations.

"I want a chance to be close to him," Kessara said, letting her voice go syrupy-sweet. "Perhaps a proper kiss on the cheek? And a few minutes to talk. Can you give me that? No one will know, I promise."

"I'm not sure that's—" Wes started.

Kessara turned to him, her jaw set. Even in the dim light, he could see that her eyes were filled with ice.

"Oh no," Moorn said, throwing up his hands. "Oh no, no, no. I'm not turning my back while you two, er, indulge in some kind of premarital... amorous congress."

"An amorous *what?*" Wes asked, his voice cracking

Kessara shushed him, smacking her palm against her forehead. "You men are impossible. I assure you, I was not suggesting anything untoward."

"It's not my place to judge a Princess, I suppose," Moorn put in.

"Indeed it is not," she said primly, raising her chin. "At any rate, all I want to do is spend a few minutes with my betrothed. Come on, Moorn. I'll—I'll make it up to you."

To Wes' amazement, Moorn took the key from the hook and unlocked the cell gate. "Ten minutes, Kessara. I mean it."

Kessara squeezed his arm gently before stepping into the cell and allowing Moorn to lock it again. She gestured to the chair and Moorn obliged, rolling his eyes as he sat facing the opposite wall.

"Everything okay?" Wes asked, glancing between Moorn and Kessara.

He allowed her to lead him to sit next to her on the cot, though he was certain that he was blushing furiously.

"Do you trust me?" She whispered, leaning so close that he could feel her breath on his ear. He felt even more heat rising to his cheeks.

"Yes."

What choice do I have?

"I spoke to Dorold the other day," Kessara said at normal volume, standing up without making a sound and beckoning Wes to do the same.

"He told me that the trial was probably going to begin after your return from Whitespire. There was a problem with the judge, apparently, and they've asked my father to allow the trial to be held in Galeharbor."

Wes watched in horror as Kessara's cloak fell to the floor, leaving her standing in the formal black dress. She gestured with her hands, and he turned around.

"What do you think about that?" Her voice was artificially loud. "I'm thrilled, personally. I mean, better if it's in Galeharbor, I think. My father will make sure it's conducted fairly. I trust him."

"Oh, uh, that's amazing news," he stammered. "Honey. Darling."

He watched as a blonde wig landed near his feet, the tendrils of hair sticking to his leather boots.

"And after everyone realizes that you're innocent, I was thinking an autumn wedding would be perfect," Kessara continued. He could hear the smile in her voice. *She should have joined a theater troupe.* "I'd like to do it here, though I think my mother will be disappointed. We've been bickering about it for weeks. But the forest in autumn would be so magnificent. We don't get color like that in Galeharbor, you know? Except perhaps in the west, but even then, it's nothing like the interior of Silverfell. Oh! I just had a thought."

She tapped him on the shoulder and he turned, not daring to take his eyes off of the pile of clothes on the ground.

"Now yours," she hissed. Wes glanced over at Moorn, who was fidgeting on his chair but otherwise paying little attention. *What is it with women and planning weddings?*

"I'd like to have a traditional temple ceremony, of course, but we could have the dinner outside. I just thought of the perfect location. Remember that little pond out toward Old Hill? It would be gorgeous when the leaves turn."

He began to take off his own clothes, hoping that Kessara would be equally careful to avert her eyes as he was. He doubted he needed to worry, but still, he had always been raised to be especially careful with such matters.

However awkward the execution was turning out to be, he had to admit that the plan had some merit. He was thin enough that it might actually work. *As long as Moorn stays put, anyway.*

"We will find you the most beautiful dress in Kaveryth," Wes said, playing along as he struggled to get undressed as silently as Kessara had. His weight loss had not served to impart any new grace in his movement, and for one horrible moment, his boot got caught on his pants and he nearly fell backward.

Finally, his clothes were in a pile on the floor of the cell. He scooped up the women's attire and turned his back, relieved. He heard Kessara do the same.

"There's this dwarf designer that's supposed to be incredible.

Gwendolynn Deepmaul, I think her name is," he added, hoping that the genuine grin on his face added to the realism of his acting.

"Does she work in human sizes?"

"Oh, yes. She specializes in them, actually. She makes dresses out of...of..."

He trailed off, finding it surprisingly difficult to put on a woman's dress and to think at the same time. The fact that Kessara was known to speak several languages became even more impressive in his mind.

Why did she need to wear something with five hundred buttons? And where does one even purchase a wig?

"Fine silk, dotted with jewels from the mines?"

Kessara prompted, tapping him on the shoulder again. He turned, relieved to find her fully dressed in his prison garb, his cloak covering her bright blonde hair, which she had done up tightly in a knot at the back of her head. He watched, wide-eyed, as she tucked a small dagger into the front pocket of what were once his pants.

"Er, right. Yes. She also does cakes! Traditional dwarven cakes. Did you know that dwarves are famous for them?"

"Two minutes," Moorn announced.

Wes grabbed the long blonde wig from the floor and attempted to put it on, trying to get the hair to fall prettily on his head. He was not having much luck, but hoped the bright cloak would mostly conceal the tangles.

"Really? Famous for mines, song, crafting tools..."

"And wedding cakes. Traditionally, the frosting is flavored with ale and smoked brisket."

Kessara glared at him and began poking about his outfit, fixing a button he had missed and replacing the tie that had fallen off the end of the wig's braid. Even the men's clothes could not conceal the feminine grace of her every movement. It was something inborn among women, one of the great mysteries of the fairer sex that was incomprehensible to him.

"Sounds lovely. Oh, how I long to marry you. To call you mine, forever, unto the eternal lands!"

"Not even death can separate us, my Princess. Or should I say, my future queen," he returned, finding it easier than he'd feared to fall into the role.

This really doesn't sound so terrible, Wes thought. Kessara leaned toward him, making an exaggerated kissing noise with her mouth. He was so taken aback that he nearly shoved her backward, tripping over the hem of his dress.

"Ow!" She hissed before she could stop herself. "Oh, darling, these scruffy cheeks of yours are something to get used to. They absolutely must be gone before the wedding."

He stroked at his prison stubble absentmindedly, thinking that surely Moorn was not stupid enough to believe this blatant charade.

"Alright, lovebirds. Are you decent?" Moorn said from across the room, glancing up at the door that led to the outer hallway. Mercifully, Wes had not heard anyone else approaching.

"We always were, like I said!" Kessara chirped, moving to sit on the edge of Wes' bed, flopping down hard enough that the wooden frame creaked.

Wes was amazed by the transformation. Her face remained beautiful and distinctly feminine, but she had so mastered his posture that he was certain Moorn wouldn't notice until it was too late. Whether or not he could muster up the proper girlish mannerisms would be another story.

He moved toward the gate, trying to keep his head down, playing with the end of the wig's braid as Moorn got up from his chair.

* * *

For a moment, Wes hesitated, his heart pounding as he listened to the click of the lock. After so much time, it was hard to imagine that freedom lay so near.

He thought of the feeling of grass beneath his feet and the smell of rain on trees. They would be covered with bright green leaves, and the fruit trees around the palace would be in bloom with fragrant, colorful flowers.

No, not the palace. He nodded to Moorn and slipped wordlessly through the gate of the cell.

He had been given no time to prepare, and suddenly, the realization of what freedom meant felt overwhelming. He couldn't go home, nor could he risk seeking a place to hide out in Stronghollow.

Nearly everyone in Silverfell knew his face, and a good number of those in the rest of the Four Kingdoms would as well. He had no food, no money, and no idea where he was heading.

I don't even have the clothes on my back, unless I feel like taking this charade home to Galeharbor. I wonder what King and Queen Manta would have to say.

He had entered the penitentiary without knowing what would happen next, but over time, he'd come to value the simple routine of his life. Someone brought him food three times a day. He had finally been permitted books to read, so he had improved his study of the old languages, hoping to make his father proud from where he rested in the world beyond.

It wasn't the most pleasant life, particularly the crushing loneliness, but it was familiar.

It was safe.

Ever since his memories began, he had lived a life governed by routine, tradition, and order. The four Feasts, one every season. The feeling of riding a great stag through the gates of Stronghollow. The turn of the forest road that led to the border. The plains of Aridmoor. The mountains of Umrym. Whitespire. The cavern. The Caravan of the Claim that welcomed him home after each trip.

Some things had changed, of course, but so much stayed the same, day after day and year after year, until Celesyria came into his life.

Here, he had been able to turn back, at least for a little while. Here, he slept at the same time each night and awoke to the gleam of dawn at his window.

Now, he could hear only thunder, and see only darkness. He was to emerge into a future unknown, with no idea where to begin.

He dared a glance back at Moorn as he made for the stairs, terrified to speak. It was dim, but would it be dark enough to conceal his identity? What if it was brighter past the door, with more guards?

He hoped Kessara had thought that far ahead. Furthermore, now that she was in the cell herself, how did she plan to get out? Moorn had stuck his neck out for her, and now their lives were both in peril.

I chose to trust her. He tried in vain to silence the hammering of his heart, sure that Moorn would be able to hear it. *I guess that means I have to trust the High One all the more.*

What was done was done.

There was no way to go but forward, come what may.

Just as he wrapped his fingers around the door handle, Moorn spoke.

"Remember," he started, as Wes forced himself to turn and face his friend. He hoped that his hood shadowed his face. It would be enough. It had to be enough. "Not a word of this to anyone. I'd be in for it with the army, not to mention what the Septemvirate would say about the... impropriety."

Wes' cheeks flushed again. The urge to correct his false assumption was strong, but not strong enough to take the risk.

"Not a word," he choked out, trying in vain to imitate Kessara's feminine lilt.

Before Moorn could comment further, he was through the door, relief flooding his heaving chest like cool water in the wilderlands of Boneshire.

Chapter Nineteen

Lightning seared the sky as Celesyria flew, claps of thunder sounding every few seconds. She could scarcely see the ends of her wings. The rain was pouring, and thick clouds covered the stars and the moon. There were no constellations for her to navigate by, and any potential landmarks below were shrouded in darkness.

"We have to go back!" a voice cried from her back, barely audible over the storm. "We need to wait for daybreak."

If this is going to work, I'm going to need to teach you to speak properly. She strained to hear him. Still, he was probably right. Even if the weather were better, she needed time to think of a plan.

Wes was down there, somewhere near Stronghollow, and he needed her.

"Hold on," she said, turning sharply and heading to a lower

elevation.

When she had burst out of the prison, it had felt so good to be free that she thought of nothing that lay ahead, considering only the joy of jumping into the air. It had been glorious after so much time locked away. Every beat of her wings felt magical, as though she was flying for the first time. She could still feel a sting of pain every time wind rushed against her wounded wing, but it was bearable.

It was the manacles that bothered her.

The Aridmoor soldier, whom she had found out was named Alder, had attempted to remove them, but he had only been given the keys to the cell's door. It seemed that they were too strong to break, but there hadn't exactly been much time to experiment.

When they fled the dungeon, they had been intercepted by several other guards. To Celesyria's astonishment, they had ignored her in their rush to subdue the traitorous soldier.

Though the hall leading toward the lower dungeon had been large enough for Celesyria to move through, King Ursa's men had trouble mounting an effective sword attack.

Alder had jumped on her back, pressed himself as close against her scales as he could, and waited as Celesyria bowled past them, leaving a clatter of metal and moans of pain in her wake.

As they made it through to the outside, the soldiers scrambled to regroup, trying to pierce her and her rider with arrows.

It had been useless. Celesyria was too big, their arrows and swords too small, and their numbers too few. Without deceiving her into cooperating, there was little they could do to control her. The realization had filled her with renewed hope.

They flew away from Stronghollow as quickly as they could.

Things would not end happily if the army was given time to bring in reinforcements.

She could barely make out the thick forest below her claws. She hoped she was still in the general vicinity of Stronghollow. The last thing she needed was an unknown mountainside to appear out of the mist.

"Any brilliant ideas?" she called to Alder over the rushing wind, hoping that no one on the ground could spot her bright orange scales flashing between the clouds.

* * *

Running in a dress was not as difficult as he'd expected.

It's keeping my wig straight that's the problem. Wes raced down the hallway outside of his cell toward the next flight of wooden stairs that led to ground level.

It was darker here, and it looked like the other cells were all empty. He saw one guard sitting at a small wooden table, a pack of cards spread out before him. He gave a bow of his head in greeting, which Wes returned, saying nothing.

The next level was busier. He could hear the snores of dozens of sleeping men filling the rows of cells that lay on either side of the main hallway, but fortunately, the candlelight was dim enough that they paid him no notice.

He could see the door leading outside, the memories of his capture flooding back all at once. A surge of anger jolted through his limbs. *So much time wasted. They left me here to rot.*

But there was no time to dwell on it. Two soldiers stood there, one at either side of the door, with Aridmoor longswords at their waists.

Wes peered out from under his large hood, noticing that their thick gray cloaks lay on hooks off to one side. *Here we go.*

"Gentlemen," he started, keeping his voice barely loud enough to hear.

"What can we do for you, my Princess?" one of the soldiers said with a quick bow, giving him a smile that revealed his rather crooked teeth. The other man was older, with thick eyebrows and a dour expression. He grunted in agreement with his companion, pulled out a small knife, and began cleaning his fingernails.

"I was wondering if I may borrow a warmer cloak," he said, smiling, but keeping his face pointed toward the floor. "It's a cold night."

"Of course, my lady, it would be an honor," the cheerful soldier said, reaching behind him and plucking one of the cloaks off of the wall.

"That's mine," the other man said, glancing up from his fingernails.

"It will fit her better," the soldier protested, handing the cloak to Wes. He took a tentative step closer and grabbed the cloak, pulling it around himself.

"I am in your debt," he said, bowing toward the friendly soldier. The other man swore under his breath. Wes ignored him, though he wondered if Kessara could have resisted the urge to demand his respect.

The soldier opened the door, releasing a burst of freezing wind into the hall. As he stepped over the threshold, he could hear several of the prisoners yelling at the guards to hurry up and shut the door.

Wes gave a quick nod to the soldier and slunk away along the prison's wall until he found a small alcove where the wind could not reach. While keeping the cloak in place as best he could, he took the bottom of Kessara's dress and stuffed it into the top of the white cotton underpants beneath.

He considered removing the decorative cloak, but since it was hidden well enough beneath the second one, he kept it for an extra layer of warmth.

He yanked the blonde wig off of his head and stuffed it into the back of his partially see-through makeshift pants. *Why do women's clothes never have pockets?*

He would have to get rid of it as soon as he was away from Stronghollow Penitentiary. He supposed it was in a way fortunate that he had no other possessions. They would only slow him down.

He looked to the eastern sky, wondering how much longer it would be before the dawn came. Though he was much warmer with the help of the guard's cloak, it was still miserable weather for traveling, and he did not know the area well enough to be eager to navigate by night.

Not to mention the small fact that I'm an escaped fugitive.

He listened for a moment, leaning up against the wall and allowing himself several moments rest, letting his heart rate slow. Outside of the rain and the periodic crack of thunder, nothing seemed to be amiss within the prison.

With any luck, Kessara would sleep and Moorn would say nothing further until morning. After that, he hoped she had a plan, because he didn't. It made him sick to think that she was putting herself in harm's way for his sake, but she had made the choice. It would have done him no good to refuse her. As far as he could tell, this was his only chance.

"*Hey, Celesyria. Wings would be great and all, but is there any chance you can bring me some pants?*"

* * *

The sudden sound of Wes' voice in her head was so surprising that she faltered in the sky for a second before regaining control.

"*Pants?*" She managed to ask, ascending high enough that she could comfortably circle while they spoke. The weather was even more unpleasant higher up, but she needed to think.

"What's going on?" Alder asked. She ignored him for the moment, too overcome with joy at hearing from her friend to consider much else. It wasn't as though he could run off in a huff, anyway.

"*I'm free. I'm out, but I'm—uh— in disguise,*" Wes said. "*I'll explain later. Where are you? Are you alright?*"

"*You're never going to believe it, but I just escaped tonight.*"

Wes filled her in on the details of his own capture and escape with the aid of the Princess as she and Alder circled the sky.

Fortunately, the Aridmoor soldier had been able to spot the moon briefly between the clouds, so she no longer feared getting lost. Stronghollow lay directly to the south of where they flew.

"*I hope this has proved to you that the hand of the High One is upon all things.*"

"*Maybe so. I've been so lonely. I was starting to believe I had been forgotten. But not even King Ursa or the Septemvirate can truly control my fate. Or yours.*"

"*So, do you have a plan?*"

"*I didn't even plan my own escape, so no. You?*"

Celesyria risked craning her neck back to look at Alder, a difficult task while flying. "I'm not sure I got to say it, but thank you for everything," she said aloud. Her companion nodded, both of his hands clinging to the base of her wings with white knuckles as she took a sharp, fast turn.

He'd been braver than she'd expected about flying. Gramnok never dared to ride on her back, and she had a feeling that Wes would not take to it with such immediate enthusiasm. Considering Gramnok's betrayal, she furrowed her brow, wondering if Alder was truly an ally, or whether, perhaps, he was planning some wicked design against her.

There was nothing she could do about it now, one way or another. She'd trusted him to help her escape, and unless he gave her a reason to doubt, she would have to continue to believe in him.

"Let's meet at the north gate of Stronghollow," Celesyria said to Wes. She wanted to tell him that she was bringing a friend, but decided against it at the last second. Such a conversation would be easier to have when Alder could hear what was being said.

"But I'll be seen!"

"I thought you were incognito?"

"Only partially. How about the Waymere River?"

"It's too dark. I'd miss it unless I flew low over Stronghollow, which kind of defeats the purpose."

"Fine. The gate. But we won't have much time. It will be well-guarded, especially if they've figured out I'm gone."

With a brief goodbye to Wes, she took a final loop and adjusted her altitude before heading due south. The lightning and thunder had let up somewhat, but the rain continued, the clouds still thick enough that the moon was only visible for brief moments at a time.

Still, it was enough to know the way, and considering her size, it was for the best. It would be a lot easier to avoid detection in the dark and gloom.

"Where are we going?" Alder yelled out from her back. She did not turn, but she felt his weight shifting as she flew slightly lower.

"To pick up another rider," she said, flapping her wings against the pain of her wound and flying as fast as she could. Dawn was drawing near.

* * *

Wes hadn't expected Celesyria to answer.

He knew that he should be elated to hear that she was alright, not to mention the impossible miracle of her escape, and yet, something was nagging at him.

As he walked toward Stronghollow's north gate, he couldn't help but to glance over his shoulder every few seconds, convinced that at any moment, a swarm of prison guards would descend upon him, flowing out of the woods along the path like locusts rushing against a field of fresh wheat.

There should have been several guards standing alert at this point in the path, just as he'd told Celesyria.

Instead, it was deserted.

It was possible that there would only be one or two men posted in the early hours of the morning during a rainstorm. It wasn't as though anyone in their right mind would be traveling through Silverfell in such weather when the comfortable inns at Stronghollow lay so close.

Even as he tried to convince himself that everything was fine, the groans of swaying trees in the wind and the ominous fog that shrouded the narrow road conjured up images in his mind that logic could not push aside.

Once I reach Celesyria, I'll be okay. He pulled the borrowed cloak in tightly around his shoulders as a gust of wind ripped past him. He felt a pang of guilt that he had taken it under false pretenses, wondering if there was some safe way he could ensure it made it back to its original owner, however unpleasant he was.

We need to get away from here, find some food and a place to rest, and figure out what we're going to do next.

His unease persisted.

He continued to walk, his socks so thoroughly soaked despite the boots he wore that he had long since ceased to feel his frozen toes. He thought of all that had happened in the past few months, and all that remained for him to do.

He had to find a queen.

He had to find the Codex Veritatis.

And eventually, I have to burn the whole edifice of worship in the Four Kingdoms to the ground.

He and Celesyria had been given a second chance to save Kaveryth from the tyranny of deceit, and he couldn't squander it. They would have to find a way.

Before he could consider the matter further, however, a man stepped into the road ahead of him. Though he was only a few yards away, it took Wes a moment to realize that it was Dorold.

Wes looked to the woods on either side of the road, seeing no one else, but he was certain that they were there. His stomach turned with nausea. He was right. The soldiers were already watching. He heard a howl from somewhere deep in the wilderlands.

He didn't fear the ironwolves.

Men willing to listen to the demands of tyrants were a far more frightening enemy.

"My son," the Elder said, clasping his hands together in front of his chest. Through the rain, Wes could see a look of sadness on his face, perhaps even regret.

He stood stock-still, unsure whether to run or to let the man speak. As if reading his mind, Dorold continued. "It's time to stop this madness. There's no need to run. I just want to talk."

Wes watched as Dorold raised his hands as though in surrender, taking a couple of steps closer. The old man should have been shivering in the chill, but he seemed entirely unaffected, his gait steady as he ambled toward the boy he continued to call son.

Wes could just make out the high stone gate that led into Stonehollow rising in the distance behind him, mired in heavy mist.

"I wanted only to help you, child," he continued, placing a hand on Wes' arm. He drew his cloak more tightly over Kessara's clothes, though he supposed it was too late to hope that Dorold had somehow overlooked her involvement in his escape.

"I promised your dear parents that I would always look after you, and I never wanted to break that vow. I have done everything in my power to ensure your treatment was befitting to your noble blood."

"Even the lowest peasant deserves better than to be thrown in a hole for months without trial."

"It is no small matter to arrange justice, Wes," Dorold said, a sad smile making the corners of his eyes wrinkle. "Be reasonable."

Wes clenched his fists, saying nothing. Taking advantage of a moment to think, he called out to Celesyria in his mind, warning her to stay up beyond the clouds unless he told her otherwise.

"But—" he paused, letting go of Wes and pulling his own cloak tighter around his head as a gust of wind tore at them. "I know it must have been difficult for you. I want to be fair. If you come with me willingly, I will petition the Steward to allow you to await your hearing under house arrest. Your rooms in the palace have not been touched, of course. It will be much better than living in a cell."

The temptation to accept Dorold's offer in hopes of returning to his home was overwhelming. He shivered, thinking of his soft mattress and silken sheets in his wing of Stronghollow's palace.

There, he could wake up every day and look at the portrait of his family that hung over the parlor fireplace. He couldn't believe how quickly his memory of their faces had become blurred around the edges during his time in prison. The thought of leaving the physical reminders of his happy past behind forever made his heart ache.

"Wes, you need to understand that it's not only you who I'm thinking about," Dorold continued, waving his hands as he spoke. There was an edge of desperation growing in his voice. "King Ursa taking Stewardship of Silverfell has been good for our people—for *your* people! Trade is thriving. The streets are safer than they've been in years."

"I heard as much in prison."

"The guards speak the truth. I know it's difficult to accept change. I have watched this Kingdom evolve since long before you were born. Progress may not be easy, but it's for the best. It's necessary. We cannot allow our comfort with what once was to stop us from pursuing a more glorious future."

Wes gave a quick glance toward the east. Though the clouds

and rain remained, he could see that the sun was inching higher, sending a soft glow across the tops of the trees.

What he wanted to do, what he should do, was to call Celesyria to take him far away from here.

But then he looked at Dorold.

Even after all that he and the rest of the Septemvirate had done, there was a part of him that wanted desperately to listen to his mentor, to forget everything that had happened this spring.

He thought of how strange and thin he must look, so different than the pudgy boy that the Elder had raised into a man. The changes must have been hard on Dorold, too. Everyone in the palace knew that he saw Wes as a son, and now, his son had, in their eyes, become a traitor to the Dracodei. *He's putting his reputation on the line to protect me.*

Dorold looked so much older, even after only a few months. What additional weight had Wes caused to fall upon his sloped shoulders?

"I don't believe there's a trial at all," he said finally, looking at his feet. Another bolt of lightning lit the sky, sending a rumble of thunder rolling across the forest. There was no time left to step around what had to be said. Only the truth could remain. "You left me to rot. How could I ever trust you now?"

"There is a trial. The summer Feast draws near. We were planning to tell you about it as soon as you returned from Whitespire."

"After I've done your bidding, is that it?"

"Wes, I know you're angry," Dorold crooned, placing a wizened hand on Wes' shoulder once more. "I can't say I blame you. You have borne tragedies that few others will ever understand."

"Including you."

"Perhaps so."

They stood in silence for a moment, watching each other as the rain pattered on the dirt road. Wes could see the sun now, a tiny sliver of burning red fire at the edge of the world.

He thought of what it would feel like when the clouds cleared, the soft heat on his skin, the brightness that forced him to squint. Even if Dorold told the truth, and he was able to fall back into his old life, the light would be missing.

He would see the sun, but his soul would be shrouded in darkness.

He would carry the coins across Kaveryth, and the weight would crush him.

He shook his head at Dorold and shrugged the man's hand off of his shoulder, stepping past him, toward the gate of Stronghollow.

"Wes, you must know that I have dozens of arrows trained on you now," he heard Dorold say from behind him. His voice was so gentle that Wes could scarcely hear it over the rain. "I hope you will do the right thing out of love for your people, but—"

"But I don't have a choice. I never had a choice."

He was sure he could feel the moonscar burning against his skin, dragging him back to the life that had been laid out before him. Refusing to let go.

Chapter Twenty

A roar sounded, silencing the remaining thunder.

Wes could hear the flap of wings as Celesyria flew closer.

"Careful," he said, watching the armed men that moved in to surround him. As the dawn light grew brighter, he could see more and more of the men that Dorold had hidden, tucked neatly behind trees and ducking next to crags of rock, bows drawn.

Celesyria was huge, but that didn't mean she was invincible, especially at close range. Wes was sure that Dorold's men would be well prepared for this eventuality. Arrows were one thing, heavy pikes were another.

He turned to face Dorold, willing his hands not to shake as he heard the titters of men behind him, drawing closer, hemming him in on all sides.

Dorold laughed, his mouth twisting into a rictus of loathing. He no longer looked old, or tired. He stood up straighter, moving with renewed grace toward Wes, as though his rage fueled him.

"So I see. You are so predictable, my son," he glanced up at the sky where Celesyria was visible between clouds. "Of course, we knew the dragon escaped, with the help of some Aridmoor traitor filth."

Wes wondered who he could possibly be talking about. *Maybe she told one of her guards about the High One.*

"Poor Wes Cervos, never able to keep up with his more handsome, more talented older brother in swordplay, battle tactics, history, diplomacy... Your parents told me as much, how frustrating it was to have a son who failed so spectacularly in living up to their firstborn."

"How dare you speak of them."

"I thought you cared about the truth! You were willing to destroy your own Kingdom over it."

"I do. But that's a lie," he hissed, turning slightly so that he could observe the men around him, how they moved. *You're right, Dorold. I was never particularly adept at strategy. But there's one thing I can use.* In the Elder's anger, it seemed he'd overlooked it. Wes hoped the soldiers had, as well.

"Oh, but it isn't. I suppose we all prefer truth when it's said about something other than ourselves. Didn't the Dracodei send a similar message back in the fall? Oh, I forgot. You don't believe in them," he smiled again, his eyes hollow. "The truth is simple, Wes. You've always been a coward. Whenever things go wrong for you, someone else gets to die to protect your worthless life. Haven't you caused enough pain?"

Tears stung Wes' eyes.

Every rational part of him knew that what Dorold said was a lie, designed only to wound him, to make him surrender. But he couldn't help but hear an echo of his own darkest thoughts, his hate for himself, the things he confided to the ceiling when he lay alone at night.

Along with the faces of his family members, Odrigh, and Lev, he now dreamed of Zanek, half-brother of the King, lying there in the dirt, dead by his hand.

He looked up at the sky. The clouds had broken above, and he could see the orange glow of morning breaking overhead.

It was the most beautiful dawn that he had ever seen.

The world could change, men could do good and work evil, but as long as the High One held His creation together, the light would always come after the darkness.

Without warning, Celesyria was there, circling so fast and so close that he could hear the hiss of displaced air mere inches from his head. He watched as the men lashed out with pikes, but she was much too fast for them. He forced himself to breathe as he monitored the state of the battlefield. The rain had nearly stopped. It was time.

"Elder Dorold," he began, striding toward him until he was mere inches from his face. "You can try to manipulate my guilt all that you like. It will not work."

"So you admit I'm right. You are guilty."

"I am. But so are you. So is every soldier here."

Dorold laughed, but there was a flicker of fear behind his eyes.

Wes continued.

"I don't deserve the sacrifices that others have made on my

behalf. For years, I have let that guilt destroy me. But that ends now."

Dorold laughed again. Wes could scarcely recognize him. His face looked different in the breaking light. It looked warped, in a way he couldn't place.

"So you're just going to decide to stop crying? Decide to stop pondering ways to kill yourself?"

Wes flinched. He knew. Maybe everyone did.

"Don't listen to him," Celesyria said as she circled him. *"You can't change the dark things you've done, or wanted to do. You can only move forward."*

"It's not too late to be loyal to the House of Cervos, Dorold," he said instead. For a moment, he could see a flicker of doubt behind the Elder's eyes, a flash of the man he had been back when the King and Queen yet lived.

A second later, it was gone. Dorold chuckled, gesturing to his men.

Wes closed his eyes as he spoke to Celesyria.

"Now."

The dragon circled once more, coming in fast. The men had ceased firing arrows. Instead, they arranged themselves in lines, their sharp pikes pointing skyward.

Dorold turned away, shaking his head. "If that dragon attempts to burn my men, I will see to it personally that her head is served on a platter after the next Feast."

"You know as well as I do that she can't. Unlike you, she is loyal to the laws of the Four Kingdoms."

As Wes spoke, Celesyria flew over the trees at the edge of the path, so close that her claws brushed against the leaves. There was a great rushing sound as she breathed, a torrent of fire bursting from her jaws.

"But as far as I know, the trees do not fall under the protection of the dragons."

Before any of the soldiers could react, the forest on one side of the road was burning, the flames so hot that they broke ranks and rushed toward the other side, nearly crushing Dorold as they went. The fire tore through the woods, moving faster than a man could run as it devoured the trees one by one.

"No!" the man screamed as great plumes of black smoke washed over his men.

Wes tried to stay where he was as Celesyria circled back for him. He watched as she approached, his eyes streaming from the smoke, lungs heaving. He would die if he stayed here even two minutes longer.

He could see the manacle on her left ankle nearest him. All he had to do was grab hold of it.

Across the road, he could hear Dorold and the soldiers screaming back and forth amongst each other, but no one dared come any closer to the consuming fire.

Celesyria was only a second away.

He coughed uncontrollably, doubled over, the seconds stretching out before him in the intolerable heat.

And then a bough fell across the road, sending red embers flying in his direction.

Wes screamed as something hit his face, the pain sending sparks radiating through his skull. Somehow, he managed to get hold of Celesyria's manacle with both hands.

He closed his eyes, gritting his teeth against the pain, unsure if he was still on fire or if whatever had caused the burning had fallen off.

His stomach lurched as she flew higher. He prayed that she would land before he passed out.

***

They landed a few miles away, in a forest clearing that Alder had spotted as Celesyria flew. Wes knew that they could not stay long, but it was a relief to lay down.

The clouds had all but faded away, leaving a cool summer morning with a gentle breeze. As he looked at the trees and smelled the remnant of the rain, it was hard to believe what the night had held.

It was another world, here in the light.

His face was burned, but it was not as catastrophic as it had felt. At Celesyria's suggestion, he dug up some mud and pressed it against his right cheek, cooling any burning that might still be taking place beneath his skin. He chuckled under his breath as he did so. Celesyria gave him a questioning look.

"My moonscar is gone. It's been replaced."

The dragon said something, but he didn't hear it.

He was happy to see Celesyria. Happy to be free. Happy that somehow, they had found another unexpected ally in Alder—the tall, kind soldier he had seen at the border of Aridmoor months before.

But there was a deeper thing, a more complicated thing, that he had not had time to think through.

During all of his months in the Stronghollow Penitentiary, he had been able to hold on to a scrap of hope that someday, everything would go back to normal.

Whatever he'd said, whatever promises he'd made to do what was right, there was always a part of him that held something back, reserving the option to do what was easy.

To do what would bring him peace, even as the storms of the world raged around him.

Now, as they awaited an even more uncertain future, he felt that little bit of self-love spilling away, forced out of him by some great hand, pressing hard upon his chest until he could not even take another breath on his own.

He looked up at the sky, the sun warm upon his face.

He whispered into the warm sunlight.

"If I follow you, it's all or nothing. If I accept the sacrifices made for me, I must offer my whole self in return."

Alder and Celesyria glanced at him, saying nothing.

As he lowered his face, he looked back toward Stronghollow, where even the palace was hidden behind the sea of trees. There would not be much time for contemplation. King Ursa and the Septemvirate were not about to give up.

But still he was not afraid, for he finally understood what kind of sacrifice he was being called to make.

TO BE CONTINUED

Read Majesty (Storm & Spire Book 2) now!

Dear Reader

Thank you so much for reading *Magnify*, the first book in the Storm & Spire series.

If you enjoyed this book, I humbly ask you to consider leaving an honest review. It can be just a sentence or two if you like. Reviews are an author's lifeblood, especially independent authors, and *especially* those who write in smaller genres like Christian fantasy. =)

Thank you from the bottom of my heart for your support & encouragement.

If you want to stay up to date with my writing (including Storm & Spire book two!) please consider signing up for my newsletter. I'm also working on some fun exclusive content just for subscribers.

You can sign up at https://authorstefanielozinski.com/newsletter

In Christ,

Stefanie Lozinski

Behind the Scenes

I've written several novels, but this is the first time I had to actually *publish* one.

Unsurprisingly, being a one-woman publishing house is a lot of work, and I made a lot of mistakes while getting Wes and Celesyria's story ready for the world.

Somehow, it all came together in time, but at certain stages in the process I thought I would never get all of the moving parts to work together.

The most important thing (outside of the story itself) that I *really* wanted to get right was the cover. Thank you, Etheric Designs!

They managed to turn my very basic vision into something incredible...

This is what I gave them to work with:

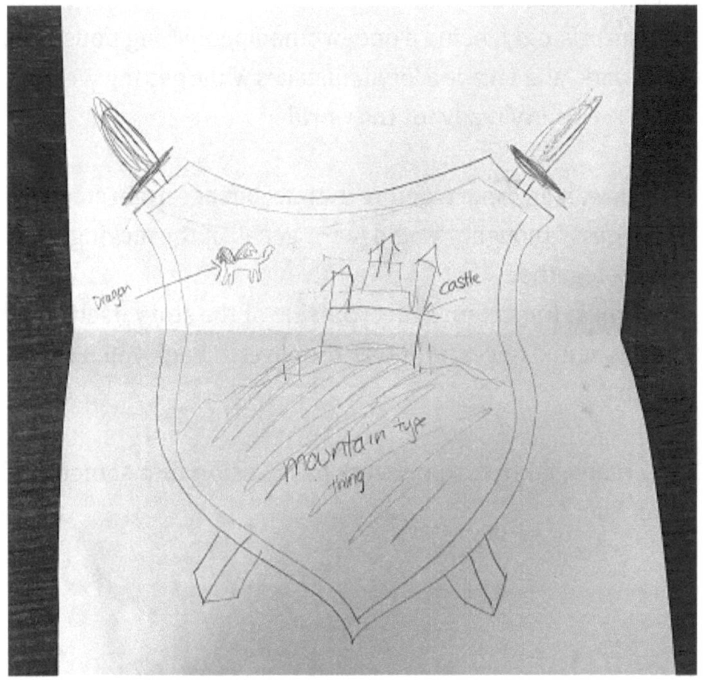

It's astonishing how much they were able to do with my total
lack of artistic talent.

I almost decided against adding a map. I love when books have maps, but if my cover design didn't make this clear, I am *not* an artist. In the end, I decided that I had to try, and I really enjoy how it turned out.

I did it myself in a program called Wonderdraft. During the actual process it seemed like it was never going to come together, either. It wasn't until the very end where I was like "Oh! This actually looks... good!"

When I wrote *Magnify*, I was adding to this very clumsy, messy map and wondering how on earth I would turn it into something that belonged in a fantasy novel.

Here is how it looked - some names were changed later:

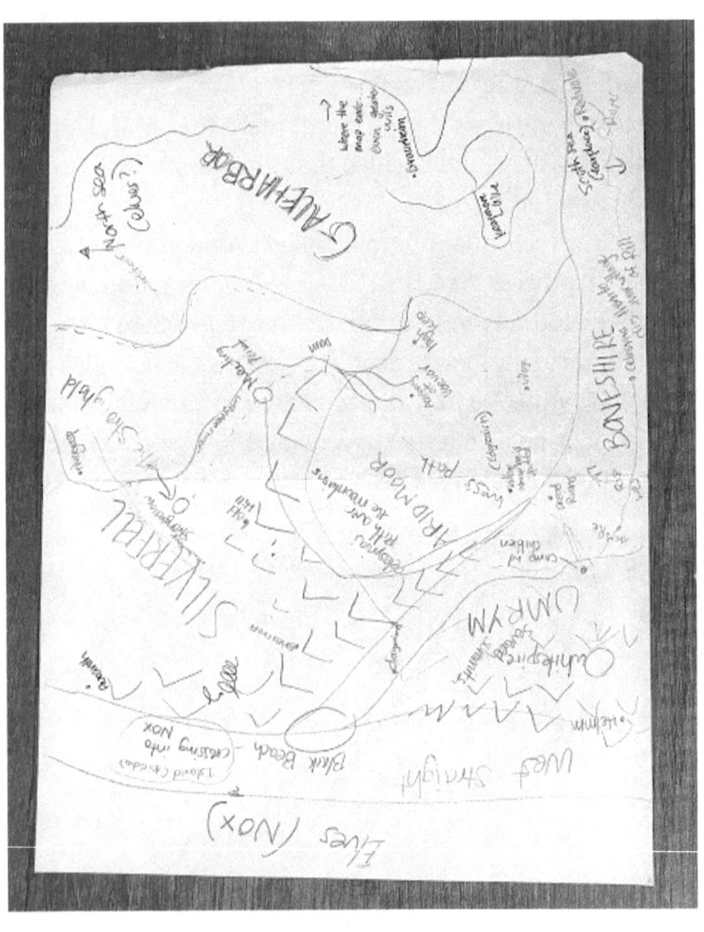

Acknowledgments

Thank you to my husband Jordan for your endless support and belief in me as a writer, and for supporting our family so that I can be at home with our kids. If that wasn't enough, you also spent hours of time proofreading and helping to edit this novel, finding all kinds of things that made the book stronger in the end. Your sacrifice and hard work mean the world to me, and I am so blessed to call you mine.

To my son Dawson – I am so proud of you for your progress in learning how to read, even when it's difficult and you want to quit! One day, I hope to share this story with you. You also ask me my word count every day, which helps me to stay on track. Thank you.

To my daughter Lucia – You're about to officially become a toddler as I write this, so your contributions to the project were a little more abstract! Thank you for reminding me that even in a busy season of life, writing is possible. Thank you for laughing and smiling and reminding me that being fruitful and multiplying is absolutely great.

To Jackie - Outside of my parents, you are my longest-term supporter. Ever since we met on Tumblr in 2012 and bonded over Stephen King, you have been there for me as a writer and as a person. Thank you for listening to my daily word counts and almost daily (oops) writing struggles.

To Jacinta - Your typo-hunting skills and encouragement were a light in the darkest part of writing and I hope that you will continue to aid me when I write the next book!

To my parents and my sisters - Thank you for always believing that I could become a writer one day. I am so thankful that I was homeschooled and surrounded by stories from birth.

To all of my readers - I'm completely amazed that you took a chance on my story. I hope you enjoyed it, and I hope you will stick around for more.

To Jesus Christ, my Lord and Savior - May all that I do be done in You, with You, and for You. Thank you.

About the Author

Stefanie Lozinski lives in Ontario, Canada, with her husband, two young children, two cats, and a whole lot of books. When she isn't homeschooling her little ones, you'll find her on a long walk, drinking coffee, praying a Rosary, or working on her next novel.

You can connect with me on:

🌐 https://www.authorstefanielozinski.com
📘 https://www.facebook.com/authorstefanielozinski
🔗 https://www.instagram.com/lozinskistefanie

Subscribe to my newsletter:

✉ https://authorstefanielozinski.com/newsletter